Fuller's Curse

Fuller's Curse

Ann Fields

A New Thing Publishing
Dallas, Texas

ISBN-13: 978-0-9893685-1-3

FULLER'S CURSE is a work of fiction. Apart from the well- known actual people, events and locales that figure in the narrative, all names, characters, places and incidents are the product of the author's imagination or are used fictitiously. Any resemblance to current events or locales, or to living persons, is entirely coincidental.

The Scripture quotations contained herein are from the New Revised Standard Version Bible, copyright, 1989, by the Division of Christian Education of the National Council of the Churches of Christ in the U.S.A. Used by permission. All rights reserved.

Cover art by Kathy Amaral
http://designbykatt.deviantart.com

Cover photography by Lisa Bagherpour
http://fairiegoodmother.deviantart.com

Front cover model: Ariel

A New Thing Publishing
P. O. Box 170875
Dallas, Texas 75217-0875

Printed in U.S.A.

Acknowledgements

My deepest thanks to the following who provided reader feedback, editorial comments, suggestions and ideas, research knowledge, administrative support, love, encouragement and overreaching support during the twelve-year evolution of this story:

Elizabeth George;
The skilled writers in Elizabeth George's Track III writing track at the 2000 Maui Writer's Retreat;
Janice Croom;
Janice M. Johnson;
John Warren;
Detra Moore;
Dr. Robert Ilaria and his staff at UT Southwestern in 2000-2001;
The Writer's Block;
Alan and Goldie Browning of Storyteller Publishing;
and most of all, to my family, both immediate and extended.

Dedication

To being human, good and bad

The First Beginning: The Curse

Malachi 2:2 (NRSV)

...if you will not lay it to heart to give glory to my name, says the Lord of hosts, then I will send the curse on you; indeed I have already cursed them...

Lying is easy. It's the Truth that'll wear you down.

If living had taught her nothing else in ninety-some-odd years, Mattie Fuller had at least learned that fact. And as sure as those billowy, gray clouds were rolling in from the northwest to pay a visit with much needed rain, she knew that soon—and very soon—she would have another opportunity to lie. To whom? She didn't know. The exact time? She didn't know that, either. But soon.

"Gone, now. Git down," she scolded the mutts that were jumping, licking and nipping at her hands, bringing her round from the surety of the unknown to the here and now.

Now the strays, that were here tonight but might have moved on by morning, wanted water and the crushed, mutilated meat by-products in the open cans of Alpo. Mattie gave them what they begged for…and extra. A generous compensation for the lies and denials she would have to feed the prying visitors when they showed up to plague her. With empty cans left scattered in the yard—Governor would pick them up, he always did—Mattie slowly shuffled across the rock-hard dirt, eyes cast downward, searching the veins of the earth for a beginning and an end. Learning nothing from the dust, she climbed the steps of her back porch.

Lowering herself into her Mama's old rocking chair, her gray-rimmed, black eyes lifted to focus on the white Holy Bible with gold embossed lettering that was lying on a straight-back chair on the back porch next to her. It wasn't the color-infused pictures of Jesus Christ and his disciples or the maps of the ancient lands or the lyrical words of scripture that drew Mattie to it, but rather the secret concealed inside the covers of The Good Book. Inside those razor-induced slits were onion skin papers, some with her left-handed scrawl, and they contained the Truth of her family.

Her old eyes searched carefully around the backyard and beyond to the trees and woods and outlying structures that surrounded her family's home before reaching for the Bible and withdrawing the papers of Truth. Mattie unfolded and smoothed one sheet of the fragile document in her flower-print lap. As it always did, one name leaped off the page. That name, more than the others, twisted her heart, wringing a groan of agony out of her. It was the only name that made the paper of Truth a lie. Willie shouldn't be on the paper. His name should only be engraved on a headstone, not this flimsy paper weighted down with pain.

Big brother Willie, eighty years dead, along with the rest of the family, had just stirred to life in Mattie's memory. The rooster had crowed only minutes before, Mama had breakfast sizzling on the stove, and Daddy was already in the woods checking the pine tree harvest.

Helen, older than Willie, saw them coming first. Pitch-black, high-yellow, red-boned, damn-near white, honey-tan and velvet- brown in color. On foot, in carriages, on horses, and in wagons they came, crowding their big front yard. Family members all sharing the same blood, all seeking to absolve the hatred in their eyes, the fear in their hearts.

Helen had yelled and screamed, pulling the kids and Mama from their morning chores. Six of the seven residents of the house—Mama and five children, ranging in age from fourteen to three—crowded the front porch. Daddy was missing. Maybe if Daddy had been there Willie would have lived another day. Maybe not.

"Another death last night," said the leader, Uncle Jess. "We know it's your boy."

None of the six on the porch had to guess which of the three boys he meant. All eyes were fixed on Willie. Mischievous Willie, who used to pull Mattie's hair with one hand while giving her candy and fruit with the other. No one knew what to make of Willie's confusing ways.

"We're ending this right now, Aldana. Right now, it stops."

Mama pushed Willie behind her, trying to protect him from the hatred and ignorance that crowded her front yard. But Mama was a little woman and the rest just kids. What could they do to stop an intense mob—women, men, children, teenagers, all blood relatives—that pressed forward? Some held sticks, some knives, some pitchforks, some axes. All had ugly expressions on their faces.

Mama tried to reason with all that ugliness. "If he were the one, what you aim to do won't help. Only *I* can stop it."

"Hand him over." Uncle Jess stepped menacingly forward. They weren't willing to listen to common sense or family knowledge. They were too far gone; too filled with hate, fear and blood lust. "Don't make this hard."

Mama leaned down low and whispered something to Willie. But Uncle Jess must have heard it too, because as soon as Willie took off running around the side of the house, Uncle Jess and the family were right behind him. By the time the five on the porch made it to the backyard, the family had already disfigured Willie so badly, he was unrecognizable. Helen stood closest to the back porch, holding her ears, rocking, sobbing, screaming. Mattie bent low, toddling between the legs of the many aunts, uncles, and cousins who had changed her diaper, given her birthday presents, and passed her from one lap to the other in church.

Mama screamed and tried to stop the final blow of Uncle Jess's ax as it landed hard in Willie's chest, but hatred outwrestled a mother's love. Another Uncle locked Mama in his arms while Uncle Jess carved the heart from Willie's body and lifted it high for all to see. It was a deep burgundy red—not black, like they had imagined.

Hatred seeped out of the air like the sun evaporating moisture. Slowly, blindly, the dazed crowd stumbled to the front of the house. Anywhere but the place of their mistake. Confusion and disbelief clouded their faces. Regret rested on some of them, but for most, it was disbelief.

The family's loud bloodletting cries must have reached Daddy in the woods because he appeared as the last family member rounded the corner of the house. Daddy didn't need an explanation. The heart lying by the mutilated body of his first-born son was explanation enough. He fell to his knees, hands stretched wide, his chest heaving in and out, doing what it could to hold in his anger, the need for revenge, the pain. Willie had been thirteen years old and he was now dead for no reason other than desperation and fear.

And so, the family lived on. The curse lived on. But Willie was gone forever and his story...it was hushed up and eventually, it died too.

After a while, her parents had seemed to understand. She and her siblings had not. But eventually, Mattie understood—after she was given custody of the Bible and the Truth. She didn't have a choice but to understand, to accept, to protect; to do her duty to her family.

Mattie stared at the paper, wiping tears from her ancient eyes. With her crooked finger as a guide, she compared her memory to the names. Stopping at the last entry, she wondered if her unknown visitors would bring the end for her. Lord knows she prayed every day for deliverance. She was tired, heavy-hearted, and ready to leave the harshness of this family secret. Mattie was ready to be with Mama, Daddy, Helen, Willie, Floyd and Johnny in Heaven.

But Mattie's purpose was not yet complete. More names to scratch on the paper; and only the Lord knew how many more deaths before she could rest.

The same troubling spirit that had crawled into bed with Mattie crawled out again the following morning. Something's going to happen today, it nagged her through breakfast. Something that will lead to your finish, it warned her as she hung housedresses across the make-do clothesline in the bathroom. Something that will end with your death, it ridiculed her as she rocked in the living room, staring through the rain-spotted window, looking at nothing, waiting, with the family Bible lying in her lap.

Mattie had to wait longer than she wanted to, but finally they came— arriving in one of those high-riding trucks. They got out in slow molasses fashion, as if they were teasing her, taunting her. When the last door slammed shut, Mattie let the face towel that covered the small window on the front door fall back into place. Slowly, she twisted the rickety handle, letting the door fall open slightly so that a sliver of gray daylight slithered in. Her eyes squinted, straining to see through the wire screen and overcast haze, trying to see her future. A heavy sigh. Then, she unhooked the screen door and crossed the threshold to face her fate.

They didn't look scary. Actually, quite pretty. Nice-looking females. Maybe they weren't the visitors the troubling spirit had warned her of. Maybe they weren't the visitors who would help Mattie cross over from the physical to the spiritual world. Maybe they were just lost travelers, needing directions.

But the moment their feet touched the second porch step, making it groan in the spot that was rotten with age, Mattie knew they were supposed to be there. Mattie knew they were the manifestations the troubling spirit had heralded.

The same instant Mattie knew, the curse reached out and pushed her backward with Its force. The screen door caught her, holding her upright. Her aged hands clutched the area where her burgundy red heart pumped weakly, trying to protect it, to shield it from the curse. They were no protection. Mattie felt the curse riffling through the layers of her skin and bones to expose generations of family lies, secrets and Truths; it stopped at Mattie's heart. It hovered there, mocking her.

Scratching, grasping at her heart, Mattie tried to free herself of Its invasion. She banged her head against the screen, wishing she had remained wary and uncertain inside her family's house. She bent low and threw herself backward, hard, against the door, trying to dislodge the evil force, wishing someone, anyone else, had been given the burden of Truth Keeper.

Oh, it hurt! The pain exceeded that of losing Willie, of knowing the Truth. If only she had known the last time would be like this, she would have martyred herself many times before at the hands of the cursed one.

The curse played with her heart. It, too, knew this was Its last go-round with Mattie. Indeed, It challenged her to run to the woods as Willie had attempted to do or stay put and accept the unacceptable. Mattie wanted to cry out, to scuttle inside to her parent's bed and hide under the covers of their love. She wanted Governor's presence to bring her strength, to bring about peace and safety. But there was no help on earth for her. She had to overcome this—as she had lived most of her adult life—on her own.

Eyes shut tight, hands clasped fiercely together, Mattie desperately rocked her upper body. Forward, then back; forward, then back; forward, then back. Reaching past the fear and pain, she raised her "In-Me" spirit with a chorus of words of assurance: *Perfect love casts out all fear... Perfect love casts out all fear... Perfect love casts out all fear...*

After a while, her rocking became less frantic, breath steady, hands more relaxed as a sweet peace flowed through her. The words, a lullaby, soothed her flesh and spirit and lifted her higher than the fear and pain. A while longer, she felt the curse stirring, unsettling itself, then slowly, reluctantly, exiting her body, which sagged deeper into the screen door as the last bit of vapor left her. Despite the stiff, iron screen wires poking through her housedresses and raking her black skin, she smiled, savoring the lightness of her heart, enjoying the lift of her soul.

Gradually, her hands unfolded and fell to her sides; her gray-black eyes opened. Eyes that were once again full of strength. Eyes that were now fierce with duty.

Standing erect with the power of "In-Me" pounding through her aged body, she spoke forcefully, staring the oldest female directly in the eyes. "Let me go."

The woman, looking shocked and surprised, quickly heeded the command, releasing the grip she had on Mattie. "I... I...Are you okay?" She gathered herself and straightened to a height many inches taller than Mattie. A frown disgraced her pretty face. "I thought you were having a heart attack or something. I was...I wanted to help."

Mattie looked the woman good in the face. She frowned, seeing her family in the build of her face, in her mouth and eyes, but it was watered down, mixed with another family's blood. Mattie turned her head to stare at the young girl; a teenager who shared some of the woman's looks, but had taken a stronger liking for someone else's bloodline. Yes, they were her family and one of them had the curse.

Looking back and forth between the two, fear caused Mattie's scalp to tighten and her body to shiver. Instinctively, she crossed her arms under wilted breasts, readying herself for another battle, wondering if the cursed one knew she was both frightened of and grateful for the visit.

With a frown on her face and in her voice, Mattie asked the woman, "What you want?" knowing full well the purpose for the visit. It was time to record.

"Uhhhh, well..." The woman held out her hand, seeking a fresh start. "My name's Deborah King..." The woman dropped her ignored hand and circled an arm around the young girl's waist, lovingly drawing her closer to her side. "...and this is my daughter, Hope King." A tender glance from mother to daughter provoked pity in Mattie's heart. Cursed, and one of them didn't even know it.

In spite of the non-existent welcome, excitement lit the woman's face and words. She took a step closer to Mattie. "Are you Mattie Fuller? We're family...from Dallas."

Dallas. No wonder she hadn't felt the cursed one until today. The vibrations were strong, but not strong enough to reach Mattie from over a hundred miles away. But now, Mattie acknowledged the evil vibrations skipping across her skin like the indecisive touch of a fly. Mattie looked at the mother, then the daughter, wondering which one carried the curse. Which one was trying to intimidate her with the vibrations? Which one polluted the patch of air surrounding mother and daughter with the smell of blood? The smell offended Mattie's nostrils and informed her that the cursed one had already killed. It was a reminder that Mattie was going to die by her hands.

Deborah pushed the one-sided conversation forward. "Ummm, Shandra... Shandra Fuller, well, we just met her in town. She suggested we come and talk to you. She said you're the oldest living relative in the family and would be able to help."

Mattie stared knowingly at the woman, but the kind of help this woman and child needed Mattie couldn't provide. The Truth Keeper simply followed the lead of "In-Me," occasionally recorded and always hid the Truth. That was Mattie's job—a job she hadn't asked for.

"See, my daughter..." Mother turned to daughter and noticed a chill shook the girl's slender, teenage body. Deborah turned back to Mattie, frowning, "Do you mind if we come in? It's really wet out here and Hope has allergies, which the rain seems to stir up."

The spring shower *had* become mean since the pair arrived. The wind had doubled its howling and blew unanchored, lightweight debris around the yard. Not to be outdone, the rain flung itself between the thin, square columns dotting the porch, trying to batter and bruise mother and daughter with its sting. Both rain and wind joined Mattie in wanting the evil washed or blown from her front porch, from her life.

The nastiness of the weather didn't move Mattie's heart. A mother's genuine plea of concern for her child didn't shake her hold on tradition. "We talk here."

After Willie's death, Mama had not allowed outside family members inside their house. Mattie never knew if it were because of Willie or because the Truth resting inside the family Bible became a resident of their house shortly after Willie's death. She had asked Mama many times; Mama's answer had always been the same: their house was consecrated, pure, untouched by blood. Evil was not allowed inside. At the appropriate time, she learned it had been the latter reason, and she maintained the tradition; it had been easy to do. Family in town never visited, and that was better than all right with her.

Mattie shook her head. "We talk here or not at all."

Deborah drew her daughter closer still, giving Hope an apologetic smile. Mattie saw the confusion come to rest in the woman's brown eyes, but she didn't care. Family tradition was family tradition, and today it was being upheld in more than one way.

Quickly, Deborah unzipped her orange rain slicker and pulled a spiral notebook from an inside pocket. "Hope has a school project that we've been working on. It's a genealogy project for her social studies class. We're tracing our roots as far back as we can go." She flipped through the notebook until she came to a sheet of loose graphing paper. Holding the paper out to Mattie, she said, "The project is due this week, but we've got some gaps. We came to Partway this morning to spend time at the library and hopefully find and talk to family members. We were excited when the librarian...um, Shandra turned out to be a cousin." Deborah's joyous chuckle was picked up by the wind and mutilated.

Mattie just stared at her, listening and wondering if Governor could feel the cursed one from the cemetery.

"Shandra told us all she knew, even printed off some news clippings and old Census reports for us. She suggested we come here and interview you—"

Mattie cut her off with tight eyes and tighter words. "How you a Fuller?"

Deborah blinked quickly. A moment passed before she caught on to what the old woman was asking. "Oh, my father is a Fuller. But he couldn't offer—"

"Name some names." Mattie wanted to know just how ignorant they were or weren't.

"Excuse me?" Another confused blink.

Mattie stared at her. She didn't repeat herself. Just looked back and forth between mother and daughter, wondering how much they knew about the family's curse, wondering how the vibrations could be so strong, stronger than she had ever felt before, wondering how she would be killed.

"Well, ummm, looking at this diagram..." Deborah pointed to a name on a carefully drawn out family tree. "...it appears Hope and I come from Helen Fuller-Grant's line." Deborah looked up from the diagram to stare intently into Mattie's face. "Helen Fuller was your sister, right? You're my...our great aunt."

Since the end of slavery to now, the cursed ones had taken so many Fuller lives. So many innocent people had paid for bad blood. Helen had been one of them. Even though she had moved away to Dallas to try and escape, she hadn't really escaped. There was no escape.

With her mind retreating to the past, Mattie dully quoted, "Helen was my sister. Helen died. Lots of Fullers died."

"Could you tell us about—"

Mattie's back and the closing, locking of the door left Deborah's question quivering in the cool May air.

Inside the sacred house, Mattie leaned against the door, sliding down it to sit on the floor, legs spread out in front of her. Shoulders rounded, breathing shallow, a funereal look on her face as vintage images of Helen's death scene played in Mattie's mind. Outside, the young girl's whining served as background music.

"See, Mom, I told you this would be a waste of time. That old woman's crazy. Can we go home now?"

A few moments of silence, then the creak of the porch step. The slamming of doors. The start of an engine. The cursed one was gone—for now, but she'd be back. They always came back to Mattie.

The rain that helped wash the cursed one from Mattie's porch turned on her as she walked up the country lane to the FM road that led to the town cemetery. Mud sucked at her bare feet; heavy drops pelted her eyes; mad winds tried to push her down. Teasing air whipped her thin, cotton housedresses around her legs, restricting her forward movement. Still, Mattie marched on, determined to get to Governor.

A procession of long, dark cars streamed past her as she crossed under the cast iron archway that separated the dead from the supposed-to-be-living. The front of the cemetery had long been filled with permanent residents. A widespread case of typhoid fever in the nineteen-thirties had seen to that. Governor had to be in the back by the south wall—the only spaces still available for the recently deceased. She stomped that way and soon saw him. His tall, lean, crooked body propped on a shovel, smoking in the rain and staring at the dark hole in Mother Earth. He looked up, feeling her presence.

"Sit here." Governor Fuller ushered Mattie under a tarp to a folding chair that had been occupied minutes ago by the wife of the dearly departed. "I feel it strong on you, Mattie. The next one come to you, didn't it?"

"Gov'nor, I ain't never met it so strong. It tried to get in the house. It wanted the Bible and papers." Mattie rocked in the chair, arms wrapped around her middle, holding on tight. Her eyes fixed on the rectangular hole above which a smoke blue, stainless steel casket hung. A shame something so pretty had to be covered up with dirt. "Such pretty girls. Pretty and young."

"More than one?" The gathering of his brows showed an amazing level of confusion.

Mattie continued rocking, bobbing her head. "Don't know which one. The other's love was too strong to tell. But Its force ain't never been this strong. Never. I'm too old Gov'nor, too tired. Don't know if I can do this one."

"You got no choice, Mattie." His sympathetic, watery eyes stared through Mattie. "Cain't help 'til you're gone. You know that. You the one told me."

She stopped rocking and cocked her head toward Governor as if to see him better. With her old eyes full of fear and sadness, she stared at him, admitting, "It entered me. It hurt me. Hadn't done that b'fo... ever."

Except for the splashes of rain against the overhead tarp, there was silence while Governor seemed to fasten his mind around her words. That done, he stubbed his cigarette against the sole of his shoe and carefully tucked the butt in his monogrammed shirt pocket. With a gravelly voice formed by a pack a day for more than sixty years, he murmured to himself, "It comin' against her with all It got. It don't want the Truth recorded. It wants to destroy the Truth."

Even though they were meant for him, Mattie absorbed Governor's words and acknowledging them as true, she resumed rocking. Then, she finally spoke. Not to Governor, but to Heaven, to herself, sorting through the past so she could understand her ending. "I done all's been axed of me. Served longer than any b'fo me and all I prayed for in return is a peaceful death. In all these years, that all I axed for. But it ain't gonna be so. I'ma go like Helen, Willie, and all the others. Painful like, vi'lent. It gonna hurt real bad." Slow-running tears mixed with rain splotches on Mattie's black face. Her shoulders sagged; her head bowed. "Don't want it to hurt, Gov'nor. I done my duty and I done it good. Why do I got to go like the others?"

She knew that Governor didn't have an answer for her—not that Mattie was really looking for one. Comfort, that's what she needed, and she knew he would try to give it to her. He did, wrapping his long, wiry arms around her, pulling her into temporary safety. Her eyes closed, shutting out the open hole that called to her as she leaned into his strength. Images of Helen's, Willie's, and other closed casket services flicked through her mind. She knew her death would be bad and that she, too, would have a closed coffin.

After a few moments of accepting pity from her nephew, Mattie stiffened and pulled away, taking up once again the heavy cross her mother had left her to bear—record keeper of the Fuller family history. "It from Helen's line," she spoke softly, factually and went back to rocking and staring at that open hole that represented her future. "Never had one from Helen's line b'fo." Mattie sighed deeply. "Guess it was time. Guess it only right." She thought it appropriate to be killed by someone from her sister's line. Keep it close, in the immediate family. That would be the cleanest handoff to Governor. "I'll mark that on the paper." She spoke by rote, as if speaking of trivial, daily living matters.

Governor struck a match, lit a cigarette. "Thought the distance would break the connection, but blood is thick. Poor Helen. She should have known the curse couldn't be thinned out by distance." He paused to inhale deeply. "What they ask you? How they find you?"

"Shandra sent them to fill in blanks on a school paper." A short, bitter burst of laughter erupted from Mattie. "Silly girls. Tryin' to get good marks with bad blood, and they got the nerve to call *me* crazy."

Governor grunted his agreement. "It gonna be somethin' with the power bein' so strong." He took a long drag and then exhaled. "Wonder if it knows I'm next...after you."

"Closer I get to death, it'll know." Mattie looked around at the nearby headstones. She spotted one that looked like Mama's. "Right b'fo It killed Mama, It announced Itself to me. I knew and It knew." Mattie shook her head, remembering the bullying force of the evil one, barely an hour ago. "Still, all these years..." Mattie stood up, took a couple of steps toward the headstone as if she'd heard her Mama calling. "Never this strong. It might already know you."

She stood at the perimeter of cover, mindless of the savage rain that plastered the flower-print housedresses to her ashy black skin. With a calm expression on her face, she reported to Governor. "It killed three, maybe fo' times, already. Couldn't make out a death. All fam'ly...of course."

Governor's cigarette stopped partway to his mouth. He stared good and hard at Mattie. A long draw and a jumpy right eye told her how badly that news took him. "That tough, Mattie, real tough," he drawled. He sucked the last bit of nicotine into his lungs. The sole of his shoe put out the flame and his shirt pocket once again became a repository.

She wasn't sure if he referred to the deaths or her bad luck in having to deal with such a sure, strong force. Seconds later, she knew.

Governor stood and moved beyond the tarp's shelter to grab his shovel. "Be best if you hang 'round here 'til I'm through. I'll carry you home."

"I'll be fine. It gone back to Dallas. But..." she exposed herself completely to the weather, looking up at the dark sky, "...It be back. It cain't stand bein' away from fam'ly too long. 'sides..." Mattie held up her crooked finger, the one a gray cement brick had crushed when she was fighting a cursed one, "...the tables could turn and she could die b'fo me." She wagged her triumphant finger and smiled sadly, remembering the cursed one hadn't left her with a choice. It was either her or him, and Governor hadn't risen yet as her replacement, so Mattie knew it had to be him.

Mattie left Governor with that happy thought, but she knew and he knew and the evil one knew this was her last battle for the family. She would not win this one, but she also knew she wouldn't die until the final tasks were complete. She had a little bit of time. Not much, but enough to make sure Governor was ready to take the Bible and the papers.

Strutting over and around the headstones, being careful not to walk on the bodies six feet under, Mattie whispered words of assurance. Prayers slipped past her lips as she paid respect to those who'd passed through the spirit gates before her. Her prayers asked God to forgive her for her sins of lying, murder, almost suicide, swearing, and disobedience. She could have gone on, but as she scaled the list of sins, she thought about the scars—

physical and emotional—she'd collected for the sake of keeping the family secret just that—a secret. She thought about this last fight to come. But mostly, she thought about going to her heavenly home to be with Mama, Daddy, Helen, Willie, Floyd, and Johnny—the family she really loved and missed.

A silent house. A sink full of dirty dishes. Ten hours to fill.

Deborah King was not happy with the way her life had turned on her. Ignoring the top-of-the-line, stainless steel automatic dishwasher, she ran crisp, clean city water in one of the double sinks, added to it a little bleach, a lot of soap, and the mindless task of cleaning breakfast dishes began.

With six years of advanced schooling and studies toward a Ph.D. stuffed inside her brain, she stood at the sink with soap bubbles covering her wrists. What had happened? Oh yeah, she remembered. The stress and demands of being a research scientist had greatly diminished her good health, forcing an early departure from the profession she loved, followed by the birth of Hope eighteen years ago. Those two events had changed her life. At the time, she had hoped not forever. But as the days stretched into months, then years, Deborah had lost Deborah.

Now, all she knew about Deborah was that she had a daughter who would be a Spelman girl in three months and a husband who had no expectations of his wife other than a hot meal and hot sex every once in a while. In a few days when school let out, Deborah wouldn't have PTA, school assemblies, the Booster club, or chaperon opportunities with hormone-driven teenagers— Hope's high school activities that had helped to fill her ten hour days. In a few days, her life would be even more wasteful and unfulfilling; the days even longer. How could she get back to being Deborah? Who had Deborah been? What had made Deborah happy? What used to make Deborah get out of bed in the morning?

Instead of letting the tears fall, she held them in with a tenuous sigh. Activity. That's what she needed. Something to take her mind off self. Carefully folding the dish towel, she positioned it just-so on the bridge between the deep sinks and mentally began sifting through activities to fill nine hours and fifteen minutes. The bills were paid for the month; the financial accounts reconciled. Yard work was never an option; she hated it. Samuel had not left a list of errands for her to handle for him. There were no upcoming birthdays to plan for and Hope's graduation festivities had long ago been planned down to the tiniest detail. She didn't need anything from the grocery store and even with five hundred plus channels to choose from, there wasn't a show worth watching on television.

Activity to fill nine hours and fourteen minutes. Maybe phone talk. *Who's at home I can talk to?* Mother, daddy, husband, daughter, sister, nephew, brother-in-law, friends—most at work, some at school. She was the only person home during the day, the only one devoid of definition, of content. The only one lacking a purpose.

Activity to fill nine hours and thirteen minutes. *Reading. I've always enjoyed reading.* Deborah poured a fresh cup of coffee and settled in at the kitchen counter. While searching through the pile of Samuel's medical journals to locate her Journal of Biological Chemistry, Hope's social studies notebook fell to the floor.

Deborah moaned to the silent house. "Oh Lord, not again." How two professional perfectionists managed to have such a careless and irresponsible child, Deborah didn't know. After her sixteenth visit, Deborah quit counting the number of trips she had made to the high school to deliver abandoned homework assignments, school books, or lunch money.

Following the previous set pattern, she ran upstairs, changed into street clothes and raced downstairs to the garage. Deborah sped to the school not only to turn in her daughter's school project, but also to get away from eight hours and forty-two minutes of emptiness. She got all the way to the school and was walking up the wide cement staircase when she remembered Hope had turned in the genealogy project over a week ago. At the end-of-the-year school dance last Friday night, Hope's teacher had told Deborah how impressed she had been with Hope's family tree and that Hope had gotten an A.

Reminded again of how pitiful her life had become, Deborah returned to her SUV. Sitting inside, desperately gripping the steering wheel, she tried to avoid the mirrors so she wouldn't have to see her sorry self and was successful at doing that until she started the truck and checked her rearview mirror for traffic. There she was looking sad and useless and that's when the tears gushed out. They came and came, each wave heavier, more forceful than the last until finally they reached a climax and petered out. Feeling less desperate, but still empty, Deborah sniffed, reaching for tissues to smooth and pat her face, blow her nose, and mop the last of the tears. When all the damage had been cleared, she tried smiling, cheering herself on, "You're okay, Deborah, you're going to be okay." But it was a lie; her smile, fake; her words as hollow and empty as she. Deborah couldn't even maintain eye contact with herself. Her head dropped and her shoulders drooped as she cried out, "Help me, please, help."

The tears were on the cusp again, but Hope's smart comment from last week trumped the deluge. "I'm turning my project in with blanks and all. And I *bet* I still get a passing grade because *I'm* sure the other kids' moms didn't *force* them to go to some dusty old town that's stuck in a time warp to meet relatives they could care less about. If *you* don't think this family tree is complete enough, *you* finish it." The girl had contemptuously tossed the social studies project at her mom and stomped out of the room.

"If *you* don't think it's complete enough, *you* finish it." Hope's careless words filled the truck.

"*You* finish it." Hope's sassy words planted a seed.

"...finish it." Hope's command caused a seed to burst open.

"...finish..." Hope's directive generated new life.

Purpose and meaning sprouted from the verbal manure of an eighteen-year-old girl-child. Deborah gunned the motor and yanked the stick into drive. An illegal U-turn and a speed in excess of what the city allowed facilitated Deborah's arrival at the downtown Dallas public library.

It didn't matter that Deborah was the youngest person in the genealogy research room. It didn't matter that Deborah was one of few persons of color in the room. It didn't matter that she had a daunting number of blanks to fill in on their family tree. It didn't matter that she had never done *this* type of research before. What mattered was that life had purpose. Deborah had meaning.

This was Mattie's place. Her sanctuary. Black Hill.

Black Hill, with its rusty old crooked-hanging gates that held open year round; its chipped, leaning, and fallen headstones; its thick-based, venerable oak trees, stationed like lookout towers throughout the cemetery, watching the going-in and the coming-out of the physical and spiritual beings. This place warmed her, made her smile, comforted her. Walking into this holy piece of land felt like walking into her mother's arms. She visited this place every day and always it renewed her, providing a temporary pardon from the sentence of living.

Mama was here. Daddy, Helen, Willie, Floyd and Johnny. Everybody was here, except her. So, she came and talked to them. Cared for them. Rested with them—their remains below the earth and she above, head to head, her stomach flat against the fertile ground. In her favorite place, in her favorite position, she talked to her Mama, asking her questions that she sometimes got answers to. What was dying like? Does the spirit separating from the body hurt? Is there really a light and angels to guide the way? Is there a long check-in line at the Pearly Gates? Who checks the Book of Names? ...St. Peter? ...Gabriel? ...Jesus, himself? Does hell really exist? Are all of the BlackHearts in hell? Does God really forgive all sins? ...including her sin of simultaneously loving and hating her family?

Mama never talked long. Her days in heaven—whatever timeframe that was—were as full as her days on earth had been. And now—as in the days when Mama physically walked the earth—she grew tired of Mattie's endless questions and gently encouraged her to go play with her sister and brothers.

Mattie got up from her mother's grave, not bothering to brush the crushed leaves, small sticks and clinging ants from the front of her housedresses. She stepped across the narrow grassy aisle, went one row back and one row over closer to the creek and lay down between Helen and Willie. They were more talkative than Mama. Probably because as the oldest, they felt the need to guide her in life lessons. And, of course, Willie had to tease her relentlessly...

still. Those two had plenty to say all the time.

She hadn't started her visit good when she felt the intruder. Mattie went still, reluctant to turn and acknowledge with her eyes what she knew in her heart. Troubled company had just arrived in that high-riding truck.

"She here," Mattie whispered to her sister and brother.

"We know," they whispered back to her in an awesome, unified voice.

"Take care, baby sis." Willie expressed his concern gently.

"She's beautiful," Helen's wondrous voice exclaimed. "She's mine." She claimed the visitor, declaring what all of them already knew.

For Helen's sake, Mattie turned onto her side to face the front of the cemetery. She watched as the woman got out of the truck. "She does look like you, Helen."

Even the birds and crickets silenced their songs as the living and dead watched the woman walk through the gates, her eyes searching for Mattie among the icons of death.

"Make yourself known, Mattie," Helen spoke reverently.

Mattie slowly stood up, her eyes staring through the woman, trying to see her heart.

"Let's go, Helen," Willie spoke in a pressing manner, "This is livin' folk business."

"I just want to feel her, touch her," Helen pleaded, love in her voice.

"Let's go, Helen," Willie urgently repeated.

Mattie felt his spirit depart, followed moments later by Helen's loving presence. She would have given anything except the family Bible and papers of Truth for Helen not to have to leave. Helen had so desperately wanted to wrap her down-the-line relative in love. Mattie understood that, empathized with Helen's heartache, knowing it was her line that killed this time. She was sure Helen wanted to counter the killings with love, but as Willie had said, this was living folk business. Helen had to give up her intention. Helen had to go.

Alone again. Alone with the burdensome task of family record keeper and handler of the Truth. Mattie trudged forward, knowing what the visitor wanted.

"Good morning..." The woman's voice floated to Mattie from several feet away.

Mattie stared at the woman, watching her as closely as a mother watched a sick child. As she waited for the woman to reach her, Mattie thought about building her defenses, conjuring "In-Me"—just in case. But the residue of Helen's presence and the love her sister had left behind anchored Mattie's defenses. She stood unprotected as Helen's blood child smiled in her face.

"Shandra said you'd probably be here. I'll have to tell her she was right." The blessed smile she gave Mattie would have been downright beautiful if she didn't have evil attached to it.

"I don't know if you remember me, but my daughter and I were here a few weeks ago. We're researching our family tree."

Mattie nodded, thinking how silly of the woman to think the recorder of Truth could forget meeting the BlackHeart, the cursed one.

"I think you were ill at the time and couldn't help us. But I really would like to ask you a few questions. You see, those of us in Dallas, we've been estranged for so long. I don't know anything about Daddy's people, and when I asked him, he didn't know much about this..." Deborah waved her hand to encompass the general geography. "I really would like to know."

Helen's ever-presence moved in Mattie's heart. It stomped out the resistance that reared within her. *Mattie, please give her a little of what she's asking for. Please, before she dies.* Mattie heard Helen and obeyed.

Without rearranging her cast-iron facial features, Mattie motioned for the woman to follow her. She crossed the main aisle—a beaten down, trodden footpath—to start at genesis.

"Fullers've been here since the beginnin'," she recited, leading Deborah to a weathered old tombstone that read: CHARLES FULLER – *Born a Slave – Died a Free Man* – *1790-1867*. Most people knew him as the progenitor of the family, but few knew he was the man responsible for the curse.

"Such beautiful roses," said Deborah, admiring the bush of red American Beauties that bloomed in front of Charles Fuller's grave.

Mattie ignored Deborah and continued her lecture. "Fuller the name of the plantation man who owned great-great-granddaddy. He got his freedom. Started a town." Mattie pointed her crooked finger in the general direction of Partway. "Fullertown."

"Fullertown? I thought the town was called Partway?"

Mattie stared hard at the woman, telling her silently with her eyes that she shouldn't interrupt her history lesson, a history lesson normally reserved for the record keepers, a history lesson that Mattie shared because it was Helen's wish for her to do so. Mattie's hard, black eyes told Deborah she should be thankful she had given up visiting time with the family she *really* loved and cherished, and that Deborah should show her thanks with a shut mouth. All of this communicated with one look.

"When the 'ficial gov'ment folk come thru, they couldn't stomach a town named after a black man. Changed it to Partway 'cause it part way 'tween Dallas and Austin. Got a big laugh 'outta that. White folk started movin' here after the name change." A deep pause punctuated the sadness of that long ago time. "That was the end of that and the beginnin' of sumthin' else." Mattie stopped at this period of Fuller history. She could have gone on and told Deborah *that* was the start of the family curse. She could have explained *what* caused the curse and *how* it led to the killing and estrangement of family. She could have told Deborah *how* to eradicate the curse. But that part of history was sealed tight in the hearts of the past and present recorders of Truth and in that Bible in her living room.

Deborah opened her mouth to speak, must have seen the wickedness in Mattie's eyes and closed it.

Returning to the beginning of their family tree, Mattie continued her oral lecture. "This stone's his wife. Thems over there and by the gate…" Mattie led Deborah to an uneven row of flat stones with first names crudely chiseled into the smooth surface. "…they chillen."

Deborah knelt to study the evidence of her bloodline while Mattie moved on, returning to the main path, anxious to get this woman out of her sanctuary. She'd done what Helen had asked her to do. Give her a little bit. And that's what Mattie had done. Obligation met. Now she wanted the woman gone.

After several minutes, Deborah apparently realized she was alone. Looking up and around, she spotted Mattie on the other side of the cemetery staring down at two headstones so close together they looked like one. She rushed over to where Mattie stood. Forgetful of Mattie's rule to be quiet, she spoke, nearly out of breath, "How do you move so quickly without shoes? Aren't those rocks and sticks hurting your feet?"

Mattie just stared at her blood relative, wondering how the woman could be so concerned about a simple thing like shoes when family lay dead and were dying around her.

Unaware of Mattie's harsh thoughts, Deborah smiled in Mattie's face, offering, "I have some extra ones in the car. Shoes I use for driving. I can go get them. You can have them."

"I got shoes." Mattie didn't need her hand-me-downs. It was Deborah who needed pity and help, but she'd learn that soon enough. Mattie continued with her lesson. "Yo' daddy from Helen's line." Mattie picked up on their family markers, skipping generations. "She buried here." Mattie pointed to Helen's grave.

The outline of Mattie's body, where she'd been lying and enjoying her sister's and brother's spirits before Deborah had interrupted, was still visible. Ignorant of that outline, yet drawn to the spot, Deborah knelt and fingered the headstone as if it were a priceless family heirloom. And indeed, it was. "So, this is my great, great, great grandmother."

Mattie could have told her Helen was murdered by the BlackHeart and that two rows over lay the black hearted cousin who had beaten and choked the life out of Helen. Because she had responsibility for the Bible and papers, she could not point out the grave markers for every family member who had carried the curse. She could not show Deborah the headstones for every cousin, aunt, uncle, mother, father, sister, brother, niece, nephew, granny, or grandpa who had died at the hands of the cursed ones. That knowledge remained where it should be.

Deborah didn't know there was more, and so awe and excitement quelled within her, spilling onto her face and seeming to reach out to Mattie to try and draw her into this important moment of discovery. Mattie rejected the bond, shook it off as easily as a fly and stood immovable like one of the oak trees that guarded the cemetery. She surveyed the plot of land, turning her mind to practical things like wondering where the current BlackHeart would be buried. There was still room on this private piece of land, but considering the Dallas lineage, more likely burial would be in Dallas. That was fine with Mattie. She had her own death and burial to ponder.

The woman's voice pulled Mattie from her sure future. "I've spent a lot of time tracing our roots, researching our tree and connecting the lines. And I've been pleased and surprised by the amount of information available on our family." Deborah reached into her shoulder bag and pulled out a notebook. She flipped through several pages, finally landing on a page she liked. "I haven't had any problems. No roadblocks uncovering names or dates like some of the folks in the genealogy room. Information on our family seems to be everywhere."

A feeling of unease started rising in Mattie. Where was this leading? What was she up to? Perhaps trying to make it seem that the cursed legacy was publicly known? On their first visit to Mattie, the BlackHeart had been crafty in trying to get in the house to steal the proof of their family's murderous ways. That hadn't worked, and neither would anything else the BlackHeart devised. As long as her eyes opened to see the rising sun, Mattie would never give the Bible and papers of Truth to a BlackHeart. She would never disappoint herself or the Fullers in that way. Because even though she both hated and loved her family, as long as she remained strong and held on to the Truth there was hope that one day the Fullers could be freed from this life-stealing curse.

Unease moved out of the way for sudden darkness. It was the middle of a yellow-washed June day, yet Mattie felt like someone had pulled the power cord on the sun. The landscape inside her mind and the landscape of Black Hill went dark. The smell of blood penetrated her nostrils, and she knew someone—a family member—was going to die soon. A high-pitched scream echoed through her head. The victim's name materialized. Then, a violent tremble shook Mattie's small frame, almost pitching her off her feet. Tears conceived from sadness, frustration and defeat formed in Mattie's wise eyes and tracked down her cheeks.

Deborah's head was buried in her notebook, totally ignorant of Mattie's premonition and of the role she performed in the ongoing play of the cursed family. She spoke, obviously unaware of anything but the need to keep her own purpose alive. "Lots of public records, but I was wondering..." She finally looked up, but the sun's highly-watted rays prevented a serious study of Mattie's face.

She squinted, eyes more than halfway closed with a hand shading them. "...if you know of any family kept records? ...a journal, bible, scrapbook. Shandra mentioned something about a collection of records passing from elder to elder. She wasn't sure if it was myth or reality, though. If family-held records exist, I'd like to use them to validate the public records."

Wrapping her arms around herself, Mattie closed her eyes, rocking in time to her silent mantra, to her words of rightness. *Perfect love casts out all fear... Perfect love casts out all fear... Perfect love casts out all fear...*

Finally sensing the change in Mattie, Deborah rose from her crouching position, deep concern networking itself across her face. "Ummm..." She touched the old woman's arm. "Are you okay?"

Mattie backed away from the woman. She didn't need sight to plan her steps. She knew this place as well as she knew her family home. Four steps back and she would be at the edge of Benny's grave. Benny was a cousin who died naturally. Nothing important about his death. Somehow, that thought comforted her, helped her get right. The rocking stopped abruptly. The cantations droned to silence. Turmoil and uncertainty fell to pieces like wet newsprint.

Anger took its place.

How dare this woman come into Mattie's holy sanctuary and tarnish its peace with such trickery! How dare she try to manipulate Mattie into acknowledging the existence of the Bible and papers!

Oh, yes! This BlackHeart was not only strong in spirit, but also smart. Smart enough to try and use other's weaknesses and innocence. Smart enough to lean on strong family relations to get what she wanted. But the BlackHeart had misjudged. She had succeeded in doing nothing but making Mattie very, very angry.

The urge to pick up a rock and smash the woman's head filled Mattie, but "In-Me" warned her that wasn't the way it would be. Although it was likely they would both die—Mattie for sure—now was not the time. And a rock was not the way. "In-Me" would tell her when and how.

The woman's voice interrupted the guidance of "In-Me."

"I can take you home. You don't look very good."

Mattie looked at worry lines grooving the woman's face. Pity and a fresh surge of anger engulfed her. Pity that for all her smarts and college degrees, Deborah couldn't discern evil. Anger because Deborah allowed evil to use her.

As the woman took hesitant baby steps toward her with hands stretched out to help, Mattie retreated. "No," she hissed. Another second in this woman's presence and Mattie might give in to temptation and split the woman's head wide open.

"It's no bother. I'm on the way to town to review some autopsies. I can drop you off. Get you settled." Quickly, the woman dropped to the ground, feverishly stuffing notebooks and writing tools into her bag.

Mattie watched for a split second, tethering her anger. Then Indian quiet, she slipped off toward the closest oak, over the fence and carefully down the cliff face to cross the creek, headed for home. Home to the paper of Truth; it was time to record.

The Bible lay open on her lap, the paper of Truth on top of it. Mattie stared at the paper, smoothing it over and over as if trying to rub the casualties out of existence. She forced herself to stop. Stop wishing things could be different. Stop worrying about her own death. Stop thinking about the unfairness of it all. Stop troubling herself about Governor and the yoke that would eventually be his.

In her poor, left-handed penmanship, she scrawled the name of the current BlackHeart, along with the current date. She stared at the name, wondering how much longer before the final tussle between her and Mattie. Wondering if any others would die, excepting the three that were known and the one that would be happening soon. Would the curse ever willingly leave their family? And if so, would it then go on to terrorize another family? How much longer for the Fullers, oh Lord, how long?

Mattie flipped the aged paper over and tried to write the blood names. Her hand faltered over the first letter of the first name. It was blurry, unclear, probably because it had been a little baby, not too long out of the womb, unable to speak and make itself known to Mattie. It had died within months of living; suffocated. So sad, but necessary for the curse to go on. Closing her eyes, she leaned her head back, welcoming the spirits, welcoming family. A vision rose in her mind. A sweet baby bundled in a pink blanket, fists balled tight, big, bright eyes. *Rachel King*. The name appeared. Mattie wrote it on the paper of Truth.

Now, an older person, a woman, came to Mattie. Deborah's sister, one of the twins who were younger than Deborah by eighteen months—killed by the BlackHeart, but written up by the police as a drowning accident. Mattie knew the truth. She wrote the name *Anna Fuller* on the paper.

The third name, a teenage boy, athletic, smart and handsome, a few years older than Deborah's child, Hope. His smooth face showed no sign of fright or disbelief when he introduced himself to Mattie. *My name's Curtis Matthews, Deborah's nephew. I had just signed a letter of intent to play ball for Georgetown when the BlackHeart killed me. I saw it coming, but didn't think she would actually pull the trigger. I thought she was playing.* Mattie peered at the boy's temple, the point of the bullet's entrance. In the transition from the physical world to the world of spirits, everything was made new again and the once torn and jagged flesh lay smooth. No sign of violence. Mattie liked that. The police had written it up as a gunshot accident. Shaking her head, a sad scowl on her face, Mattie recorded the Truth.

Mattie knew the fourth name. The premonition had come to her hours ago at Black Hill. This relative was closer to her in lineage and in distance, so close that even though the young librarian and cousin of Deborah wasn't dead yet, Mattie could feel death stalking *Shandra Fuller*. The mother of two and wife of no man anymore would die next weekend at the graveside cleaning service at Black Hill.

Three—soon to be four—family members killed by cursed hands, sacrificial monuments to the BlackHeart.

Emotionally wasted from the recording exercise, Mattie lacked the energy to fold the paper and place it back inside its slot at the back of the Bible. She dropped her head to her chest, clearing her mind. Rest.

Time passed.

She stirred, feeling the presence of Governor. Time for another lesson. Not too many more lessons to go and soon, Governor would know all she knew.

Though they knew him, the dogs made a big noise when Governor shuffled into the backyard. They always thought his picking up the empty cans of dog food scattered among the dirt and weeds was a game. Dumb dogs. They didn't know Governor was addicted to order and rightness.

The back door creaked open. Governor's scraping steps marked his passage into the kitchen and then the small dining room to the living room where Mattie sat in her rocker, the family papers still resting on her lap.

"Spirits've been here," Governor stated unnecessarily. He grunted as he sat on the sofa.

Mattie didn't open her eyes or stop rocking. "My time's 'bout gone." She pointed her crooked finger at him. "You next," she reported needlessly.

Governor nodded his head at the paper. "Got it all down?" He eased into the lumpy cushions, settling in as if paying a polite social visit and not here to learn more of the horrid past and future of his family. He dug in his work shirt pocket, producing a freshly rolled cigarette.

Mattie tapped the paper. "It all here. Her name. Their names. Ever'thin's in order."

Lifting her heavy eyelids, she stared at the wall in front of her. The cheaply framed pictures of Dr. Martin Luther King, Jr. and President John F. Kennedy encouraged her, gave her a little bit of hope. If those two men could dream of a bright, harmonious future for all and believe in the ultimate goodness of man, why couldn't she dream the same for her family? Why couldn't she believe that one day the generational curse that suffocated her family would be lifted? Why couldn't she entertain visions of a "good" Fuller family, a family devoid of black hearts that pumped evil? Why couldn't she dream that one day the Fullers would be free to live like other families with only drug addiction, alcoholism, incest, adultery and financial problems to worry about? She sighed, negating belief and hope. The dreams of those righteous men might come true one day, but not so for the Fullers. Their future, their goodness died a slow death under the weight of a murderous pact. An agreement that left no room for dreaming or hoping or wishing. A second sigh full of heartbreak filled the room. No matter how many times a day she dreamed or fantasized about breaking free of the curse, she knew in the deepest corner of her soul it would never happen. Her family had sinned too grievously. Her family had disgraced God and turned their back on him. And for that, they had to pay.

Finally turning to Governor, she reported, "She came to see me today. At Black Hill."

Governor grunted low and long. "Which one got it? Mama or daughter?"

Mattie handed the paper of Truth to Governor. He read, and then slowly shook his head. "Gonna be tough. They mighty close." He fired up a match and lit one end of the unfiltered, homemade stick. "Say anything important?"

"Pokin' about for some way to get her hands on that..." Mattie pointed at the paper in Governor's prominently-veined and scarred hands. Hands that would someday have to kill, she was sure, but for now, those hands just buried the dead.

Governor handed it back over and this time Mattie slid the paper home. Reverently, she closed the Bible and got up slowly from her rocker to place it on the heirloom roll-top desk against the short wall in the room. "She talked public records. Was headed into town to get death records and all. This BlackHeart is slick. Slickest one so far."

"You can handle her."

"May just hafta kill her next weekend. Stop her 'fo she get holda sumthin' she don' need to get holda." Mattie spoke her thoughts aloud, wondering if this plan was seconded by "In-Me." She turned her senses inward, waiting to feel a response, hear a message from her guiding spirit.

"We all gonna die eventually, anyways," Governor stated, "Might as well get it over with 'fo too much harm done."

Mattie heard, but didn't hear Governor. She was tuned inward, waiting for "In-Me" to tell her what to do. She, like previous record keepers, knew not to make a move without the guidance of "In-Me." To avoid insanity, they never took a life, never saved a life, wouldn't lift a weapon to change destiny unless "In-Me" clearly directed them to.

"In-Me" spoke. *"Not yet,"* it told her. *"More time to pass."*

Disappointed that she had yet more time on earth but relieved that the painful death she feared would be delayed, Mattie gave herself back to the physical world in time to hear Governor say, "Saw Shandra yestaday. Po' girl's all excited 'bout the graveside service. She went on and on 'bout the relatives in Dallas comin' fo' the first time since..."

"...since Helen was murdered by the BlackHeart. Shandra ain't got sense 'nuff to stay away from the BlackHeart." Mattie spoke in a censuring tone, uncaring that the girl had no idea she was next in line for murder. It was better that way for Mattie. The heartache and frustration of knowing, but not being able to do a thing about it went down easier that way. The pain, less wearying that way.

"I'm goin' next weekend. See fo' myself."

In the early years of living, Mattie had attended the annual family gathering at Black Hill where descendants of the original Fullers would gather to remove trash, tree limbs and rocks, anything they felt didn't belong in Black Hill, the private, family-only cemetery that sat on original Fuller land. Even after Willie's massacre her family attended. But with the passing of her immediate people and the daily visits with them, there was no reason, no need for Mattie to attend. She wasn't interested in knowing Uncle Jess's folks or Mable's grandchildren or cousin Delia's nieces and nephews. Those people simply represented names that could end up on her thin sheets of paper and faces that could end up in her memory.

Even with Shandra's death at the graveside, her mind asked, *you still don't want to go?* Mattie shook her head. Even with Shandra's death as the highlight of this year's gathering, she still didn't feel inclined to go. No need to go when Shandra, in spirit form, would come and tell Aunt Mattie all about it.

"Be a good time to start feelin' out yo' replacement," Mattie spoke softly while fixing Governor with a hard stare. She had to stare at him; she needed to see in his eyes that he was ready. Ready to be by himself like she had been for more years than not. Ready to carry this heavy load by himself. Ready to serve his family in a difficult way. Mattie was glad to see no hesitation, no uncertainty, no confusion or fear in his eyes.

She smiled, pleased with the celestial selection of Governor as the next-in-line recorder. Her mind traveled back, taking pleasure in a momentary escape from her everyday world of curses, black hearts and family secrets. "I 'member when I first felt you. I was so glad. I was gettin' worried, thinkin' I was gonna hafta do this forever. Then, I felt you—at Black Hill."

§

Governor grunted mildly; his ghostly smile said he remembered, too.

It had been an average day in January—cool, say the 50's, but dry. No wind. A major snowstorm a few days before had stripped some of the oaks of their magnificence and now limbs, branches, and twigs mixed with snowdrifts to make Black Hill downright scary-looking. With no dead to bury, Governor had taken the free day to clear the cemetery. After plowing several paths, he'd loaded and hauled off one pickup bed of downed timber and was nearly through loading a second when Mattie walked up on him, quiet even though she wore sturdy work boots. Mattie had raised that crooked finger to his face, stared through him and declared, "You the next keeper of the fam'ly records. Come to my house tonight fo' yo' first lesson."

Until that moment, she'd had no words for him, had not exchanged a head nod or careless wave. She in no way acknowledged his humanness, yet in spite of years of being slighted, Governor found himself nodding his head, and soon thereafter staring at her back as she walked away without even a farewell or goodbye.

For some time Governor stood there by his old work truck, staring at her departing path, wondering why he'd agreed. He didn't understand her invitation, didn't know what she'd been talking about. Keeper of family records. A lesson. Alien talk to him. And not only that, he wasn't keen about going to her house. As far as he or any other Fuller knew, she never received company. Of course, there were the necessary visitors—the men who bought her pine trees and turned them into Christmas tree profit. The men who sported deer and wild hogs on her property—for a fee, of course, payable to Mattie Fuller. But social visits, family visits or the like, Mattie highly discouraged with a rusty butcher knife, and everybody in Partway, plus the surrounding counties, knew it.

So why had he agreed?

All that afternoon while he cleared his family's cemetery he searched for an answer. And in between searching he changed his mind every minute about going to her house or not going. One minute he decided to go and satisfy his curiosity. The next minute he said no; he didn't owe her anything. The next, he decided to go; then not. At nightfall he found himself tromping through the high snow in her front yard, up those aged steps and knocking on her screen door, still of a mixed mind.

The first knock met with no response. After a considerable time, allowing for her age, he knocked again. Still, he heard no rustling about, no shouts of "hold on" or "I'ma comin'." Nothing.

He raised his hand to knock a third time, wondering if she had played some mean-spirited trick on him. But no, he was supposed to be there. That much he knew, or else he would be at his own house in front of the warm stove, reading or tinkering with some mechanical device. Yes, he was definitely in the right place, or else he would have stayed home and not risked his life driving over the slushy roads of downtown and residential Partway, then finally traversing two patched and weary blacktop county roads that were now treacherous because of hidden slick spots. Something more compelling than his good common sense had forced him here.

He heard dog sounds coming from the back and decided he might as well check the property since he was there. He didn't imagine she would be outside since the weather had dropped a full twenty degrees since he'd last seen her, but something was causing the dogs to yelp, whine and bark. If not Mattie, then some wild animal. Might as well investigate.

Stopping by his truck momentarily to get the shovel, he gripped it securely and then rounded the corner of her house. Sure enough, there was a pack of dogs and in the middle of them, Mattie Fuller. Bent over, she was scooping food from an open can as quickly as she could and yet could not keep up with the canines' demands. Governor didn't say a word. He strode forward, snatched the manual can opener that hung from her coat pocket and opened a second can. Then a third and a fourth and by that time, they had a routine. He opened, she scooped, and soon the dog sounds decreased to a pleasing level.

Finally, Mattie straightened, looked at Governor and nodded toward her house. He followed her, picking up the empty cans and lids and dumping them in the waste container outside by the back porch. Yet another routine established.

For the first time ever, he entered Mattie's house. There was nothing special, demonic, or odd about it. It was normal—plain old walls upon which hung vintage photos of Fullers, dead and gone, intermingled with wall plaques of favorite sayings; plain old wood floors upon which stood outdated appliances, woven rugs and antique furniture; and plain old home smells of the usual sort.

Mattie stopped in the living room, gestured to the sofa for Governor to sit and then picked up a heavy white Bible with gold-edged pages. Governor thought it the most beautiful Bible he'd ever seen in his life. He couldn't seem to look anywhere else but at it, even when Mattie carried it with her to her rocker. He swore he heard it speak his name, but perhaps that was the squeak of Mattie's rocker as she settled in.

"You got inner strength. Strong ties to what's in you," Mattie said, opening the Bible from the back, which Governor thought odd. "'In- Me' what the people like us call it. Reg'lar folk call it Holy Spirit, but it ain't the same. Reg'lar folk can ignore it. We cain't. Cain't never get away from it. That good *and* bad." Mattie fixed Governor with a hard look that he soon came to know as her most earnest look. "You gettin' this?" she'd asked harshly.

No, he didn't, and although he didn't admit it, she must have read it in his eyes because she elaborated. "You got insight you cain't explain. Know things you oughtn'ta. Feel and sense things others don't."

Now, Governor became nervous. *How did she know that?* How did she know that since childhood he could envision a certain Fuller's death? Not the manner of death—although sometimes that, too—but the name, for sure. How did she know that at times he could sense the presence of good and bad spirits? That some of his decisions were based on nothing more than a "feeling from inside." She, who had never interacted with him and yet she knew this most intimate thing about him. He leaned back in his seat as far away from her as possible and automatically dug for a cigarette. He needed something to keep his hands moving, busy, so his mind would settle.

"You got a gift and a responsibility, and ain't neither one easy." She finally released him from her hard stare. Laying her head against the rocker she began rocking back and forth slowly. Her eyes focused on the wall before her.

They sat in silence for several seconds. Governor, because his head buzzed with so many questions and thoughts he could hardly acknowledge one before another crowded in. Near to overwhelmed, he lit the cigarette, took a drag, and that helped to force his mind to stillness.

"You got questions," Mattie told him, keeping her eyes on the wall.

That he did, and just hearing her say it lined them up nice and neat in his head. "How come I got it? This gift. Mama didn't. Daddy didn't. None of my brothers or sisters had it, that I know of."

"Why some babies got two heads, one body? Why some people got one eye brown, t'other eye blue? 'Cause that the way God wanted it. He chose you. You special."

"You got it too?"

"Yes and my Mama." She sighed. "They only a few of us. Right now, jus' me 'n you."

"What you do with it? Is that the 'sponsibility, the lesson you talked about?"

"Yeah, but we save that fo' 'nother time. Tonight, you got to be com'table with what the Lord give you." She turned to him and pinned him hard again. "You okay with bein' on speakin' terms with Death? Can you follow orders, hold your peace? You al'right bein' alone and lonely?"

He exhaled smoke and said, "Seems like I got no choice."

She continued staring at him. He returned the stare, and she finally nodded. "You gonna be all right."

§

That had been the end of the first lesson and now, almost twenty years later, Governor sat in Mattie's small house, still in awe of the emotions that he'd had when he left Mattie's place that night—relief and fear. He'd been relieved to know that his ability to sense people and spirits and to know things by tuning inward was a gift with a purpose. He'd been relieved to learn that he was normal in that every so often a Fuller child was born with this gift, and that the gift allowed him or her access to both worlds—the spiritual and the material.

It had also scared him. Scared him so badly he had not been able to sleep that night and for many nights after. He feared the future lessons, sensing they would not be as gentle as the first one. He feared his own future, wondering if this gift meant he would end up like Mattie, separated from family, alone with straggly mutts for company. It scared him that he might not be able to live up to the responsibilities of the gift.

However, over the years as he gained more knowledge and experience, those feelings had lessened, and now he viewed his gift and approaching duty as ordinary, as commonplace as waking and rising. He didn't take it for granted, though. He would never do that, but after witnessing a few cursed deaths, it had become normal. A while back, when he'd mentioned his observation to Mattie, she'd simply said, "Grown into yo' position. Near 'bouts ready."

She was right. Governor had developed a mind and a stomach for death, assisted no doubt, by his chosen career as a cemetery caretaker. He didn't tremble at pools of blood, didn't sicken at the smell of decay. Would not hesitate to kill or allow killing if so instructed by "In-Me." He knew where all of the killed and killers were buried. Could recite the family history and the story of the curse in his sleep. Knew how to call and talk to the spirits and his own "In-Me." He had grown strong, creating a shell around his heart and mind that was as tough as Mattie's. Mattie had even complimented him, saying, "You better at pinchin' off yo' 'motions and feel'ins than me."

That had been a bittersweet compliment for it reminded Governor of the life accessories, a wife and children, he had given up because of his gift. Like so many prophets in the Bible, Governor had forsaken his desire for love and marriage, but that did not stop him from thinking about "her" or what their life together would have been like.

Cora Jean Williams being the "her." The love of his life. The woman he'd bought a ring for but never presented to her because in his twenties, when he'd thought about claiming her, something inside had held him back—his gift. It had known, even though Governor hadn't at the time, that his life would be best lived alone. So, he shelved the ring and Cora Jean had gone on to marry another, even though she and Governor both knew their hearts were entwined forever. Throughout her marriage to the other, up until her death, when they passed each other on the streets of Partway their greeting was always kind and their parting always entailed a backward glance.

Here in Mattie's house, as he reflected upon the only thing in life he grieved because of his gift, he also admitted gratitude. After witnessing the cruelty, the never-ending pain, and learning that he, like any other Fuller, could sire a black hearted child or raise a child that could be inhabited by the BlackHeart, the thought of loving was unbearable. It was much better to focus on his duty, on his gift that served his family.

Unknowingly.

As Mattie fed Governor in Partway, Deborah fed her family in Dallas.

Different menus.

While Mattie fed Governor tales and tidbits of the Fuller family legacy, Deborah fed Samuel and Hope catfish, fries and white bread, picked up from a neighborhood joint.

"Awwww, Momm..." Hope whined, "I thought we were going to have that chicken and rice casserole tonight. I don't want fish."

Deborah ignored her daughter and set the Family Meal Deal on the table. "I didn't have time to cook today. I'll fix it tomorrow." Deborah thought about all the goodies she'd brought back from Partway just forty-five minutes ago and tacked on, "Maybe." Tingles of excitement flirted up and down her spine as she thought about her successful day of research. Photocopies of more newspaper clippings, Census reports, copies of death records and Almanac sheets waited for her upstairs. The family tree waited for her upstairs. Notes from her tour with Mattie waited by the computer in her study—upstairs. She was dying to get upstairs to her treasures!

That non-committal "maybe" seemed to shatter Hope. "*Ma*-ma, we haven't had a decent meal in weeks," she exaggerated.

Deborah sat down to enjoy her dinner. Her ten-hour days of rushing to, fro and from Partway, as well as researching and creating, had blotted out the depressing boredom that had previously been her life. The uselessness of her life was over, a memory. She smiled at her daughter, more cheerful than she'd been in a long while. "Your father isn't complaining, and he pays the bills."

Both mother and daughter stared at the head of the household whose face was buried in his plate. Realizing something was expected of him, Samuel raised his head and shifted from consumption to conversation. Grease made his lips shine. "Tastes good to me," he declared and lowered his head to finish devouring the fish steak on his plate.

Hope rolled her eyes disrespectfully, pouting, "You used to cook *every* night." Dissatisfaction with the menu didn't stop her from drowning her fries with ketchup and stuffing them in her mouth.

"I'm busy now, Hope." A dash of Louisiana hot sauce, a dollop of ketchup, a quick prayer of thanksgiving and Deborah joined her family in the feast.

"Doing what? What's more important than taking care of me and Daddy?"

"Hope, you *know* you and your Daddy are the most important people in my life. But you guys can take care of yourselves. You'll be leaving in a few months for college, and I won't be in Atlanta to cook or clean or wash for you, and your Daddy is rarely here. I had to do something to fill my life. *I had to do something.*" Some of the past desperation seeped into Deborah's consciousness, making her voice quiver. It hadn't been that long ago. Not enough time had passed for her to forget the long, unfilled hours, the feeling of uselessness, the emptiness of her existence. Never would she return to that. Never.

"But my school project, Mom? That's so, so sad."

"Shut up, Hope!"

Deborah's vicious outburst shocked everyone at the table. Samuel's head yanked up; Hope paused in dipping her fries and Deborah stared at her plate, struggling to stuff her anger in a safe, hidden place.

In a regret-filled voice she apologized, "I'm sorry, Hope. I've had a busy day and I guess I wore myself out. I'm tired." What else could she do but apologize? She couldn't tell the truth. She couldn't admit to her selfish teenager and work-engrossed husband that Hope's assessment hurt. She couldn't convey to the two people who had purpose-filled lives that Hope had just threatened her reason for getting out of bed in the mornings.

Hope, with her life just starting, and Samuel, with his abundant life now, didn't have the capacity to understand what it was like not to have a life. To be in your late forties with nothing to do, nothing to look forward to, going out of your mind with nothingness. They couldn't understand the dismal, desert existence of mother and wife. They wouldn't understand the rainbow of promise an unfinished school project offered.

Deborah didn't and wouldn't lie to herself. The family tree would not have been her first choice. Resuming her career as a research scientist would have been. But the decision to have a life now rested not on the criteria of preference, but on immediacy. The family tree offered her a life now. Work as a scientist meant updating her knowledge and credentials, then landing a job. Steps that required time. She'd needed a *now* project. Something to do *now*. The family tree. Hope's unfinished school project.

Her apology didn't dispel the heaviness in the air. It twisted around Deborah like flannel sheets in the summer—exceedingly hot and extremely uncomfortable. She cleared her throat, determined to fix everything. Determined to put all back to normal in the King household.

"Hope, let me explain." She leaned toward Hope. "This isn't just a school project anymore. For a long time, we didn't know anything about Daddy's side of the family. When I told him I was working on our family tree, he was...*is* so excited. He and Mom can't wait to go with us this weekend to Partway for the graveside cleaning. He can't wait to meet the family we've been estranged from. And just think, Hope," She squeezed her daughter's hand, "You started it, the reunion with family we didn't know. You started this."

A sort of smile lifted Hope's mouth. All pouting gone. "Yeah, I guess I did."

"Try to understand what this means to us old folks, okay?" Deborah smiled lightly, affectionately.

Hope's return smile was light and breezy; a proud gleam lit her eyes when she said, "Grandpa's excited about this, huh?"

"Oh, yeah," Deborah confirmed sincerely. "I don't know how he's going to get through the next few days." Her smile widened, thinking about the conversation she and her Dad had shared.

Samuel interrupted. "That trip is *this* Saturday?" The little bit of dark pigmentation he had inherited from his ancestors faded. "I thought you said in a couple of weeks?"

"No, you *heard* in a couple of weeks. I *said* this Saturday and Samuel—" Deborah started a threat that Samuel cut off.

"I'll be there, baby. I'll be there. I can switch with Roberts. He won't mind."

Deborah cut her eyes at him. They promised murder.

Samuel correctly interpreted the promise. "I'm going, baby. I swear on a stack of Bibles."

Deborah looked at her husband and daughter. "We're *all* going to Partway this weekend. No exceptions, excuses, or signed notes."

When Deborah put her foot down, Samuel and Hope knew it was down and that was that.

"So, Mama," Hope sat forward, hunched over her food, a secretive twinkle in her eyes. "You went and talked to that weird old lady again? She's spooky."

"Hope, that's not nice," Deborah scolded gently. "She's just..." Deborah wrinkled her brow, searching her vocabulary for an acceptable replacement word. "...different and old. Shandra said they think she's a hundred years old, or close to it. That's a lot of living. She deserves to be eccentric."

"Humph."

A "reprimanding mother look" put to death any future disapproving sounds.

Samuel stood, taking his plate to the kitchen sink. "Is that the same old woman who left y'all standing outside and made my baby sick?"

Hope jumped in, responding before her mother could. "Yep, one hundred years or not, Daddy, she was mean to us."

"Uhhhh-huh. Sounds like old age pickled her manners." He walked by the table, quickly kissing both girls on the tops of their heads. "Good dinner. Game on TV."

Deborah and Hope knew the implications of that. Baseball and napping had Samuel for the rest of the evening.

"Did she say anything useful this time? Let you in the house?" Hope asked, pushing her plate aside.

"Actually, she was extremely helpful. She gave me a lot of good information. Took me on a tour of the gravesites. Told me about the beginning of our family." As she talked, Deborah recaptured the excitement. An itch to get upstairs to begin reading, validating and recording started anew. The family tree may not have been her preference, but it had a lot of the same elements as science research—reading, taking notes, analyzing, compiling, testing and following paths that sometimes took you nowhere and sometimes back to the beginning and sometimes to a new path. And of course, recording. Always recording. Similar methodology, different subject. Deborah was happy.

"She knows everything about the Fullers. Even stuff Shandra didn't know, like the original name of the town and why it was changed. And did you know—"

"But did she let you in the house?" Hope interrupted harshly. "Did she admit to having private family records?"

Deborah jerked back. Hope's unexpected and forceful intrusion surprised her. "I... Well... We were at the family cemetery. At Black Hill."

"Sorry, Mom, didn't mean to throw you off." Hope smiled, prompting, "Private records?"

"No, I…You know…" Deborah leaned on one elbow thinking about her time with Mattie. "She got sick again. Maybe it's me." Deborah furrowed her brow and frowned, thinking how odd for Mattie to take ill on both of her visits. If she didn't know any better she would be concerned. But it was a coincidence; nothing more.

Hope stood, gathered her plate and used napkins and headed for the kitchen. "I was just curious. No big deal."

Deborah smiled, glad her daughter showed some interest in family history. She decided to capitalize on it. "Hope, since you're in the kitchen, please do the dishes for me. I'm going upstairs."

"Awwww, Mom…" Hope's whine drifted, missing its target. Deborah was gone, up the back stairs to her study.

Traveling highways, blacktop, gravel and dust roads they came. Down the same roads that had brought generations of Fullers to Black Hill for the annual family event. Some Fullers arrived as early as 6:00, if assigned to barbeque detail, while others pulled up to the narrow strip of yard at the front of Black Hill as late as 9:00, if unfortunate enough to draw cleanup duties.

Because the faces changed every year with only a handful remaining the same, no Fuller gawked or pointed a curious finger when the Fullers from Dallas filed out of the Suburban. Deborah, Samuel, and Hope King, escorted by Daniel and Imogene Fuller, stretched to work out the kinks and then headed for the official-looking table set up under a mature oak tree, its branches spread wide in welcome.

Cousin Shandra's excited squeal caused the pier and beam of earth to tremble as she jumped up from the table and ran to her previously estranged family. "I'm so glad to see you. I was afraid you would change your mind and not come." Skinny arms circled Deborah's neck. The hug was long, meaningful.

Using her memory of past conversations with Deborah as a reference, Shandra stood back and matched names to Deborah's immediate family. She got it right. "I feel like I already know y'all. Deborah and I have talked so much. Is Hannah and her family coming?"

The mention of Deborah's younger sister elicited disappointing murmurs and excuses.

Daniel, the father of three girls—one deceased—explained. "Both Hannah and Reggie returned from business trips late last night and Shawn has some big basketball camp this weekend. You're stuck with just us this time."

"That's a shame. You'll tell them they're welcome anytime, won't you? They don't have to wait 'til the next graveside service. That goes for all of you. Come back whenever you feel like it. We'll be here."

Just that easily, the bridge home was laid. And easier than that, wholehearted acceptance into the Fuller clan.

Along with acceptance came introductions. A Fuller didn't just give a name, shake a hand and quickly connect the family tree limbs. Oh no, no. Fuller kinfolk told stories and near-truths with made up beginnings and speculated endings. Fuller kinfolk liked to tease and point humorous fingers at other family members. Fuller kinfolk liked to sing out tales and act out fables. Fuller introductions took time and patience.

Only half of which—time—Daniel and Samuel had. At the tail end of Uncle Roy's third fib, they eagerly accepted the garden tools that were shoved into their hands. With a cold beer planted in the other hand, they ambled off, following male relatives to an unkempt part of the private land. When Hope opened her mouth to protest having to stay and listen and meet folks she wouldn't remember, Deborah silenced her with a mother look that told her: "You *are* going to learn about your grandpa's family."

The three women were left with the job of tracking the maze of family roots, tsk-tsking over the illegitimate branches, and chipping through the Fuller bark to get at the real Fuller facts. And Deborah loved it! She was beside herself when she met some of the names already inked on her chart. She was thrilled when the dates and names told to her orally lined up with the public records she had reviewed and recorded in her notebook. Her pen whizzed across her notebook pages recording in narrative how Fullers were impacted by The Great Depression, the first Juneteenth, the World Wars and the Great Migration to the North and West. Empty passages still mocked her chart and accompanying chronicle, but not for long. She scribbled like nobody's business, hand and mind as one.

To no one in particular, Deborah quipped, "This is so good. As good as the information Aunt Mattie shared."

Descendents of Fullers stopped what they were doing. Rakes rested. Hoes halted. Side conversations and fooling around ceased. Even authentic cemetery sounds died out—no birds chirping, no summer breezes, no debris tumbling. Silence.

The stillness of humanity and nature destroyed Deborah's excitement. In its place—anxiety and confusion. Faces, once friendly and open, now projected distrust and...was that fear?

A shiver of unknown origins shook Deborah into subtle defense mode. Carefully, slowly, she closed her notebook and clipped her pen to it. Disappointed. "What did I do?" Her eyes surveyed the ebony, ivory, and every shade in between faces, some who resembled her and some who did not. She searched their faces looking for a hint, a clue, anything to explain the sudden silence. "Did I say something wrong?" she asked, struggling to understand her unknown transgression, wanting to know the unwritten, unspoken Fuller rule she guessed she had broken.

Step-Uncle Billy, not really a Fuller but married to one so long he thought he was, disturbed the silence. "You met Mattie? You talked to her?"

Some light, though not enough to move her out of darkness. Deborah mumbled a shaky yes and then turned to Shandra, her eyes pleading for help. Nothing came out of that plea. Shandra was busy shooting real nasty looks at nearby relatives.

"How did you learn about Mattie?" Step-Uncle Billy moved closer to Deborah, his intentions unknown.

Shandra moved, placing her petite self between Step-Uncle Billy and Deborah; her face and body tense in defiance. "*I* told her about Aunt Mattie. She told you earlier she's putting our family history on paper. Who better than Aunt Mattie to send her to?"

Tsk-tsking. Hissing. Head shakes. Frowns. Signs and sounds of disapproval from family as some of them returned to their previous activity. A few, the more guarded ones, the outspoken ones, plus the ones who liked mess and smelled a big pot of it simmering, refused to let Shandra off. They moved in. Deborah, the family tree, the good time they had been having before Mattie's name passed a pair of lips—forgotten.

"Everyone in Partway knows what Mattie knows. Why you want to put the girl in harm's way by sending her to *that* woman." An elder, Cousin Clarice—a blood Fuller—challenged Shandra.

The brightest, the most loving Fuller in Partway stood at the center in a close circle of Fullers, not afraid to defend herself or the oldest member of the Fuller clan. "There's no harm in visiting Aunt Mattie." Anger transformed her voice into something ugly, harsh. "She's just a little old woman with some unusual habits. She wouldn't hurt a soul."

Step-Uncle Billy's "Naw" was startling enough to send the birds flying from the secure branches of the oaks. "*Unusual??!!*"

Shandra skewered him with a hard look. "Yes, unusual!" Her voice escalated to scalding hot. "None of us are perfect. We all have something that makes us seem strange to others. Look at me—a ninety-pound nerd who sleeps with books. And you, Uncle Billy, with one good hand. Clarice, green hair at *your* age. There's something unusual about each of us, but that doesn't mean we're dangerous or ready to be locked away."

"Naw, naw. They's mo' to Mattie than jus' strange," Step-Uncle Billy declared, flapping that one good hand around. "The woman is downright crazy. Possessed!" He made a meaningful verbal sound that translated into "I-know-what-I'm-talking-about."

A background of church-inspired "wells" and "amens" supported Step-Uncle Billy's claims.

Cousin Clarice threw her measly two cents into the pot, probably figuring that bought her some talking rights. "The woman needs help. I ain't concerned about her walkin' around God's creation all the time. Shoot, I need to exercise mo' myself," she patted her belly that pooched out like a pregnant woman's, "but *without shoes!*" Cousin Clarice appeared scandalized, her face twisted like a confused circus clown. "And in *two* thin cotton housedresses." She held up two fingers to make sure her relatives understood two was two.

Cousin Clarice barely finished her seek-and-destroy mission before Step-Uncle Billy rolled his destructive dice. "And what about her layin' around here all day? ...in a cemetery? ...with dead folk?" Step-Uncle Billy shook his head violently. "Naw, naw, Shandra. That ain't natural. Oh, hell naw, that *beyond* unusual."

Deborah's head snapped back; her mouth fell open. She had assumed that on the day she found Mattie at Black Hill that her visit had been a coincidence, and that Shandra had just guessed right in telling her where to find Mattie. Not in all the Fuller lifetimes combined would Deborah have guessed this place was on Mattie's list—a short list, Deborah felt sure—of frequent visits. But curiosity overrode the discomfort of the earlier shutout from her relatives and she spoke up. "You mean she comes here all the time?"

"Ev-e-ry-day." Step-Uncle Billy pointed to the ground at Deborah's feet. "Just like you standin' right here, she be here tomorrow and the next day and the next." He raised a finger on his good hand, pointing it at her. "'Cept you standin'; she be lyin' down. Near 'bouts over there." He pointed in the general direction where Mattie had abruptly ended Deborah's tour earlier this week. "And when she come, she stays loooooong hours." Step-Uncle Billy sucked on a decayed tooth—loudly. "Only time she miss a visit to Black Hill is bad weather, real bad and..." he stepped a little closer to Deborah, making sure she didn't miss any of his precious words, "...when other folk is here, like today. You won't see her at none of these family things. Naw, naw, unnn, huh, that Mattie's a strange ole bird."

Deborah's mind worked diligently at trying to validate Mattie's behavior as logical, reasonable, but it defied commonsense. She couldn't make it work. If Step-Uncle Billy's words were true and not mere gossip, then she feared she would have to agree with Step-Uncle Billy's assessment. Aunt Mattie's behavior was not commonplace and represented yet another quirk to add to an expanding file.

§

Cousin Clarice couldn't stand to be outdone. After all, she was a true Fuller, and if anybody was going to spread truths and lies about a Fuller it needed to be a true-blood-Fuller. With an interested party in Deborah, she took the plunge, wading waist deep into the family's most discussed, most hushed, most joked about and feared subject— Mattie Fuller.

"And what about all them rumors about Cynthia's death? The po-lice went out to Mattie's house fo' times to question her." Cousin Clarice rolled her eyes and held up her hands to heaven as if preparing to pray. She did. "Lawd, lawd, please hep that woman if she did have somethin' to do with that po' girl's demise. An' if she didn't, hep her anyways. And thank you God that it wasn't my daughter who was kilt."

Step-Uncle Billy forced his words into the pause after the prayer. "And a whole lot more than just Cynthia. Remember Tate and Sally and Maybelle? Somethin' ain't right with them deaths neither. Naw, naw, Mattie know somethin', more'n she tellin'."

"Yup, un-huh, sho' do." Cousin Clarice seconded, vigorously nodding her green head of hair. "Ain't no tellin' what kind of evidence she got holed up in that house. Ain't nooooo tellin'."

"And she don't talk to *no-bod-dee*. Naw, naw."

The two were on a roll, dishing dirt so quickly no one else could squeeze in a word and tumbling over each other's words.

"Nope, un-huh, sho' don't." Cousin Clarice shook her head, emphasizing her words.

"Seen her in town t'other day and she didn't even return my greetin'. Naw, naw, naw, just kept right on walkin', pushin' that grocery cart full a Alpo, eyes hard as life and focused on somethin' I couldn't see."

"Shoot naw, she didn't speak. You ain't Gov'nor. She only frat'nize with Gov'nor," Cousin Clarice puffed accusingly.

"Naw, naw, I'm thinkin' there a whole lotta truth to that Fuller's curse and ya'lls'…" Step-Uncle Billy chose this moment to exclude himself from the family. "…*Aunt* Mattie is smack dab in the middle of it."

Cousin Clarice's eyes lit up in agreement. Her mouth formed a pouty "O." "Sho', yeah, that it—the Fuller's Curse."

§

"Stop it!" Shandra shouted over them. "Just stop right there!" She yelled at Step-Uncle Billy and Cousin Clarice, full up with their tattling words and angry at herself for not stepping in sooner. She planned now to end it. "All this stupid talk is ridiculous. Y'all should slap yourselves for the garbage coming out of your mouths. And you ought to be embarrassed for bringing up that silly curse." She pinned the village idiots with an icy stare, stepped threateningly close and pointed a finger in their faces. "We're family, and there's not a thing we can do about that. But what we can do is be nice and stop cannibalizing other family members." Breathing heavy, finger shaking, yet radiating with peace, love and unity, Shandra demanded, "You two owe Deborah, Imogene and Hope an apology."

Step-Uncle Billy and Cousin Clarice stepped back, away from the petite dynamo, obviously planning to ignore her.

But then, Shandra's voice turned opposite its natural tone and she stepped toward them. "Don't let them drive back to Dallas thinking we're barbaric." Her dark eyes flashed in anger, her hands clenched.

Cousin Clarice mumbled a quick but meaningless apology. Shandra knew Clarice didn't want to hear from Shandra's mother, Mary, later. Mary didn't mind getting in somebody's face; she liked to get physical. But worse than that, Mary Fuller had more money in Partway's branch of Central Texas Bank than all the other Fuller checking and savings accounts ten-keyed together. With that kind of money and her ex-boyfriend's criminal connections, she could mess you up. She knew that Cousin Clarice didn't feel like being messed up.

But Step-Uncle Billie wasn't that smart. He broke free of his conscience, ignored the Shandra/Mary threat and issued a threat of his own. "Look a here, Miss United Nations, you can try and paint a pretty picture for the newcomers here, but it ain't like that. Naw, naw. If you send this girl to Mattie again and she come up dead, it gonna be on you." He flapped his good hand in the air, prophesying, "It already on you."

"Forget you, Uncle Billy." The young librarian gave up on love and peace and unity for Step-Uncle Billy. Disgusted with him, she grabbed Deborah's arm and swung her around into the presence of Governor.

The lone, smoke-gray cloud passing over and blocking out the ninety-plus degree sun rays should have alerted them to Governor's arrival, but every nearby Fuller had been immersed in the Billy and Clarice show and had missed the coming of the future record keeper. When he spoke, guilt and bad manners ate them alive.

"'Whole lot easier to hold the mirror up to another and avoid yo'self, ain't it, Billy, Clarice?" Governor stepped into the broke down circle of Fullers. "Shandra here done worked hard, pullin' all these folks together." Governor raised a thin, muscled arm in a wide arc that included all of the Fullers who gave up a Saturday to honor those lying underground. "Why you wanna mess it up wit yo' trashy mouth?"

In every family there is one member everybody respects. That one for the Fullers was Governor. Not because he was one of the oldest living male Fullers. Not because he was educated through eighth grade yet checked out from the library and read three books a week—one on theology, a second on economics, and the final on history. Not because he'd never been caught in a lie or missed a day of work or stayed to himself, minding his own business. Not even because he gave admirable advice when asked. It was a simple reason; more simple than the character of a man. Fullers respected Governor because he was the only Fuller Mattie talked to. The one person Mattie spent time with was worthy of undeniable respect.

Billy and Clarice knew and subscribed to this Fuller principle. They dared not rebuke or rebut Governor and instead, showed good sense by dipping their heads and staring at the fertile ground.

"Go grab some work," Governor commanded, the hard edge of anger in his voice softened by love.

Without another sloppy word, Billy and Clarice skulked away. Their taste for reckless talk frozen until another time.

Suddenly, work became the single most important reason for living as the other Fullers turned back to clearing the grounds and paths—raking, pulling weeds, carting away limbs and fallen branches, planting flowers and ivy. Governor scanned the sorry lot of skin and bones, momentarily questioning why he loved them. Wondering why God loved them so.

Shandra's quick hug brought him out of his thoughts.

"Thank you, Governor. You always help me." Gratitude filled her eyes and framed her soft voice. Forever mindful of her manners, she guided the newcomers forward toward the tall, crooked man. "These are our kin from Dallas. This is their first graveside cleaning service. Isn't it good to have them with us?"

Governor turned to his kinfolk, his expression neutral. He'd felt their presence. Knew evil was with them, but his eyes, his thoughts were fixed on Shandra. Today was her death date. She had no idea that the people she introduced him to would be guilty of her death.

If she knew that in a few minutes she'd be dead, Governor wondered, would she have invited evil to visit them? Or would she have closed them out as Mattie had? If she knew that in less than an hour her soul would be taking its permanent journey home, back to God, would she have lived differently? Maybe traveled more, played more, sang more, talked less, worried less, done less?

He looked long and deep into her dark brown eyes, and his tears almost escaped their holding place. He wanted to pull her close now while her blood was warm. To cradle her tight like her mother would be doing soon. Unfair. It was unfair to take *this* child. Why Shandra? Why not Billy, Clarice, or one of the others who contributed so little to the world? Why not the ones who took, destroyed and made ugly the world? The questions had been asked before by Mattie. In the silence of night in her small living room surrounded by spirits, memories, names and that Bible. The questions had been raised by past record keepers. Now he—a future Truth bearer—asked the same questions. Never to receive an answer—at least not on this side of life.

Sadness fell on him. It landed on his shoulders, making them droop; it saturated his face, making it longer; it blanketed his soul, making it cry.

Pinch off yo' 'motions, Gov'nor. Easier that way. Mattie's voice schooled him from her wood frame house a few miles away.

He nodded his head, sure she saw him. Doing what Mattie said, Governor cordoned off his feelings. He emptied his mind and then filled it with the mantra Mattie and other record keepers had used throughout the years: *Perfect love casts out all fear... Perfect love casts out all fear... Perfect love casts out all fear...*

His relatives in the physical world didn't know the transformation Governor underwent. They looked expectantly, waiting, waiting for this gentle man. When time seemed to grow uncomfortably long, Shandra placed a hand on his arm and queried, "Governor?" Rattling on to cover the awkwardness, she said to him, "This is Deborah, her mother Imogene, and her daughter, Hope. They're the relatives from Dallas I told you about. Deborah's the one working on our family tree. She brought some of it with her. It's exciting to see our history on paper. And it's good the family's back together again after such a long separation. Aren't you... Isn't it good to have them here with us?"

Governor came back to awareness as Shandra's prattling petered out. He blinked, bringing the new relatives into focus. He lifted his hand to shake Deborah's belatedly. "Welcome," he offered in his gravelly voice. "Shandra's been talking about y'all for weeks now. Good to meet you." His smile was as crippled as his lie.

Mattie had told him she was pretty. Oval brown face. Easy, sunny smile. Broad features, well-spaced. But those eyes. The eyes told him what he sought. They validated the paper of Truth.

Deborah, her voice church-nice said, "I'm *very* happy to meet you. I was hoping I could interview you for the project."

As Deborah swooped to the ground to fetch another notebook from her shoulder bag, Evil responded to the presence of Truth and rose from Its secret place. It floated through the air to Governor. Not to enter him as It had Mattie, but to wrap Itself around him just tight enough to be under the threshold of pain. From the top of Governor's tightly-woven hair to the soles of his work boots, the BlackHeart did just that.

And the second It touched him, he knew who and what It was. The second It hugged him tight, he understood, without experiencing it himself, the abundance of pain Mattie had felt the day she met the current BlackHeart for the first time. His own "In-Me" warned him the BlackHeart was initiating him, teasing him. Even with this knowledge, even knowing his heart was out of danger, Governor clutched the skin, layers above his heart, shielding it from a pain that wasn't there, an invasion that wouldn't come.

"Governor?" This time it was Deborah touching his arm, trying to reach him through his distraction. "Governor, are you okay?"

The anticipated keeper of Truth didn't respond. He couldn't. The BlackHeart's invisible shroud tightened more, forcing him to stay focused on It and not human words or touches. In a humanless voice, It mocked Governor, telling him It knew he was the future and the future started after Mattie's death. It boasted about their matches to come. It challenged: *Not much longer before you and I square off. I've tired of old women. Mattie, Aldana, Mae. Good opponents. Passionate. Strong. Committed. All of them. But it's been a while since I've been up against a man. Gonna be good.*

Deborah screamed at seeing Governor's coloring change, his body grow tense, his hand on his heart, the fixated bug eyes. "I think he's having a heart attack!"

Living Fullers popped up from among the many headstones, looking, straining to see the cause of all the ruckus.

"Mama, Samuel has a bag in the truck. Hope, go find your Daddy," Deborah directed as folks figured it out and rushed toward the emergency scene.

The BlackHeart's sick laugh floated on a level of atmosphere that only spirits and gifted ones could discern. Its vaporous bindings unraveled; Governor was free.

Free to crumple to the ground on his hands and knees, inhaling large amounts of air. His eyes saw nothing real. Didn't see the crushed leaves clutched in his hands. Didn't see the fire ants marching toward his fingers. Didn't see the root of the oak tree peeping from under the ground. Dark, dark eyes were open only to fear.

Since she had been cradling his waist, Deborah fell with Governor and within seconds, family had gathered near them, some knelt beside her, some beside him. Others bent low, crouching. All faces showed worry and questions.

"Please, someone," she screamed again, "I think he's having a heart attack. Please get my husband."

I'm scared, Mattie, I can't do this, Governor cried inside his mind.

You'll be fine, Gov'nor. Mattie's presence was there to calm him. *The first time is always tough.*

It has so much power. I couldn't move. Couldn't protect myself.

That's the way it seems, but ain't so. You got all It got and more.

I'm not ready. I thought I could do this. I can't, Mattie. He shook his head vigorously, sure he was right. Sure he would not succeed, that he would let his family down and waste his gift.

"Would someone please go find my husband?" Deborah cried louder, almost out of her mind with fear. "Find Samuel!"

It's just tryin' to get the upper hand. Did me the same way. But once you get started, scaredness goes right on by. Yo' natch'ral self takes over. All you know starts workin'.

Governor hushed, mulling over Mattie's words, thinking her words rang true. Frowning, he recalled the night Mattie had to kill Tate, the then-cursed one. They had arrived just in time to witness Cynthia's last few breaths and as soon as he saw them, Tate went straight for Mattie, syringe held tightly in his hand. Governor had given no thought to danger, entertained no notion of fear. He'd just set about to save Mattie and himself. By the end of the tussle, he and Mattie had survived. Tate, the BlackHeart, lay dead by Mattie's hands.

Afterwards, after the cover-up and clean-up, back at Mattie's house, some of the action he could recall. But not enough. He knew this was the truth Mattie spoke of. That night with Tate served as confirmation that when it happened again, "In-Me" would take over. He wouldn't have to think. Just act. Just do.

Told you, you'd be fine. Ev'rythin' you need is in you. You gon' make us proud.

Governor was silent, thinking about the Truth handlers before him who had done their duty, who had carried off their responsibility. His heart and soul told him he would do the same. By the grace of God, he would be a credit to those before him. He would not go crazy. He would not kill himself. He would control the fear and bandage the physical pain. He would learn to master the loneliness and isolation. He would do his job and survive until his own replacement was felt and trained. All would be okay and continue on as it had for ages.

So resolved, Governor eased to the ground, trading hands and knees for his tailbone, crossing his long, thin legs yoga-style. He closed his eyes, blinked several times and joined the madness going on around him on his behalf.

Some man's head was bent in front of him, listening to his heart. At the same time, he had a hand on Governor's wrist, counting the strong beats there. The man moved back; their eyes met, locked. Governor beat him to the words. "I'm okay. Heart was jus' burnin'," he truthfully explained.

The man, younger and much lighter in color with a special gift for healing, nodded his head. "It appears that way. Do you know who you are?"

Governor thought about telling Samuel he was the man who might kill his wife or maybe his daughter. He thought about confessing to being the next Mattie. A number of answers ran through his mind, wanting to escape through his mouth, but he clamped his lips together.

Telling the truth wouldn't do a thing but make it ugly, faster. Besides, nobody wanted to hear the truth, especially not members of a cursed family. To hear the truth meant taking action, being accountable and responsible, and nobody really wanted that. It was too hard, too much discipline required, too much sacrifice. No, it was better to answer the question in an acceptable version of the truth so this blind, sorry, false-dealing group hovering around him could break up. Give him some air and give Shandra over to Death—their sacrifice for forgetting the truth.

"I'm Governor Fuller." He answered the doctor's question while his eyes searched the crowd for the murder victim. She wasn't far away. In touching distance, next to Deborah and Hope. Her sweet face showed concern and worry. Governor felt bad for delaying her future. It would be better for her when she left this family.

"Governor?" Shandra gently asked, "Do you know where you are? Do you remember what happened?"

He was going to miss her voice. Miss her helpful guidance in picking out books at the library. Miss her love. The family was losing somebody special, but thank God her soul would be free of this family's legacy. Emotions started stretching inside him, straining to get free, but he hardened his heart, clamped down on his emotions.

"Graveside cleaning for Black Hill."

Heartbreak was hidden from his eyes as he shifted his gaze from Shandra's precious face to stare hard into Deborah's eyes. "Must'a been the beans and ice cream. Bad combination for a black man," Governor lied, thinking about the destruction Deborah had brought to the family.

A relieved chuckle rotated around the huddled mass of family. Everyone smiled, glad something serious turned out not to be. Even Governor managed a half smile as he held out a hand to officially meet Samuel King.

Samuel took the extended hand and exchanged looks with his wife. "Good, strong beat. Eyes clear. Breathing regular." He turned to Governor, smiling. "You look and sound healthy, should live a long time."

"Probably," he replied, thinking about Mattie.

"But he grabbed his chest and fell to his knees. Shouldn't he go to the hospital?" Deborah insisted.

"No," both men answered. Governor had to stay here, had to be near Shandra. He couldn't say that though, couldn't explain his reluctance. Then again, he didn't need to. The doctor had more pull with his wife than he did.

"It's easy for people to confuse severe heartburn with a heart attack," Samuel explained in his "It's-going-to-be-alright" doctor voice. "The symptoms can sometimes look alike. And as good as they are, beans and ice cream..." he shook his head "...nothing but acid and gas."

"Shouldn't he be examined more thoroughly? Or give him a pill or... or something?" Deborah seemed determined to make this a medical case of tremendous proportions.

"Look at him, honey. He's fine. He looks better than I do!"

Deborah wasn't convinced. Frown marks broke the smooth finish of her skin and she crossed her arms over her chest.

"Okay, okay," Samuel relented. He reached in the dark brown leather bag Imogene had brought from the truck and pulled out a case with pills of various colors and shapes. "Here... Here's an antacid. This'll clear out any remaining gas." Instead of seeking Governor's approval, Samuel asked his wife, whose rear had not occupied nearly as many chairs in medical school as her husband's, "Are you okay now?"

She smiled weakly, somewhat appeased by his action.

Governor quickly swallowed the pill. No more time to delay; Death stood waiting.

The sound of a jangling cowbell split the air, tolling the Fullers to lunch. Those hungriest took off, anxious to be first in line. Others, more than a handful less than two, lagged behind looking at Governor, waiting for him to get up off the ground while also taking baby steps toward the lunch line. An intimate group—Shandra, Deborah and Samuel—gripped Governor, helping him to his feet even though he didn't need the help.

Death is waiting. Mattie's voice reminded him of something he knew.

Shandra had to go to the creek. Death waited for her there. And Governor had to head there as well so he could be nearby. It wasn't that he wanted to watch Shandra die. He didn't want to stand at the top of the bank, ripped in two with wanting to help, but not being able to. It was just that he couldn't shake the need to be near Shandra as she took her last breath, as she made the transformation. He needed to feel her soul as it passed by and know she was okay. He needed this so he could go on.

Governor reached in his mind for an excuse to get away from the nurturing ones. Shandra had to believe he was fine or else she'd continue to flit about him and delay her date with Death. "I'm going to the privy. Gone ahead. I'll be right on." He eased out of their hands and with a long, steady stride and erect back, he marched confidently to the outhouse.

Shandra looked doubtful and Deborah started to say something, but Samuel, sensing Governor needed time for himself, grabbed as many womanly arms as he could and steered them in the opposite direction.

With his back to them all, Governor heard Shandra say, "Oh! I forgot the kids! I need to tell them it's time to eat." Seconds later, she yelled to the crowd. "Go ahead and bless the food. We're going to get the kids."

Governor didn't need eyesight to know she was heading to her destiny and the BlackHeart was with her.

He walked inside the confining, stale space and pulled the door to, leaving a crack yea wide. His eyes tracked the two women and teenager as they cut through the cemetery, taking the shortcut to the creek. After verifying Samuel and everybody else had merged into the serving line, Governor closed the door and waited long enough for grace and for Shandra, Deborah and Hope to make some progress. Then, he slipped out of the john as quiet as a tiptoe, thankful that no one had been willing to exchange him and his continued good health for their place in the long food line.

Behind the toilet, through the thigh-high weeds, to the thick trees lumped together, he trekked. It was the long way to the creek, but there was no other way he could go undetected and he had to be there. Finally, he reached the end of the trees and arrived at a twelve foot drop off straight down to the creek where water flowed briskly but not aggressively this time of year. There was no safe way to slide down the bank—too steep and rocky. The only practical way to reach the creek was to travel east. In that direction, the topography declined until it merged with the creek. But Governor didn't need the creek; he needed a vantage point from on high.

Moving slower than he wanted, but figuring he was still on time, he followed the ragged edge, being careful not to send an avalanche of pebbles to the creek bed announcing himself as a witness. The closer to the east he moved, the stronger the intensity of the Evil One.

During a past visit with Mattie, he'd questioned her about his knowledge of certain Fuller deaths. Why should *he* know such things while *she* served as keeper of the Bible? Mattie had opened her knowledge to him, explaining that the closer she moved to death the more pronounced his gift would become. *It meant*, she'd finished weakly, *that her death was near.* Governor had been sorry he'd asked. But it explained why he was now able to feel the BlackHeart, was now able to sense It, even though he could not see It, and he knew Its actions, although he was blind to It.

He reached the point he had pre-selected in his head, leaned against a tree trunk and turned his senses inward. Still. He was so still.

§

To the east, Shandra, Deborah and Hope approached a group of kids of various sizes, colors, ages, and temperament. They were not happy with the interruption of their play—skipping rocks, building dams and "playing the dozens"—until the reason was given. Like the adults, some of the children responded immediately and headed straight away for the cemetery, while a few straggled behind throwing their last handful of rocks.

"Look, kids! A mockingbird. Our state bird," Shandra squealed excitedly, her finger pointed toward a bird in flight. It c a m e t o rest high above their heads on a leaning tree branch.

Hope looked up, saw the bird and shrieked delightedly. "Let's climb up and get a better look."

"No, Hope! It's too high up." Deborah's motherly concern nullified the suggestion before it caught on with the few remaining children.

"Please, Mom. I'll be careful."

"No, Hope." Deborah turned and moved forward thinking the discussion was closed.

Inclined to spoil any child, Shandra, moved by Hope's crushed face, offered, "I'll go up a little ways with her, if that's okay with you."

Deborah turned around, looked at Hope's expectant face, examined Shandra's sturdy sneakers and then glanced up again at the bird which had dropped to a lower branch. "No, thanks for the offer, Shandra. I don't think so." She didn't like the look of that jagged cliff face.

"I've got two little boys, remember. I'm used to rough-housing it with them. We'll only go up a short ways. Not all the way."

Hope, taking her mother's split second of silence as agreement, dashed off, scrambling toward the cliff.

"Hope! Come back." Deborah's words were lost in the breeze; the two or three steps she took were halted by Shandra's hand on her arm.

The younger woman smiled assurance. "I'll go. We'll be right behind you." She winked, a sign of further assurance.

Deborah delayed for a few moments longer, then found herself gathering the last of the kids and guiding them back the way they had come.

Using exposed tree roots, rocks, foot holds and flat landings of earth, Shandra climbed carefully up the cliff face, dodging the skittering of rocks Hope's feet and grasping hands dislodged. She followed the footprints of the BlackHeart whose agile, flexible body maneuvered the tricky, steep face naturally. Just the two of them. The rest of the family was swallowed by the bend of the water's course, out of sight of what the BlackHeart planned for Shandra.

§

Evil vibrated in the air. At this distance, It hummed against Governor's skin, making the hairs on his arms and chest curl inward, trying to grow back under his skin to escape the dark vibrations. The BlackHeart was close to blood, to conquest. It was about to have Its hate tempered by the act of killing.

§

At the top of the cliff, Shandra bent over at the waist, hands on knees, greedily gasping for air. "I...told...your Mom...we'd only go up a little way." She paused, straightening up. "I see you're as hard-headed as my boys." She turned sideways to look at Hope and stilled.

The transformation had happened quickly—from eager, sweet-faced teenager with a perfect complexion, a long bouncy ponytail, clear brown eyes, and a girly smile to Evil with hard, black eyes, a wicked twist of the mouth, and a black glow that radiated around Hope like an aura.

Seconds ticked by with only the sounds of nature filling in the gap between shock, realization and fear.

The BlackHeart stared Shandra in the eyes and asked innocently, "You don't believe in the curse?"

Shandra wanted to answer. Her mouth moved, her eyes showed signs of wanting to respond, but a sudden trembling took hold of her. Unconsciously, she took a step away from the BlackHeart.

Hope moved toward Shandra, keeping them close. "I'm real. And I hurt." She balled a fist and beat it against her heart. "Within me...the struggle hurts. I have to ease the pain. I *have* to."

Shandra's trembling became spastic, almost epileptic. Her head shook, her mouth formed a silent no. And yet, even deep in fear, she acknowledged surprise that Hope's evil transformation had not changed her voice. It remained pure, light, appealing.

"Goodbye, Cousin Shandra. Your death serves your family well."

The BlackHeart's hands rushed out and in one graceful movement she yanked Shandra's arm and flung the lightweight woman with such strength that Shandra felt intense pain in her arm before even registering that she was airborne. When she did, she exhaled one hearty scream before hitting her head over and over on the huge rocks that formed the cliff from which she fell. That was enough to silence her forever.

§

In less time than it took to climb up, Shandra's body, once brimming over with life, came to rest at the creek bed. Like a discarded puppet, she lay with arms and legs splayed every which way, head awkwardly crooked and one hand being baptized in the water.

Once the disrupted rocks settled on and around her body—stillness.

Governor's chest heaved. The pain was great, burning hot like someone had run him through with a branding iron. Big, heavy tears plopped on the leaves at his feet.

But Evil wasn't through yet. The eagerness on the BlackHeart's face told him so.

It shimmied down the cliff, sure-footed as a mountain goat, intentionally grazing and bruising Itself along the way as evidence for Its story. With supernatural strength, It lifted a giant rock and brought it down on Shandra's head. Once. Twice—until the skull cracked open.

Tossing the rock aside, It smiled, a sick, satisfied smile that spoke of Its release from pain. With eyes closed and inhaling deeply, It savored the absence of pain, loved the feeling of peace. It clasped Its hands above Its head and danced victoriously. After moments of rejoicing and dancing and celebrating death, It turned in Governor's direction and stared as if seeing him up high among the brush and trees.

It pointed a finger at him, challenging him silently. Then, before another tear hit the ground at his feet, the BlackHeart screamed and screamed and screamed—so loudly Deborah and the other kids came running.

Another accident—which wasn't an accident.

§

Somewhere in the center of Texas, part way between Dallas and Austin, a soul separated from the physical shell that had been its home for twenty-seven years. Human eyes didn't see, couldn't see the ascent of the soul—except for three. Those three watched with spiritual eyes as the soul shimmered over the pure, cold creek water, up the cliff face, through the brush, past pine trees to a little wooden house. A house that was home to stray dogs, secrets and truths.

Inside the house, Mattie sat in her rocker in the living room. She opened her arms, inviting the soul to snuggle within her heart for as long as it needed to. It accepted the invitation and Mattie closed her arms, hugging herself, merging with the soul. They fused for long moments while it told Mattie of its fate—as if she didn't know—and together as one, they cried and prayed for the family.

Sometime later, when both Mattie and the soul felt somewhat healed, somewhat right, the precious soul separated from Mattie, sifted upward through layers of atmosphere to a place humans called Heaven.

Mattie, old and tired and lonely, sighed to take its place, but duty kept her bound to the rocker, to the house, to the family. Slowly she got up, retrieved the Holy Bible with the tale inside and wrote the name. With the last curve of the last alpha-letter, she knew there would be more, and she hated that knowledge.

She made everything right—sliding the paper into its slot, reshelving the Bible—then returned to the rocker, waiting for Governor to come and be comforted.

Five days passed and the family came back together. Same location. Different occasion. This time when they met, it was to say kind words, offer righteous prayers, sing going-home songs of Zion and pass judgment on others beneath delicate hankies. This time, instead of honoring the long-time dead with sweat from hard labor, they memorialized the recently dead with sweat from the sun's rays. This time, it was Shandra's funeral and interment at Black Hill.

On the first and only row of chairs facing the casket sat Mary Fuller, her two elementary-age grandsons and Shandra's brother, Sap, who everyone had been surprised to see since no one, including his Mama, had heard from him in some time. Behind the row of chairs stood the rest of the family—aunts, uncles, nieces, nephews, sisters, brothers, cousins, grands— interspersed with friends, associates and co-workers. All shuffling for space under the tarp out of the sizzling Texas sun.

The interment was short. Fifteen minutes max. The preacher appeared just as anxious as those who missed out on the shade to leave and find someplace indoors—cool, comfortable, with food. At the last "Amen" folks scattered slowly, knowing not to move too fast in the Texas sun, else you might faint.

The first row occupants didn't move at all; the weight of their emotions anchored them to their chairs. Still numb. Still shocked. Probably thinking a mistake had been made in Heaven. That it couldn't be Shandra in that steel cargo box. She was too young, had too much future left in her. Surely, surely, God had called the wrong child home.

But no mistakes existed in the heavenly order of things. All was as it should be.

One of the unfortunate ones who had been left without protection from the sun during the service was Deborah. She moved forward now, snailing her way through the crowd. Imogene and Hope followed as they made their way to the first row occupants. They waited patiently in the sympathy reception line for their turn to offer comfort to the grieving family.

"Please, let us know if there's anything we can do. Anything." An overused funeral platitude, something she'd said many times before, but this time Deborah's words held real meaning. This time, Deborah spoke sincerely. For Shandra, the cousin she'd only known a short time, had come to represent a sister she'd lost, and because of this, Deborah would do anything Mary Fuller asked of her.

She stooped down and kissed Mary's smooth cheek, then slowly moved down the row to hug Shandra's thin boys and her haggard-looking brother. She wanted to linger, to hang on to the boys, to give them a piece of herself and take a piece from them, but others behind her in the sad procession wanted their time with the downcast family too. She had to move on, but...

Her time in Partway would be incomplete without a final word to Shandra. The casket, stainless steel rose pink, hovered above the open hole as if by magic. Deborah moved closer, her waist level with the colorful spray the family had selected—all Shandra's favorite flowers. Deborah's words were soft and low, spoken from an overflowing heart.

"Our time together was too short. But special, very special because of you. I don't know if I'll ever walk into a library, any library, without thinking of you." Deborah paused, needing time to suppress her tears, to wipe her wet nose. "Thank you for making time for me and for welcoming us into the family. Thank you, Shandra, you'll always be my special angel."

Two tears escaped, ran down her cheeks and dangled at her jawline. She dabbed at them, swiped their tracks, removing evidence of her sorrow. The rag-tag tissue in her hand had long ago stopped being useful. While she dug in her purse for a new one, two more, then four, then a stream of tears cut the same path as the original ones.

"Here, Mom," Hope handed her mother a soft cloth monogrammed with Imogene's initials.

"Thank you, honey." Deborah blew and wiped, staring at the flowers lounging on top of the casket. "Where's your Grandma?"

"She went to the car. You know she can't stand the heat." Hope fixed her eyes on the casket, a symbol of finality. "I can't believe she's really gone."

Deborah nodded her head, unable to make words right then. Hope reached out, her fingers gliding along the polished exterior of the casket. Inching her hand up, it hovered over the spray, then dropped into the mass of flowers to pluck a red rose from the bouquet. As soon as the rose rested in Hope's hand, it turned from brilliant red to black, curling into itself.

Dead.

Deborah witnessed the rose's transformation from live to dead, frowning in consternation. She'd never seen such a thing, and she was so ensnared by the spectacle that she missed Hope's own transformation.

§

From no smile at all to a bright one, accompanied by a puffed out chest and a gleeful gleam in her eyes. Pleasure radiated off the girl as if she'd achieved a monumental goal—which she had—that goal being the taking of a Fuller life and relief from pain, even though only temporary.

§

These things Deborah missed, but what finally drew her attention from the rose's mysterious change was that loving title softly spoken by her daughter. "Mom..." Deborah looked into Hope's face and seeing the tears in her eyes, her dispirited smile caused Deborah's own sorrow to magnify. "...I know I give you hell at times, but I'm glad you're my mom, and I'm glad you're here." She spoke to her mother, but her eyes were on the two small boys frozen to their chairs, looking like little men in their dark suits, but projecting a lost and frightened air.

Tears clouded Deborah's vision, but through her distorted view she saw a daughter-to-mother love in Hope's eyes, so intense it lit them up, made them sparkle. Her heart swelled and then burst with a corresponding love, a love so abounding, so innate, Deborah couldn't begin to contain it or determine its beginning or end. She pulled her daughter close, fiercely crushing her to her bosom, rocking her as if she were a babe again.

Eyes closed, Deborah's mind went to the woman who, instead of hugging her child, was burying her child. She knew from experience that was the worst nightmare a mother could endure—saying goodbye forever to a child of your womb. It had been years since Deborah had sat where Mary was sitting, but she remembered. One never forgot the soul-deep pain, the overwhelming darkness, the never-ending struggle to get up each morning and try to make sense out of disorder. It was awful, too awful to even think about.

So she didn't.

Instead, Deborah guided herself to the ritual she'd started after baby Rachel died of SIDS. She held her remaining daughter close and prayed for her. Whispering, her lips moving in a desperate, frantic way, brushing against Hope's ear, she asked God to give her daughter a long life of health and happiness and peace. She petitioned for few life trials and many life accomplishments. She prayed that Hope would never feel what Mary was feeling right now and what she—and her own mother—had felt before. She ended her prayer asking for blessings and mercy for her daughter and for the entire Fuller clan.

Sealed in this moment with Hope safe and secure in her arms, Deborah sank deeper into her own mind, the world forgotten.

The BlackHeart stood content, still in Hope's mother's arms, a vague smile teasing Its lips. With eyes closed, It accepted the goodness of Deborah's prayers, hoping all of it would come true. Hope wanted a husband and children. She wanted a career as a medical researcher—a hybrid of her parents' careers. She wanted a good and happy life, free of pain and strife. But mostly the BlackHeart wanted to go on killing Fullers until It got the one thing that would ensure Its permanent control and existence—that damn Bible with the papers of Truth inside. This, Its true life's purpose.

It couldn't remember at what age Hope had understood and accepted her purpose—at perhaps five or six, It guessed—but the vision of whom It was and what It needed to destroy had come to Hope during the night. *That* It did remember. Months later, after the vision, It suffocated Hope's baby sister, Rachel. That had been Hope's initiation, the BlackHeart's first step toward achieving Its life's purpose. *That* It remembered clearly.

Thinking back on that memory, It remembered that the pain had awakened Hope in the deepest part of morning. Sitting up in bed, she had wrapped her arms about her chest, moaning until the strongest voice within her—stronger than her natural voice, stronger even than the voice of her parents—whispered clear instructions.

Following that voice, she tiptoed out of her room and headed for her sister's nursery at the opposite end of the long, curved hallway. Entering with not a creak from the door, she padded on noiseless bare feet until she reached the antique crib. As she'd seen her mother do, she lowered the side panel and stared at Rachel, noting the infant's skin, which was darker than her own, and the cap of thick, black wavy hair, which was also different. This was her baby sister—but right now, it was her enemy—the source of her pain.

Then, following the instructions of the voice, Hope picked up the bright yellow pillow lying to the side of Rachel, fixed the pillow to the baby's face and pressed down and hard until the infant stopped squirming. Minutes later, when she lifted the pillow, she saw her sister as she'd been before—eyes closed, body relaxed. Minor differences—no more rise and fall of her tiny chest and no more sucking movements of her tiny lips.

A sick, evil smile had darkened Hope's face as the BlackHeart replaced the pillow in its original location. Walking backward, Its eyes never left the face of Hope's baby sister until It entered the hallway. Then, back in Hope's bed, It smiled sincerely, feeling warm and free. The pain had dissipated and that's when, at such a young age, Hope had *made* the connection between relief of pain and killing.

Over a decade later at eighteen years old, she now *understood* the connection. Not only understood it but knew at a soul level she would be freed of the connective constraints once the BlackHeart secured and destroyed the Bible and the papers of Truth. She also knew and accepted with remarkable clarity that each pain-driven kill drew It closer to the prize.

The BlackHeart's smile grew bolder as It continued resting in Hope's mother's arms, thinking about Its kills since Rachel—Anna, Curtis, and now Shandra. Yes, It'd experienced great success all these many years, aided in some small measure by Deborah's loving prayers for long life and success. Unable to thank her outright for her contribution to the BlackHeart's success, It hugged her tighter, a payment for the support and well wishes throughout the years and the future.

With thoughts of the future, there was no getting around thoughts of Mattie. Dear old Aunt Mattie was proving to be stronger in spirit and more devoted to family and righteousness than the BlackHeart had originally thought. Beating the old woman would not be as easy as drowning Aunt Anna in the pool or putting a gun to Curtis' head and pulling the trigger. No, this was going to be a struggle to the end just like times before. But once the dust cleared this time, the BlackHeart had no doubt that possession of the Bible and papers would fall to It. And with possession would come destruction. With destruction, permanent and unfettered rule. The thought of that pleased It, gave It joy.

For her role in this, for bringing two halves together to make one whole family, Deborah deserved another hug and kiss. The BlackHeart gave her both. Hope's poor mother would never know that her need for purpose and meaning had led the BlackHeart to the prize sooner. Yeah, sure, the BlackHeart would have gradually found the "missing" family. It would have eventually landed in Mattie's front yard, demanding the Bible and papers of Truth, but Deborah's hollow living had sped up the process and made the discovery more natural, less suspect. "Thank you, Mom," It whispered again in Deborah's ear.

Turning Its head to give Hope's mother yet another well-earned kiss, the BlackHeart froze. *A threat*, Its senses warned, *go within*. It did so, closing Hope's eyes and converging everything spiritual in It to understand the danger. *Yes...there...by the back fence—the record keeper.* The BlackHeart stiffened in Deborah's arms, drew in a sharp breath.

"Hope?"

It heard Deborah's inquiry and felt a minor shifting of her body. But the BlackHeart was not interested in appeasing Hope's mother. It opened Its eyes, wrenched Itself out of Deborah's embrace and turned to the back part of the cemetery where Aunt Mattie journeyed forward toward the grouping of family. The BlackHeart's face showed no emotion, no awareness of others as It tracked the old woman's advance.

Moments after It sensed Aunt Mattie, others became aware, and a disbelieving hush descended. All watched as the bearer of Truth skimmed past headstones, stepped over rocks and teeming insect life, making a crooked path to Shandra's final resting place. The BlackHeart watched closely as the self-imposed outsider passed the perimeter group of family and friends, and being curious, nosy people, they followed in her wake, but not too closely. Others who blocked Mattie's pathway to Shandra's coffin moved smartly out of the way, giving the old woman a wide, open path. Squinting Its eyes at Aunt Mattie, the BlackHeart noticed the elder did not look to the left, right, up or down; she stepped with purpose until finally, in the hush, she reached the casket and stopped. A few feet of steel separated them.

From Its side of the coffin, the BlackHeart looked through the old woman, trying to engage her, but Mattie had fortified herself, effectively blocking Its efforts to feel her out, to sense her intentions. The BlackHeart smiled at this, content to give the woman this trivial victory, fine with letting Mattie alone for now to stare down at the hole to be filled later by Governor. Still, It didn't trust Mattie. It figured the old woman had her butcher knife with her and wouldn't waste a second of explanation before using it. Figuring that, It kept Its senses sharply focused, finely tuned, ready to decipher any plays Its adversary attempted.

Minutes passed with the BlackHeart staring at Mattie and Mattie staring down at the hole. When finally Mattie looked up, it wasn't to challenge the BlackHeart. Her dark eyes roamed rapidly through the throng of people, settling upon one. It didn't need to follow Aunt Mattie's line of sight to know who Hope's aunt targeted—Governor. The BlackHeart could feel him standing outside of sacred family land, leaning against the hearse, waiting for everyone to leave so he could finish the last act of burial.

The BlackHeart smirked when It saw Mattie offer her replacement the smallest of nods. Its smirk died, however, when Mattie turned her attention to the BlackHeart. Her black eyes were hard as pebbles and carried a message of hate so strong it caused the BlackHeart to falter and tremble for a second or two. It'd been unaware the record keeper could hate as fiercely, as completely as the BlackHeart. Quick to recover from Its lapse, strong again, the BlackHeart met the hard stare, matching it.

And so began the silent duel of strength versus strength.

Deborah believed her old auntie was not really seeing Hope, that her mind was saying bye-bye to Shandra in her own special way while Hope simply provided a backdrop. But who really knew? The old woman was impossible to read. But Hope wasn't, and the expression on her daughter's face told the world she didn't like this woman, that she didn't appreciate being stared at, that she could give as good as get. And give it to her grand-auntie she did—a bold look filled with challenge.

When it started feeling uncomfortable, when it seemed like the two were going to stand and lock eyes all day, Deborah wrapped an arm about her daughter's slender waist and whispered to her, "Don't be rude."

Turning to Mattie, Deborah attempted a smile, but it dissolved as quickly as it formed. If she hadn't been weighed down by death and sorrow, she could have sustained it. But given her state, the best she could offer her elder was a somber, "Hello, Aunt Mattie. I hope you're feeling better." She referenced their last time together at Black Hill when Mattie had looked strangely ill and run off before Deborah could give her a ride home.

"Things is comin' to an end. Yo' work. My work. But a change starts it up again." Mattie spoke at Deborah, but stared at Hope.

Deborah crooked her head, a puzzled look etched on her face. She had expected an *I'm fine,* a *how-de-do,* a *right as rain*—not an acoustic crossword reply. Too tired in spirit to try and discern Mattie's response or form a suitably vague reply, Deborah simply offered a wisp of a smile and nodded her head like a good little girl.

The small effort was wasted on Mattie. Ignoring Deborah still, Mattie broke off from Hope to look down at the family spray sprawled across the top of Shandra's casket. Deborah watched as the old woman's face took on anger. Her eyes sparked flames of indignation and Deborah could almost see steam curling from her ears. Wondering what had set the woman off, she looked down to where Mattie was staring and saw the black rose laid mockingly on top of the colorful, fresh spray. Obviously, Hope had carelessly dropped the rose there and it was that—either the dead rose or the fact that a dead thing overshadowed the living flowers beneath it—that stoked Mattie's anger. Before Deborah could react, Mattie reached out, snatched up the dead object and flung it to the ground. With the offensive thing out of sight, Mattie returned to staring at Hope, hard and mean. But for a brief moment, before the family elder had adopted the angry look, Deborah could have sworn she saw a wisp of sadness in her eyes. Of course, Deborah would never be sure, because now there was nothing in her gray-rimmed, black eyes. Nothing. Blank.

Similar to the words she had spoken earlier—empty, without meaning. "A shame. You can stop it." And just like the words she spoke now.

She pinned her lifeless stare on Deborah for several moments.

Then, that was it. Mattie was through. She stepped backward, turned in slow fashion and again focused straight ahead, affording no one a side or passing glance. She just traipsed back from whence she had come, past grave markers, past oaks, bending to slide between the fence railings and then curved out of sight following the creek's twists.

When nothing could be seen of Mattie, not even her back, the oppressive hush lifted as people rustled back to life. Muted conversations reached Deborah's ears, the loudest of which was that between Cousin Clarice and Step-Uncle Billy.

Cousin Clarice's whisper, which really wasn't a whisper, expressed what most of the family was thinking. "I cain't believe she came!"

"Me neither. Naw, goodness. Let's go see."

Deborah heard the scurrying of two pairs of feet and knew they were coming her way.

"What'd she say? Why'd she come?" Step-Uncle Billy's words hammered Deborah's ears even as his good hand yanked on her elbow. Unconcerned about the occasion or the grieving people scattered under and outside of the meeting tent, he demanded answers.

Deborah pulled out of his grip, frown lines bisecting her forehead. Honestly? Even if she wanted to answer his question, she didn't know the answer. Like all of her encounters with Aunt Mattie, this one had also been unusual. She lifted her shoulders, her face conveying her own confusion.

"What'd she say? Why you?" Cousin Clarice added to the list of unanswerable questions.

Irritation with her relatives—these two at least—worked its way to the surface, past the tangle of other emotions. Deborah managed to contain it before it broke totally free. Still, her words were severe, her glance at Billy and Clarice uncharitable when she said, "I assume, like the rest of us, she came to pay her respects."

"Yeah, but *why*? She ain't never done that before." Step-Uncle Billy continued drilling.

Not to be outshined, Cousin Clarice asked, "What *exactly* did she say?"

In her mind, she repeated Aunt Mattie's mysterious phrases. Not to provide answers to the pair of relatives who invaded her and Hope's personal space, but rather to answer for herself. An end. Work concluding. Easy to fix. The fragments didn't make sense. She had heard Aunt Mattie's words. Hearing had not been the problem. They had been simple words, words any second grader could understand. Comprehension had not been the problem. So why did she not understand? Again, her shoulders lifted, her head shook. "I don't know. I honestly don't know."

Cousin Clarice shouldered Step-Uncle Billy out of the way, moving in closer to mother and daughter. "Did she say something about Shandra's death? Did she see anything? Is she gonna raise Shandra to life?"

Deborah reared back as if physically hit. She could feel the shock and astonishment play across her face, and in her mind she questioned herself: *Did I really just hear that?* She turned to look at Hope's face to confirm. Yes, her daughter's reaction mirrored her own. She couldn't believe it! The gall, the nerve, the ignorance. It took several seconds for her mind to recover from the unexpected slam, but when it regrouped, the words came spewing forth.

"What kind of stupid question is that? Are you out of your mind? That is the craz—." Deborah stopped, remembering where she was standing. Remembering Shandra's mother and boys sitting close by. Remembering the warning about Billy and Clarice that Shandra had given her: *"'tween the two of them, they don't possess a quarter teaspoon of social skills. And they love mess. Just ignore them, if you can."*

Snatching them each up by an arm, yanking and pulling on them like she used to yank and pull on Hope when she was a young child and she'd done something that required correction, Deborah bullied them from under the tarp and into the hot, bearing-down sun, far from the civilized, heartsick people.

A silent Hope followed the threesome, an amused grin on her young face, which she had the sense to hide behind her hand.

"What's wrong with y'all?" Anger had a good hold on Deborah, making her spit words at them. "How can y'all be so disrespectful? Shandra's family is right there. *Right there...*" Her finger pointed the way. "Don't you think they heard you? Don't you think they're suffering enough? Show some respect!"

Tugging on the seams of her Sunday best dress, her nose hanging in the air, Cousin Clarice hotly defended herself. "They probly wanta hear, too. Ain't nobody in this family ignorant to Aunt Mattie's ways, 'cept you and yours," she ended nastily.

Just as hot and vile with her words, Deborah slapped her opinion in her cousin and uncle's face. "I'm *sure* the only thing they want to know right now is that Shandra's in a better place. I *know* they don't want reminders of the accident and I'm *positive* they don't want to hear about any black magic silly stuff. Shandra didn't believe in that mess."

"She may not have, but Mattie do and old girl went straight for that casket."

Step-Uncle Billy inserted himself into the fight. "Took a flower and said sumthin.' Naw, naw. Sumthin's goin' on. First, she show up and then she talk to you. Ain't no family tree done all that. Naw, naw. Sumthin's up." Step-Uncle Billy nodded his fat head, thinking he was smart, knowing he was on to something good.

A pin of reality popped Deborah's anger. It fizzled out, allowing discouragement to take its place. Discouragement born of the reality of seeing Step-Uncle Billy and Cousin Clarice stripped to their real selves. It was so clear to Deborah why Shandra had always been so hard on these two, why she hadn't cared for them. Instead of focusing on the good, they focused on the bad. Instead of unifying, they divided. Instead of uplifting, they tore down. Those had not been Shandra's guiding principles, nor were they Deborah's.

Carefully, she flipped through her vocabulary seeking non-offensive, inclusionary words, words that built bridges not fences. She spoke slowly, using her hands to help explain. "Clarice, Billy, I believe you have *reasons* for thinking the way you do—"

"See, see, this is how I figure it..." Step-Uncle Billy interrupted, as if he hadn't heard Deborah's calm voice in his ear. He was excited, hot on the trail of some dirt. "...see, her lips. They didn't move much and she didn't stay long, so she couldn't have said much, no time. Naw, naw. But..." that good hand paused in this, his dramatic climax, "...a spell don't take long, do it? I bet she put a spell on Shandra to reverse the *Fuller's Curse*. I *know* I'm right; I can *feel* it." He ended on a flourish, his good hand balled into a victorious fist.

Cousin Clarice caught onto Step-Uncle Billy's passion and righteousness. She moved in close, tightening the circle, including Deborah in their plot, but excluding others by lowering her voice. "Ummmm-hummm, Billy, you'se right. Had to be, 'specially since she..." Cousin Clarice pointed a leather-clad finger toward Deborah, "...didn't know what Aunt Mattie said. That 'cause she reversed the curse in a strange tongue."

Again, Deborah reeled back, slayed by their ignorant words, their idiotic deductions. How they could stretch Mattie's visit and words—words they didn't even hear—into something this silly, this ridiculous, was amazing. And crazier still, the serious expressions on one dark and one light face. They actually believed their conclusion. They actually saw nothing wrong in their flawed analysis.

Deborah cupped her face, not knowing what to do. Should she be mad at them, laugh at them, shake them out of their stupidity, or speak fact and logic to help their pea brains understand reality? She settled on that at which she excelled—facts, logic.

"Look, Billy, Clarice, I don't even know what the *Fuller's Curse* is and I don't really wanna know…" She rushed her last few words lest they think that an invitation to inform her. "…but I do know that *I* was the one who heard the words and Aunt Mattie *was* using English. She was simply talking in riddles. She was probably confused from the heat and she is *old*."

Cousin Clarice's glove-encased hand landed on the side of her face; her eyes bulged uncomfortably in their sockets as she sucked in the air Deborah had been using to support her words. "Oh Lawd, girl, you was nearby when she made the curse. You better hope none of it spilled over on you. You better watch yo'self, if you don't want to end up like Shandra." She glanced decently over at the casket, clasped her hands in prayer and recited, "God rest her soul."

Step-Uncle Billy said, "Amen," then nodded his head vigorously. "Double curse. By that strange, possessed woman. Better watch out. Naw-naw."

Strange? They had the audacity to label Mattie strange! An ironic laugh urged to be free, but Deborah pressed her lips together to keep the laugh from erupting in their faces. True, their old aunt was strange, but she wasn't the only Fuller who walked on that side of the street. Obviously, Billy and Clarice didn't see themselves through the lenses of the rest of the world.

Billy, a disabled army veteran, spent his days writing—and mailing—letters to his favorite characters on reality shows like *Dog the Bounty Hunter* and *Hoarders*, telling them of the surprises and dangers that awaited them on future episodes; surprises and dangers he gleaned from previews, teasers and internet gossip. When he wasn't doing that, he was busy sniffing into other folks'—and not just family—business, so he could keep the mess going. He absolutely lived for drama.

And Clarice, a semi-retired beautician, was no better. She seemed to have an aversion to matching colors and patterns and in matching clothes to the proper season. Deborah looked at her and wondered if she owned a mirror and some form of media—TV, radio, internet, anything that would give her a weather report. If she did, she could not have consulted either before she left the house or else she would not have worn virgin white leather gloves in one hundred degree weather, nor would she have ensembled those gloves with that orange dress, peacock feather church hat, green hair and yellow skin.

Yet there they stood, passing judgment on another, labeling others as strange.

Strange. Judgmental. Messy. Disloyal. Opinionated. Rootless. Destructive. Adjectives for those two materialized in Deborah's mind like flashcard answers. Objectionable…that was the sum of what those two were, and settling on that she told herself, *now is a good time to walk away from them and save my energy and intelligence for a nobler cause.* But she couldn't. Something in her—perhaps the research scientist she was trained to be or being a mother with the natural desire to teach and correct—wouldn't let stupidity go by without countering with a good, strong dose of reason.

"Billy, Clarice, listen to what you're saying. You took a bunch of assumptions and came up with the wrong conclusion. Aunt Mattie didn't come to cast a spell. She simply came to offer condolences, and it doesn't matter that she hasn't done it before. She's doing it now, and instead of making up stuff about her you should have welcomed her. She *is* family."

"Oh naw, naw, shoot! You soundin' just like that Shandra. That ain't right. With all them degrees you got you s'posed to be smarter than Shandra. All that talk 'bout fam'ly and welcomes and love and stuff. 'motional. That what it is. You 'motional like Shandra, and looka where it got her. Laid out short. Naw, naw, naw. You best open yo' eyes 'fo you be the next dead Fuller."

With both hands on one non-existent hip and nose still pointed to the sky, Cousin Clarice supported Step-Uncle Billy's pronouncements and added some of her own. "He right. You don't live here. You don't see the things we do, don't hear the stuff we hears. You say yo' little piece, do yo' little research and run on back up the road. You don't know the real deal." She swiveled her gloved hands to the other curveless hip, her neck rocking indignantly.

Deborah rubbed her forehead where a dull ache was promising to grow out of proportion. Why had she allowed herself to get caught up with these two? She should have stayed mad at them or left as soon as their knuckleheads came together. Oh well, nothing to do now except finish it.

"You know, Billy, Clarice, you're right. I don't live here. But I do know fact from fiction, truth from groundless, faulty conclusions. Shandra's death..." Deborah choked as the scene of Shandra's fall filled her mind. Horrible. Horrible. Her younger cousin shouldn't have had to die like that. No one should. She backed away from the mental scene, forced herself to go on. "... it was an accident." Again, Deborah's words were stymied this time because her mind latched on to the word "accident," which invited a rehash of the phone conversation she'd had with Mary earlier this week.

Feeling guilty that she hadn't been more forceful in keeping Hope and Shandra off that cliff and preventing another Fuller death, she'd called Mary apologizing and asking for forgiveness. She'd explained to Mary that she too had lost a daughter and knew the pain Mary felt. Mary had assured Deborah she harbored no ill feelings toward Hope or Deborah. In fact, several kids had reported to Mary that Deborah had tried to stop the pair, but Shandra had insisted.

Mary had surprised Deborah, saying, "I'm surprised she lived this long. She was always puttin' herself out for others. Always endangerin' herself, just like her daddy. I tried to talk to her about it, especially after the boys were born, but I was wastin' my breath and decided to change my tactic and start prayin' for her, instead. I left it to God, and this is how He chose to handle it. So you know that means the good Lord got the brunt of my anger. And Shandra got the rest. But we're good. No need for you to feel guilty. And please, tell your daughter I said so."

Deborah shook her head, shaking the phone conversation back in place in her memory bank. Back to Billy and Clarice, she finished, "It was her time to go and my death, your death, and every Fuller's death will be on God's time. No one in this family, including Mattie, will have a thing to do with stopping or reversing it."

"I see you gonna hafta learn the hard way. See for yo'self that the deaths 'round here ain't so cut and dry. I see you gonna hafta learn for yo'self there's other forces 'round here. Naw, naw." Step-Uncle Billy hiked up his beltloopless pants with his good hand and stared hard at Deborah. "You got all them papers from Shandra. You got that death stuff. Compare it to the *Fuller's Curse* and see if they don't stink."

He would have to bring that up. The newspaper clippings, death and birth reports, autopsies, and the like sat where they'd been sitting—abandoned. Every time she passed her study at home, every time she walked by that door, those papers called to her. Since Shandra's death, she had ignored the call, pretended like she didn't hear. Shandra's death had stripped the excitement and interest out of the project. There would be no more phone chats to discuss the progress of the family tree, no more encouraging words when she felt discouraged by the false trails and dead ends, no more help from the librarian in Partway. Deborah didn't realize, until the young girl passed, how dependent she'd become, how dependent she'd always been on another human's life, and how much hurt those dependencies could cause.

She had to go back in her mind and access what had gotten her through the previous hurts and remember how she had forced herself to move on after the deaths of Rachel, Anna, Curtis, and the loss of her career.

Responsibility. Debt. Purpose. Yes, those were the beliefs that had pushed her forward. The living had a responsibility to the dead to keep on living. The living owed the dead their best. The living had a purpose to fulfill.

As a living Fuller, Deborah owed it to Shandra and the others marked in this graveyard—and a similar site in Dallas—to stay on the path of life.

Love and life-giving energy passed through wood and dirt, sticks and stone to touch her, a gift from those six feet below who shared her blood and approved of her thoughts. Deborah sensed it; no, better than that, she felt it kindle and erupt within her.

Renewed commitment and passion for living, for completing their family tree sizzled in her words. "Okay, Billy, Clarice! I see I'm going to have to *show* you. As soon as I finish putting our family's history on paper, I'll do a study of deaths and it'll prove to you, scientifically, factually, that we're a typical, normal family in death and in life."

She didn't wait for Cousin Clarice or Step-Uncle Billy to counter or agree. Grabbing Hope's arm, she stomped away. But she wasn't fast enough to miss a parting shot. It came from Billy's mouth.

"I doubt it, but while you're provin', check that daughter of yourn's. How many Fuller deaths she been 'round? We all knows she was 'round that last one."

Deborah kept going, letting his words drift on by.

The Second Beginning: The Study of Death

Isaiah 65:20 (NRSV)
...for one who dies at a hundred years will be considered a youth,
and one who falls short of a hundred will be considered accursed.

At the exact moment when a passing hand changes one day into the next, Deborah's sleeping mind was viewing a nightmare.

A man was chasing her and Hope through a labyrinth, trapping them where two walls came together in a dingy, spider-webbed corner. The man stood over nine feet tall, glowed neon orange and had only one discernible facial feature—two black coals where eyes should have been. In one hand, he gripped a gleaming instrument of death—an axe, a knife, a pitchfork—she wasn't sure what it was, but she did know with surety that he intended to use that tool on them for utter and lasting harm.

Just as he raised the weapon to bring it down on them—

Deborah woke up, heart slamming against her chest, a terrified cry on her lips, nightgown twisted every way but right. Instantly, she realized that she was alive; there was no immediate or real threat.

In the long moments afterwards, as her heart returned to a resting rate, her mind insisted on replaying the nightmare sequence, adding different spins and twists to make the ending less terrifying, less real. The dream editing didn't work, however. The dark dream still frightened her. She covered her eyes with the heels of her hands and wedged herself against Samuel.

It came to her quietly at first, whispered words so faint she thought she had imagined them. So, she ignored them, thinking it a prelude to the same or a different nightmare. When it came a second time, its plea was desperate, causing Deborah to remove her hands, open her eyes, and lean on her elbows. She listened intently, her ears strained, and soon she received confirmation. Yes, the Fuller family tree whispered to her, offering a distraction from the dark images, relief from the scary. She sat up, fully awake, attracted to the idea so much so that when it called to her a fourth time, she rose to answer.

Many hours later, when the sun's rays had overpowered the darkness and her side of the bed had grown cold many times over, Deborah sat back in her well-stuffed leather chair and gave a satisfied sigh. With a smile curving her lips, she admired the fully blossomed Fuller family tree, all Fullers accounted for, not a one missing. She dallied over it, patting herself on the back for a job well done and wishing she could show it off now to Samuel, Hope, her parents, and of course, her kin in Partway. But there would be plenty of time later for show-and-tell. Now, it was time to prove Billy and Clarice wrong. Time now to study the Fuller deaths.

Even though her background in research science was stale from years of washing dishes, running errands, serving on high school committees and playing hostess to all kinds of service people, Deborah knew it would be as simple as a finger snap. Indeed, as she delved into the study, reading news articles, obituaries, death records, autopsies and such, marking and compiling data, pity for Billy and Clarice puffed up inside her like leavened bread. It didn't seem fair that facts and applied research piled high on her side when all they had was conjecture and imagination. *Oh, well.* She shrugged as she input data, made notes and validated. *They started this lunacy, and I'm ending it.*

Oh, but it didn't take long for a change to come. As Deborah waded deeper into the study, pity for Billy and Clarice slowly backed away, leaving the door open for frustration and second-guessing to creep on in. Deborah had forgotten that agonizing, step-by-slow-step methodology and detailed note-taking had been two of the reasons she'd worked such long hours during her tenure at the Southern Region Science Institute or "The Lab" as employees, clients, and other invested parties called it. Now, hours later and not having even scraped the top layer of the death study, those reasons came pounding back, making her head hurt and causing groans and curses to spill out of her. She entertained one dark moment during which she thought about quitting, but struck down the thought. She was honor bound. At Black Hill, on the day of Shandra's funeral, she'd made a commitment to Shandra and the other Fullers who had died that she would prove them a normal family, that they were not a cursed family or subjected to any other black magic. Besides that, she would sacrifice her life before she admitted defeat to Billy and Clarice. So, injecting determination into her veins, she focused her mind, sharpened her eyes and pushed on.

Progress came and went like a child's game. Forward two baby steps, back three giant steps. Forward one giant step, back two baby steps. Slowly, the study of death took shape, pulling theory and principles out of Deborah she thought had died ages ago. She would have continued pushing, making slow, steady progress except Samuel entered her study, bringing her coffee and a breakfast sandwich, announcing, "Time for church."

Deborah smiled, a non-verbal "thank you" for the nourishment and noting the time, she calculated the hours she'd been shut away in her office— nine. Nine long, backbreaking hours. Yes, it was time for a break from death.

§

Later that evening, after precious time with family at church and dinner followed by a long nap, Deborah returned to her death study, renewed and eager. But as before, it didn't take long for the high gloss to wear off. Too soon, the study had her grappling for a hold.

By the time Dr. Ester Ross' call came, Deborah's study of death lay still with barely any life left in it. Thirty minutes later, when Ester showed up in person, Deborah's study still held on, but just barely. Even though it was choking to death and smelling foul, Deborah refused to give up.

While massaging life into her death study, she was aware of her best friend's presence and yet not completely aware. She knew Ester lay on her tan colored couch in her office, the two of them—woman and couch—matching in pigmentation. She knew the couch was plenty wide enough to hold the curvy, attractive statistician, yet not wide enough to hold all her problems.

Deborah heard her friend speak. "I think this separation will be good. We need time apart to evaluate our problems and decide if this marriage is worth saving." But the usual empathetic comebacks: *I'm so sorry; Yeah girl, I understand*; *Are you sure this is what you really want to do?*; *What about counseling?* did not fill the air. The study of death had ninety per cent of Deborah's attention.

Apparently aware of the missing response and puzzled by it, Ester lifted her hand off her forehead and opened her eyes into slits. Turning her head to stare at Deborah's back, she declared, "Deborah, you're ignoring me. I came over to talk to you and get advice from an old married lady, and you're not even paying attention."

Deborah murmured, "Yeah, un-huh."

Ester swung her legs off the couch, and sat up. "So, you think it's okay if I throw this pillow at your head?"

Silence.

More desperate action was needed to pull Deborah away from death; Ester went right to it, marching over to Deborah, coming to a halt at her back. Leaning over Deborah's head, her eyes squinted through her glasses at the conglomeration of categories, numbers and percentages glowing on the computer monitor.

"Okay, what am I competing with? What is this mess?" she demanded to know, indicating the undisciplined pile of papers on Deborah's right and the busy blur of lines, boxes, and markings on the screen. The statistician leaned forward and asked, "What are you doing?" Her testy tone ensured a reply.

"Studying death," Deborah answered, although still focused on the screen. She had input two more causes of death on the Excel worksheet and now studied the recalculated numbers and chart. She frowned, not liking the results at all. Delaying not a moment, she moved on to the next Fuller death.

"What?" Ester snagged a nearby chair and rolled it close to the computer, as close as she could get without bumping Deborah out of the way.

This time, Deborah did blink herself out of death's trance. "I'm sorry, Ester." She shook her head, letting go of the final tendrils of death to face her friend. "I'm trying to figure something out."

"I can tell *that*. What *I* don't understand is how *that…*" she flung the word and her hand at the jumble of words and figures on the screen, "…whatever the hell it is, could be more important than my problems."

Ester Ross possessed a personality you either loved or hated; there was no "in between," no "so-so" with her. Either you loved her, or you hated her. Deborah loved Ester and Ester loved Deborah. Their friendship had taken seed on the campus of the University of Texas at Austin thirty years ago; it had rooted when they landed jobs—with Deborah as a research scientist and Ester as a statistician—at The Lab; and their friendship had held fast during the vicious obstacles life had hurled at them: Deborah's forced retirement by Samuel—who had lost patience with her long work hours and compromised health; the breakup of Ester's first marriage; the birth of Hope; the mountaintop and valley experiences of Ester's second marriage; the human losses in Deborah's family; the death of her baby girl from Sudden Infant Death Syndrome; and now this, Ester's separation from Lewis, her third husband.

Because Deborah loved Ester, she cared about her friend's marital problems, even if it was the same old story with a different male name inserted. But the timing…the timing was bad. If only Ester had waited a few more weeks before putting Lewis out or at least long enough for Deborah to clear her mind of death—ones that had happened years and years and years ago. Names and faces she didn't know, except that they were Fullers, her people.

With motherly patience and care, attributes now ingrained thoroughly because of eighteen years of practice, Deborah explained, "Ester, this is *not* more important than your problems, but it is something I have to finish. I made a commitment—" Ester would think her crazy if she finished her thought: *I made a commitment to my dead ancestors at Black Hill. That's why this work outranks your disastrous marriage right now.* Even in her mind it sounded off. Deborah could just imagine how it would sound floating on the air.

"A commitment? I thought this was some fun little project to kill time. When did it become so serious?"

The scene from three days ago at Black Hill filled Deborah's mind, eclipsing everything except the answer to Ester's question, which she kept inside her head: *when Shandra died; when I felt the unnatural approval of my dead relatives at Black Hill; when I remembered the responsibility and debt I must fulfill; but mostly when I sought meaning for my life.*

That was the real truth, but Deborah wasn't up to telling the complete truth. That would open too many doors that Deborah didn't have the mental strength to close. So, in the likeness of Mattie, she buried the truth coffin-deep, and covered it, not with a lie, but rather a humble point that grew an ego. "When I decided to prove Billy and Clarice wrong."

"Billy and Clarice?" Ester's face registered confusion. Not for long. She had not graduated number one in their class because of her looks— although she could have. She was not the most esteemed statistician at The Lab for nothing. Her male-attracting body carried a superior intellectual brain that made a lie of her inferior personal life. Given her big brain, names and relationships came together easily, quickly. "Oh, the colorful ones. Uncle and cousin."

"The nutty ones is a better description," Deborah laughed. "At Shandra's funeral they made a lot of claims."

"Like???" Ester folded her arms tight under her breasts, her face and disposition growing sourer with each sentence that carried them further away from her problems. Even still, her attraction to facts, her need to prove or disprove—traits embedded in her chromosomes—and an open Excel spreadsheet drew her into the promise of something good.

"Well, after Aunt Mattie showed up—"

"The weird old lady."

Deborah frowned, slanting Ester a censuring look. "You sound like Hope. I expect to have to correct her, but you?"

Ester impatiently waved the discipline aside. "Go on."

"Well, they claim Shandra's death is questionable, and that Aunt Mattie put some type of curse, *Fuller's Curse* is what they called it, on her so she could rise up from her grave." Deborah almost choked on the words. Not because of grief. Not because the sheer stupidity of curses, spells and dark practices of old made her gag. Rather, the stench from the Fuller deaths she had unscabbed earlier rose up, reminding her of her dying study of death, of the commitment that was slowly becoming a lie.

An abbreviated burst of sardonic laughter pulled Deborah out of her darkening mind. Apparently, that laugh was Ester's official response to Billy and Clarice's claims. "Were they for real? A curse?!" A disdainful twist of Ester's lips and a snotty glare from her eyes revealed her opinion about the hand-me-down practice from expired years.

A sober, "Oh, yes, very serious," accompanied Deborah's dour look and slow nod.

"That's the stupidest thing I've heard in a long time. Even more stupid than the stuff Lewis accused me of. A *curse*? How simple-minded can you be? I know you set them straight, reminded them we're in the 21st century?" More scorn and contempt blended with Ester's put-downs.

The retired scientist's sigh admitted defeat. "I tried. I used logic and common sense, but I might as well have been talking to myself. They weren't about to hear that, only themselves."

A moment of silence passed as Ester's big brain put two and two together to come up with four. She pointed at the image on the monitor. "That's what you're doing? Proving their stupidity with facts."

Another moment of motherly discipline was in order, but Deborah let this one slide. "Yeah, I finally told them I was going to prove them wrong, especially after they kept pushing the issue. They kept insisting something wasn't right with this family and death." Deborah's face puckered as one of the pair's loosely slung comments returned to her. "They said similar things at the graveside cleaning service. Said something about Aunt Mattie being questioned by the police about some relative's death and knowing more than she let on.

Ester rolled her eyes and snapped her neck. "Yeah, well, I would expect *them* to exaggerate a situation just to prove their point." Turning to the screen, she demanded, "Tell me what you've done. This is just the type of project I need to take my mind off Lewis. Tell me step by step, so I can check your approach." Ester moved even closer, and Deborah, feeling as if she'd been thrown a life raft, delved into the telling.

§

With their backs to the door and as engaged as they were, neither Deborah nor Ester heard the door open. Not all the way, just enough for Hope to eavesdrop. The BlackHeart leaned casually against the jamb, eating a bowl of Neapolitan ice cream while listening to Hope's mother and Aunt Ester talk about death. It felt a swell of pride as they discussed Its work, and Hope desperately wanted to warn them that all was not as it seemed, but that was just her teenage nature trying to assert itself...again. The BlackHeart understood, but squashed it just the same. The study of death, assisting Hope's mother and aunt, would not help to acquire that Bible and destroy it. Speaking of which... The BlackHeart straightened and thought It might just go pay the old girl a visit.

It's coming.

The whispered warning felt more like a caress than a call to attention. It was misleading, making Mattie think she had a choice of either waking or staying asleep, when all the hosts in heaven and two people on earth knew she had no choice.

Again, "In-Me" brushed Mattie's soul. *It's coming. Prepare.*

Experienced eyes opened, heeding the second command.

In the country, midnight was a lot darker than in the city. No street lights, no porch lamps, and for some reason the stars and moon seemed farther away, the greater distance diluting their shine. But Mattie didn't need light to prepare for the evil coming up her drive.

Her old bones unfolded slowly as she sat up, throwing back the white muslin sheet and the patchwork quilt that cocooned her at night. Although she owned several pairs of house shoes—gifts from Governor over the years, which he eventually stopped buying when he figured out she wasn't going to wear them, ever—she stepped over them and walked barefooted on creaky wooden floors to the living room. There, to wait for her company.

She was tempted to go get the Bible and its secret and hold it to her as a shield, a weapon. But she couldn't risk holding the Truth so close to evil. This BlackHeart was cunning, and Mattie didn't dare leave a crack for It to rip through. That would be disastrous, would upset the Libra balance of life and death, of innocence and guilt, of cursed and free. If the BlackHeart ever got hold of the papers of Truth, it would be better that all Fullers—and all the world, for that matter—go straight to hell from their mother's womb and not even bother with a temporary stay on earth. No, rather than risk that, Mattie left the Bible where it lay and instead, pressed her body against the front door, praying and calling forth all she knew.

Pebbles and rocks spitting under the spin of tires told of the arrival.

The vehicle screeched to a halt. A door banged shut. Heavy footsteps scarred the planks of her porch. Pounding on her screen door.

"I know you're there. Come out, you coward."

"Ain't nothin' here for you."

"I'm gonna beat you, old lady. You know that." The evil one boasted confidently in Its sweet, sweet voice. They both knew this was Mattie's last go round as the family's protector; the evil one meant for it to be ugly.

That scared Mattie. Scared all manner of preparation out of her as she wondered about her own death. How would she die? She, the keeper of the records with the longest tenure. Would it be by stabbing, gunshot, strangulation, run down, or like big brother Willie, axed to death? And where? ...what time of day? ...what day of the week? Above all the dark details, at the top of her pile of imaginings, she wondered if Governor would be there. Oh, she knew he would be nearby, but would he be close enough to hold her and ease the pain as she slipped away? She prayed so, for within his arms she would know that her commitment to duty had been appreciated, that she had been loved, and that she had been a good and faithful daughter.

"Give it to me now and I promise to make it less painful."

The compromise interrupted Mattie's wonderings. Stillness swept her mind as the offer rebounded, then settled in deep. What It offered appealed greatly to Mattie. Death and dying were not what Mattie feared, but rather the pain, the brutality that accompanied a Fuller death. She had killed too many BlackHearts, had cleaned up too many murders by the BlackHeart to know that was not what she wanted for herself. The cursed one knew this and offered an out.

Mattie thought about it, considered it. For the dirty service she had performed for her family all these years, didn't she deserve a painless death? Didn't she deserve a reward for the sacrifices she had made?

"Come on, Mattie," the BlackHeart cooed in Its honey sweet voice. "I promise I'll make it easy. I'll even let you pick your manner of death."

The temptation was just that—tempting. Mattie swayed toward it, already picturing an innocent, serene death, one without struggle, fight or strife. She liked the picture. Visualizing it made her bones melt, made her obligation to family pale in comparison. She smiled and caressed the wood of the door.

"Mattie, you deserve it. You've fought the good fight. Go home."

Home...the sound of it caressed Mattie's ears. Her smile deepened as she dreamt of home in Heaven. Her strong, committed heart wilted, thinking of permanent peace, lasting joy, eternal happiness. The hardships this troublesome, wearying and temporary world brought to her daily life would vanish, leaving her to flourish in the everlasting love of Helen, Willie, Floyd, Johnny, Daddy, and of course, Mama.

Tears splattered her foot, some dampened her housedresses as she turned her back to the door and stared at the Holy Bible.

"Go on, Mattie, bring it to me and you'll be home in a few minutes."

Mattie ached for home. She yearned for her family...her real family. Up in Heaven, where the streets are paved in gold like the gold letters on that Bible. She stood up straight, the palms of her hands the last to separate from the door. Her eyes fixed on The Good Book and the Truth within.

"In a short moment, you'll be free of all this, Mattie. Free."

One forward step, then two. The rest of the steps uncounted. She just knew she was at the desk which held the Word and the Truth. Mattie picked up the Bible. Her hands shook. She leafed through it as if searching for a particular passage of scripture, not sure why, when her focus was on going home.

In the background, the BlackHeart murmured encouragement and blessings. The gentle words reached Mattie's ear, adding to the longing, adding to the desire for rest.

"I would be forgiven," Mattie declared to the empty house as she laid the Bible on its spine. In a few seconds, the papers were free. "They know how hard this is. All would understand."

All except Governor. "In-Me" inserted the thought quickly, sliding it between the murmurings of the evil one and the tranquil images of home and family.

Governor. Shame bore down on Mattie at the mention of his name. How could she have been willing to dilute everything she had poured into him? How could she have forsaken him? And she had done it, if nowhere else but in her made-up mind.

Mattie hung her head and cursed herself. Through her selfishness, she had allowed the evil one to control her. She had given It access to her emotions, something the keeper of the records never did when dealing with the BlackHeart. Wasn't she always telling Governor: *pinch off yo' 'motions; concentrate on yo' responsibilities; never forget yo' duty?*

The elderly Truth handler leaned heavily on the desk, feeling unworthy of her calling, certain her predecessors were frowning down on her, as disappointed in her as she was in herself. She knew better, better than anyone, how smooth this one was and yet...

Don't be hard on yourself, Mattie, "In-Me" soothed, *you're tired; you're human. You will be with your family again, but not today.*

Nodding her head, accepting forgiveness, Mattie culled and squashed all her emotions. In control again, she fortified her senses, resumed responsibility and most importantly, remembered who she was. She was the keeper of the records, the handler of Truth, the burden bearer. Way back when, before she'd even formed in her mama's womb, she'd been chosen. One minor slip had not changed that.

With doubtless movements, she replaced all that was right, just, and honorable and walked through the darkness to the door, smearing all traces of tears as she went.

On the outside, the BlackHeart knew of Mattie's traitorous deed. Foul swearing from hell and beyond pressed through the door and thundered in Mattie's ear as if there was nothing material separating them.

Mattie didn't care. She spoke with hatred and anger tinting her words. "It ain't time for me to die. Get off my porch." After issuing her directive, Mattie returned to her bedroom and calmly slid under her bed covers.

The racket outside went on for a while, but Mattie didn't hear it. She was wrapped in a peaceful, dreamless sleep.

The BlackHeart was good and mad when It stomped off Mattie's porch. It yanked open the door to Hope's classic '69 Mustang, got in and took off at Nascar speed, fishtailing Its way as It went. Back out on the FM road, driving carelessly and way too fast, It simmered and steamed.

"I almost had her." It pounded the empty passenger seat. "I almost had them for eternity." It paused in Its temper tantrum, noticing two small, glowing circles in the brush ahead. The BlackHeart smiled, sick and twisted, hunched over the steering wheel and aimed straight for the orbs, hoping to lighten Its anger and disappointment by killing something. It would have preferred to kill a Fuller, but at least this—a cat, possum, dog, whatever—was living, a good substitute for a Fuller. But before It got close enough to drive the creature over and snuff out its life, the living thing scampered away, leaving everything black again. The BlackHeart screamed in frustration. It seemed nothing was going Its way tonight; everything was evading It.

Making a wild right turn onto another FM road, It slammed on the brakes. *Why, I'm no better than Mattie.* The BlackHeart threw the transmission in Park and sat up straight. *For a moment, I forgot who I was.* Rolling down the window, It closed Its eyes, calmed down with the help of fresh, although hot air and while doing so, acknowledged Its lineage.

Lucifer was not Its father in the manner humans attached to the word. Humans defined the word as someone who is emotionally attached to an offspring, and as a result, a father guided, taught, protected, provided for and loved that offspring. Lucifer did none of that. Rather, he spawned many and cared for none, including the BlackHeart. Once birthed, Lucifer's children roamed the earth, looking to devour, destroy, or manipulate with no guidance, support, acknowledgement or love from him. And that was perfectly fine with his children, for the Great Lucifer had deposited in them outstanding traits such as cunning, intelligence, tenacity, and the ability to transform or adjust as the situation demanded or even at will—traits the BlackHeart held in abundance and which It had employed to gain control of the Fuller family.

Parked in the middle of a FM road in central Texas at a little after one o'clock on a Monday morning, the BlackHeart smiled Its pretty teenage smile, reaching back in time to the day It'd met Charles Fuller, the progenitor of the Fuller family—the black Fullers, not the slave-holding white ones—the man who had set his family up to be pawns of the BlackHeart—the man who had cursed his family.

§

It had been another hot summer day, not a gray cloud in the sky, but plenty of pure white ones. It was on one of these clouds that the BlackHeart reclined, looking lazily down at earth. Floating across central Texas one year and some months after slavery ended there, It spied a black man gesturing angrily to a cluster of white men. Sensing an opportunity to destroy or control, the BlackHeart donned the shape of a mockingbird and landed on the branch of a pine tree—a prime location for catching every nuance of the exchange.

The black man wailed and hollered, "It my town. You cain't change the name. It give t' me." He spanned his arms and rotated his torso to the right and then the left. "All this, far as you can see. Mine. Me 'n my fam'ly."

"We not gonna stand here all day repeatin' ourselves, boy. The gov'ment done decided what's yours and what ain't. It's all right here." The palest of the white men shook a long, formal-looking paper in the air. "You take it now and do what it says. Here." The man held the paper out to Charles Fuller. The BlackHeart could clearly see the words DEED and WARRANTY written across the top and an official-looking stamp at the bottom.

Charles ignored the paper and restated, "Massa Fuller give it to me. Foty acres. Plus mo' fo' my wife and chillun'. Fo' hunered acres in all."

"Well, now," the shortest and fattest of the men drawled, "Funny how his will don't support that."

Charles Fuller turned to Howard Fuller, eldest son of the deceased Master Fuller and pled his case further. "You was there. You heard yo' pa."

The devious and greedy Howard Fuller, already possessed by another of Lucifer's children, shook his head and lied. "Forty's all I heard."

The two Fullers squared off with their eyes, hatred reflected in both.

"Boys, we done spent enough time here," the pale white man concluded. He threw the deed at the black ex-slave. All of the men, black and white, watched the paper flutter to the ground. "'Bide by it, boy, or else..." He let the threat finish itself.

Chuckling and small talking within their intimate group, the white men boarded their horses or carriages and left.

The BlackHeart's sly smile grew as It watched rage spilling out of Charles. The old farmer's fists were balled, hatred flashed from his eyes, and vile curses streamed out of his mouth. The BlackHeart, sensitive to white hot emotions, felt the man's pain, anger and frustration. It could almost feel the knife plunge into Howard Fuller's chest as Charles thought of murdering the man. T'was the idea of murder, not the emotions that informed the BlackHeart that It could have Charles Fuller, could own the whole Charles Fuller clan.

Speaking in a conspiratorial tone from high on Its branch, the BlackHeart baited him, "I can give you the desires of your heart." The BlackHeart smiled to Itself as Charles jerked around, trying to find the source of the voice. It was a useless hunt since the BlackHeart had projected Its voice so It sounded both near and far. It teased, "You won't find me. You don't need to find me. Just know that I can give you…" the BlackHeart paused to ensure the heartsick man listened hard, "…land, a town…murder."

Charles continued his search for the person who offered a salve to his injuries. "Are you God?"

The BlackHeart fumed; Its feathered chest puffed out; Its tiny heart hardened. Why did humans always turn to God first? It asked Itself. What had God done for them that made them such willing slaves to Him? Knowing there was no pleasing answer and not really interested in one anyway, the BlackHeart snuffed Its anger and magnified Its resolve to snatch this human from God's control.

It cooed in promise, "Tomorrow, you'll hear that Howard is dead. Tomorrow, when you learn he fell off his horse, broke his neck and was discovered by his whore, you'll know I can give you more."

The BlackHeart flew off to find Howard and fulfill the first and It hoped the only act of courting Charles Fuller.

§

The next day, pre-dawn yelling dragged Charles and his wife out of sleep. Shuffling to the front door while pulling on his work overalls as he went, Charles opened the door wide and stepped outside. He saw one of his middle sons running up and down the lane, waving his arms, yelling like a plum fool. When the boy, really a man in age but always a boy to his father, drew close Charles held out a restraining hand.

"What's all this racket, boy?"

"Howard Fuller…dead and gone…" he spoke in broken breaths. "Miss Lulu Belle… found him…broke neck and all."

Charles slumped against the porch post, hearing but not believing. "The Lawd done it," he spoke in soft amazement. "Actually smote down my enemy."

Charles knew it was bad manners to smile at death. Knew it was just plain awful to celebrate someone's demise, but he couldn't help himself. This was too good to keep in.

He shot upwards, his feet lifting several feet off the ground, a grand feat for one so old. When he landed, his knees buckled and his back spasmed, but he didn't moan or groan. He went right on dancing a jig and joining his son in whooping and hollering. When the others in the lane started easing out of their shacks and cabins to inspect the noise, only then did Charles make himself stop. It wouldn't be good for the rest of the family to see him, the well-respected elder, cutting up so. Besides, he had to go. He had a meeting with the Lord.

Without eating breakfast or slurping down a cup of his wife's good coffee, Charles high-tailed it to that bald patch of his land where two rutted paths met and showed promise of becoming a road one day. He didn't know it then, but many, many, many years later those two paths would indeed grow up to be the two FM roads that zigged and zagged to Mattie's house.

Charles arrived at the place, panting. He looked around, trying again to see God. Unsuccessful, he made up his mind to wait patiently for the Lord and for "the more" He'd promised him. Like a child at a baptismal, he eagerly shifted from one foot to the other, his eyes big, wondering how and when the Lord would show and deliver. He paced the land, searching up, down and all around, too filled with excitement to sit because finally, FINALLY the Lord had answered his prayers. After years of slavery, extreme whippings and other abuse by the evil Howard Fuller, being decreed free a whole year AFTER slaves in the rest of the country and losing his rightful land and town, Charles would finally get his just reward, his Promised Land, and a lasting legacy for the generations. His heart felt near to bursting for the love he felt toward a good God.

The first hour ticked quickly by; Charles held on to his excitement. The second, third and fourth hours rolled by too, and his excitement still held. It wasn't until the noon hour came and went—as determined by the sun's placement in the sky and the rumblings in his belly—that Charles began to feel anxious, uneasy; yet he held tight to his faith. However, when the sun began its slide to the west, meaning suppertime was closing in fast, Charles' faith and belief had thinned considerably. But, by God, it was still there! For Charles had committed to wait all day and all night if that brought him "the more" he deserved.

§

Charles didn't know that high above his head perched a mockingbird. It had been his companion all day, watching him, studying him. Through silent observation and covert tuning in, It learned what all the people in the surrounding land already knew—that Charles Fuller was a committed man, a trusting man. Stubborn or faithful, depending on whose point of view, Lucifer's or God's. The man was keen on justice and blindly determined to see his dream for Fullertown come to pass. Traits the BlackHeart could twist and use for destruction, starting now.

As It had done the day before, the BlackHeart threw Its voice so It came at Charles from everywhere. "You're a good man, Charles Fuller."

Charles jumped, startled by the bodyless voice, but he recovered quickly. After all, he'd been expecting it. As he'd done the day before, he turned to and fro trying to locate that voice. "God?" he asked.

This time, the BlackHeart was prepared for the slight. "I see the town you're building. You built the church first by the slave cemetery. I am pleased."

Charles smiled, showing few teeth and polished gums. "Thank you, Lawd, sho' 'preciates that." He paused, wanting to ask God if He'd really murdered Howard for him. But how did one ask such a thing of God? The Bible phrase filled his mind: Oh ye of little faith.

The old farmer was spared the conflict of belief versus disbelief by the BlackHeart, who knowing the cause of his lapse, stated authoritatively, "I did not lie about Howard."

"No, Lawd, I knowed you would." Both Charles and the BlackHeart knew the colored man stretched his faith with that half-truth. Through book knowledge, Charles knew God could do whatever God chose to do, but in his heart where it counted, the old farmer had not believed God would take his side or murder for him. Why would he wholly believe such a thing when this was the God of the white man's Bible?

"Do you want the rest? ...the land, the town?" the BlackHeart asked, preparing to take the final step to capture the farmer's soul.

"It was promised me, Lawd, it rightly mine." Even though he revered God, Charles felt himself puffing up in anger again.

"You must be willing to give up something."

"Anything, Lawd," Charles replied, eager to put the past behind and move closer to "the more." He even offered, "I quit swearin'. Give you mo' time on Sunday. Treat the wife and chillun' better, give up the drink. I do it all, Lawd."

In a soft, duplicitous voice the BlackHeart asked, "Will you kill for me like I killed for you?"

§

Here, Charles paused...a long pause. He suspected this was one of those faith questions the God of the Bible liked to ask. He supposed he should tell the truth which was no, he did not want to kill. Oh, sure, he killed animals on the farm and in the woods. That was different; that was necessary for life to go on. So, if killing an animal is what He wanted, fine. But now, if the Lord wanted one of those Abraham-Isaac sacrifices, Charles needed to think about that. Sure, the boy Isaac was saved in the end, but getting to that point sure seemed mighty hard. But now, if the Lord wanted him to kill an ungodly person like Howard, he could kill and not miss a wink of sleep. Couldn't he? Charles paused, doubting even that.

§

The BlackHeart knew of the man's unease and doubts and decided the righteous man needed a bit of poking and prodding to move him closer to the *eternal trap It had laid. Using Its patently paternal voice, It said, "Remember your Bible stories, Charles. Moses killed the Hebrew overseer to set his people free. And the most righteous kill of all—Jesus, son of God."*

Charles' mind and face cleared of doubt. The feeling of wrong disintegrated. *"A'course, Lawd."*

Not willing to lose this soul when so close to sealing the pact, the BlackHeart layered on even more. "You've been lied to, cheated out of land, pushed out of your town, you deserve justice." The farmer's face lit up and the BlackHeart's too as It celebrated another convert, another fool. "I'm going to protect you, give you what you deserve, but you must kill for me. Just like in the Bible. Are you willing?"

"Lawd, I'm good with a gun. Expert with a knife," Charles volunteered with zealous pride.

"Say it," the BlackHeart hissed, Its patience nearly exhausted. "I have to hear you say it. Out loud. I want you to agree to serve me, to kill for me, to be controlled by me."

§

Here, Charles paused again, but this time, in the silence, another being inserted Itself. This being was an ambassador of God who was intent on obstructing a conversion. Cleverly adapting Its voice to mimic that of the BlackHeart, It gently spoke, "Charles, there's a reason you delay. You know killing is not the way. Stand in your belief, Charles." The being swooped down from the pale blue sky, past the mockingbird, to land at Charles' side. Not that he knew. Only those with special sight could see this spiritual being. Charles was not that kind of special.

Now, Charles' confusion doubled. The same voice talking at him from two different sides? Was he losing his mind? Had the injustices of life as a slave and now as a cheated free man clawed through his mind, leaving it senseless and tattered?

"No, Charles, there's nothing wrong with your mind," the BlackHeart assured quickly, stepping up Its attack. "Say you'll serve me. Kill for me, and you'll see how fine you are. Land restored and Fullertown, your lasting gift to your family."

"Your heart, Charles," God's being urged. "Choose the heart; it will never forsake you."

Poor Charles did not realize good and bad tussled for his soul. The poor man had no idea how important he was to both sides. He only knew conflict, and that the same comforting voice spoke at him in opposition. Charles grabbed his head, pulling at the roots of his sparse gray hair as he fell to his knees. He moaned, wondering what to do: kill and obtain that which was rightfully his or refuse to serve and live in right relationship with his heart. As he battled within himself, God's ambassador crouched with him. It's comforting wings wrapped about him as It ministered to his heart with loving words and warm feelings.

While It did this, the other, smart and filled with hate, flapped Its wings, causing the DEED and WARRANTY form that Charles had left on the ground the day before to float before Charles' beleaguered eyes and land before him. Seeing it and remembering yesterday's unjust conclusion and Howard Fuller's smug, lying face infuriated Charles all over again. Then, he remembered how God had killed the man and thus proved Himself worthy of belief. At this, the unforgiveable words burst out, "I'll serve you. I'll kill for you. I'll have my just rewards."

As soon as the words hit the air, the atmosphere changed. In that square of land, the sun quit shining and the sweet smell of summer evaporated, replaced by the metallic stench of blood. Instantly aware of the change, Charles looked up and around, noticing the dark patch that encased him compared to light everywhere else. His eyes grew wide in fear, and all of a sudden he felt a profound sense of loss…and cold, so very cold.

Because he was not especially special, Charles did not know that God's ambassador had withdrawn and that being's retreat accounted for all that he saw and felt. Tears and a heavy heart accompanied the being's departure, for It had lost another. Charles now belonged to evil.

§

Chirping happily, the BlackHeart flew down to claim Its prize, changing shapes along the way, becoming a mass of tiny black dots so miniscule only the most discerning eye could detect them. It entered the old man straight away, caring not one bit about hurt or pain. Straight for the heart It went, piercing the vessel and causing two things simultaneously: Charles fell backward as if he'd been knifed through and through, and his heart, once a healthy, vibrant burgundy red—even at his old age—turned a healthy, vibrant midnight black.

§

Writhing and kicking in the dust and dirt, Charles tried to dislodge the invader. He didn't know what it was only that the pain exceeded that of any whipping Howard Fuller had ever administered. Complementing the pain were impressions that his heart seemed to stretch and grow too big for his chest, leading to a suffocating feeling, and also that his blood coursed so loudly and violently throughout him that he felt deaf as well as cold and hot at the same time. To Charles, it seemed like hours of torture. In reality, mere moments ticked by as evil took dominion of his body, his heart.

Then, in a blink…nothing.

Charles didn't immediately rise. Afraid to move, thinking it would bring on another attack, he lay with one side of his face planted to the ground, the DEED and WARRANTY paper inches from his closed eyes. If it had been solely Charles' decision, he would have stayed that way all night, so great was his desire to avoid another attack.

But the BlackHeart had a greater say, and now that It had settled comfortably in Its new shape, It directed harshly, "Get up."

Charles opened his eyes. There was no need to search for the voice; the voice now streamed from within him, heard only by him. This he knew as surely as he knew his name. Cautiously, he lifted his torso to lean on his elbow and take a steady breath. When no pain surfaced, Charles sat up and placed one hand over his heart as if he intended to pledge his allegiance, not knowing he'd already done so.

"Get up, Charles." The BlackHeart's voice was downright hate-filled this time. "Go home, Charles."

Slowly, Charles stood, fearful yet still man enough to follow his own mind, which told him to take a few precious moments to rub his aching knees and brush the dirt from his overalls. That done, he set off for home...a changed man. This, he learned from the BlackHeart as It spoke to him all the way. Charles learned he was now a bought man, one of Lucifer's legions, controlled specifically by the BlackHeart. He learned that the BlackHeart, so named by Lucifer, was a conflicted spirit, full of struggle and strife because half of its name symbolized evil, the other half, love. The existence of evil and love within one being caused conflict which caused pain which caused the BlackHeart to kill to relieve the pain. The killing did nothing, however, to remove the conflict. That would only dissolve when the BlackHeart acquired Truth. Not only acquired it, but destroyed it so the BlackHeart would never again experience the conflict and pain of both loving and hating. And the killings... At the time that Truth no longer existed, the BlackHeart would become wholly evil and enjoy unfettered rule over Its host families, unfettered hate, meaning the killings would occur at will...on a whim...frequently.

Total chaos.

Hearing all this made Charles cry big, regret-filled tears that did not move the BlackHeart. In fact, just the opposite.

Only steps away from his cabin door, Charles cringed when he heard the BlackHeart command, "Kill your wife." With every strand of his being, Charles fought to defy the order, and yet he found himself opening the door, heading straight for his wife whose back was to him as she heated water to wash— and with his bare hands, he strangled her to death.

After the deed, he fell to his knees beside her body, gathered her to his chest and cried.

§

More than a century and generations later, Hope continued Charles Fuller's—and the many more after him—legacy of killing. Killing to relieve the pain of loving while striving to obtain and destroy the Truth to remove the conflict forever and gain eternal glory.

"I won't fail again," the teen promised as she shifted into Drive. "Next time, I'm leaving Mattie's with her blood on my hands and the Truth burned to ashes." The girl sealed her promise with a sharp head nod. Then, after turning her music high enough for the heavens to hear Li'l Wayne rap about life on the streets, she spun out, winding her way to the county road and then north on I-35, headed home to Dallas.

A week and two days later, Mattie confessed her sin.

She and Governor were sitting in her sacred house, in their usual places. She in the rocker by the front window and he on the sofa, which gave him access to her same view.

It had been hard to admit she'd come this close to handing the Truth to the BlackHeart. It had been hard to admit near failure to her replacement, but at the end of the confession, Governor's face held no less respect than when he'd walked through her back door some time ago.

His forgiveness and understanding had been important to Mattie. She sighed softly, relieved.

"You said all the while she the smartest." Governor snuffed the butt of his cigarette and deposited it in his shirt pocket. Always the gentleman, always careful and orderly. "Don't matter, though. You beat her, and you'll beat her at the end."

It was a nice thought, but a false one and they both knew it. Mattie was not going to beat the BlackHeart this time. Her time on earth marched slowly to a period and her feelings about that vacillated. One minute she was happy to go home to be with her true family; the next minute, fearful, afraid of the pain of death. A minute later, worried if she'd schooled Governor well enough. Then, happy to leave the cares of this world behind. To stamp out the back and forth in her mind or at least subdue it, she'd taken to righting her life, to putting things in order.

She wrote out her will with the help of the bank manager and tucked it in the same Bible as the papers of Truth, but in the Old Testament, not in the front or back slits. Since she'd turned her back to the one man who'd offered her love early in her life, she had no husband or children to leave her land, house and everything therein to. So, Governor would inherit those, as well as the family Bible. But that one was a given. She'd also added his name to her account at the bank, and since she didn't believe in insurance—why buy insurance when the spirit world wielded so much control and power?—

there were no policies to update with beneficiary information. She did, however, believe in funerals and had taken one evening to write out her funeral plans—no church service. She'd had no use for church while living, and she certainly wouldn't have use for it when dead. No, just a simple, short graveside service at Black Hill, with no eulogy. Just a song or two, a prayer or two and remarks by Governor. Then burial next to her siblings.

Earlier, she'd been collecting her business contacts, invoices and receipts for her pine tree and hunting business when she felt Governor's presence, and shortly thereafter the dogs sounded off, confirming. She'd been thankful for the interruption.

"So, this my last lesson," Governor stated, disrupting their pleasurable silence.

Mattie nodded slowly, reminded yet again that her time on earth was drawing to a close. She sighed again and shifted in her seat. Time to share the last of what she knew and pray it would be enough to see Governor through.

"Even though Charles chose wrong, he had enuff sense to tell the truth. He gathered his people 'round his dead wife's body, told all he'd done, what he knew, how they trapped in evil, and the good Fullers fell down to prayin'. They prayed long and hard, beggin' God to help 'em. That how we got 'In-Me' and someone to go agin' the BlackHeart. That also how the Truth come to be recorded."

Mattie got up from her chair and shuffled across to the desk on which the family Bible lay. This time when she accessed the Bible, she lifted the front cover and carefully withdrew sheets and sheets of paper, some yellowed, some composition paper, some onion skin, some ruled, others not, but all contained dark writings. When she'd extracted all of the papers and shut the Bible closed, it appeared flat instead of puffy.

"The BlackHeart been crafty in claimin' us," Mattie spoke more to herself than to Governor. "But not smart enuff. It forgot that when It took someone, Its evil ways opened to that person. Charles Fuller, even in his muddled mind, had someone write down all he learned 'bout the BlackHeart and evil."

Mattie paused to return to her seat, bearing not only the papers from the front cover but the ones from the back, as well. "Charles learned how to destroy the BlackHeart. He learned how to free us." Mattie held the pages up. "It all recorded here." Mattie shook the papers hard, as if by doing so she could erase all traces of the BlackHeart or at least their family's bloodied connection to it.

"And how we do that?" Governor asked, now sitting forward in his seat, "How we rid our family of the curse and destroy the BlackHeart forever?"

Determined to make two more calls before suspending today's work on the Fuller death study, Deborah checked the kitchen clock: 5:50. Ester was still at work.

Ignoring her throbbing ear, a condition she'd acquired from having the hard plastic of her cordless phone pressed firmly against it most of the day, Deborah dialed from memory. Ester's work number was as fixed in her mind as Hope's time of birth, the colors of her wedding and the location of her sister's grave.

One ring, a second ring and then the trill of the third cut in half by Ester's gruff, "Hello."

"Hey Ester, before you start fussing about this being my third call today, I'm calling with success this time. The actuarial file will be here in a few days. He can't provide it in the format you want, but Henry Garner said if you have any problems, just call him. He's going to include his business card."

Ester growled something about a God-awful Monday and hung up.

And that was okay with Deborah. No amount of grouch could sack the smile on her face. Success felt good—even if success was something as uneventful as securing a file of death data from the Texas Insurance and Mortality Board.

Humming to herself, Deborah reached for the Partway telephone directory, a gift Shandra had presented to her during one of their work sessions. She flipped through it until she landed at the Fs.

The list of Fullers went on and on, with Mary Fuller's listing halfway through the lot. Deborah rested one finger under Mary's phone number and with her other hand picked up the cordless unit, laid it on its back and dialed.

Assured of the connection, Deborah reluctantly turned to the mundane—dinner. It was past time for her to have settled on a meal for Samuel and Hope. Hope would be walking through the door soon and Samuel within the hour, both expecting something hot and good to eat, and God bless her soul, she'd done nothing domestic all day. Even Samuel's errand list still lay where he'd left it on the kitchen counter early this morning.

Meal options auditioned in her head as Mary's phone continued its musical wail. Pizza? No, that would keep her and Samuel up all night with reflux. Thai? No, they didn't offer home delivery. Fried chicken? Not in the mood.

Sliding off the bar stool at the kitchen counter, Deborah made a level line for the refrigerator, hoping a quick inventory of the foodstuff within would jolt her culinary imagination. Cool air hit her in the face at the same time she wondered how many times Mary's phone had rung. It was dinnertime in most homes and, perhaps, Mary's non-answer meant they were sharing their evening meal and did not wish to be disturbed.

Deborah thought about hanging up and trying again later, but she was desperate to speak with Mary. She was the only relative in Partway Deborah felt comfortable talking to about such a thing as silly as the Fuller's Curse—other than Governor and Aunt Mattie, but neither of them had phones. And she wouldn't be making the call at all except Ester had strongly suggested it, had demanded it, in fact. The Ph.D. statistician had stated quite forcefully that they needed to know the tale so they could dismantle and refute it. That had made sense to Deborah, so just a few more rings…

That one minor decision paid off in two ways. While listening subconsciously to the rings, Deborah found, partially hidden behind a jar of picante sauce, a rotisserie chicken with only a few pieces missing. Plenty left to feed her hungry crew of two. Add to that a garden salad and German potato salad, one of which she found in her deli drawer, the other in the cabinet, and lo and behold—dinner.

The second payoff was more fulfilling. Mary Fuller, sounding rushed and breathless, interrupted Deborah as she placed the items on the island. "Hello."

"Oh, Mary, hello. This is Deborah. Did I catch you at a bad time?" Deborah quickly turned her back to dinner and returned to the bar where her notepad and pen lay waiting.

"Deborah! How are you?"

For a reason Deborah didn't quite understand, just hearing Mary's voice filled her with warmth. The kind of warmth that made your smile soft and your eyes even softer. The kind of warmth that lit your insides, similar to the feel you had when you knew you were in good with God. Deborah wondered why Mary's voice touched her so. Perhaps because of the natural connection of two people who shared DNA. Or maybe from the bond that two mothers with similar losses shared. Perhaps it was simply that Mary, as the closest connection to Shandra, made Deborah feel as if Shandra still moved among the living. Deep inside, Deborah knew that was it, the reason for the good feeling, and she cherished it all the more. "I'm doing fine, Mary, thanks. And you?"

"Survivin'. I tell you, I'm already seein' a big dif'rence in livin.' I been by myself for a lot of years. Now these boys here all the time... oh, Lord! They drivin' me crazy." To any stranger who might have been eavesdropping, they would not have guessed this woman had buried a daughter eighteen days ago. Her voice rang high like Shandra's in a light, teasing tone and her chuckle belied her complaints. "Just now, I had to chase 'em outta my vegetable garden. They got near 'bouts a whole playground out back, but where they wanna play? In my garden."

When Ester had given Deborah her 'To-Do' list—call the Texas Insurance and Mortality Board, call previous doctors in Partway about some questionable causes of death and find out about the Fuller's Curse—Deborah had fully agreed with her friend's rationale. Obtaining death data for other Texas families as a comparison and clarifying certain causes of death as a way to ensure accurate classification made sense. But listening to Mary, it dawned on Deborah why she had saved this task for last. She hadn't really wanted to bother the grieving mother with such a trivial matter. Not when Mary was still adjusting and adapting to her new life. But now that she could hear the strength in Mary's voice and could sense renewal in her words, she knew Mary would be fine and would not view this as a senseless intrusion.

"I imagine it has been an adjustment for all of you."

"Sap bein' here helps." A tinge of sadness grayed the edges of Mary's voice. Deborah heard it quite clearly and wondered if she had judged Mary as "strong" too soon. "He plays with the boys, wrestles with 'em. Even helps 'em with readin'. You know, Shandra was big on readin.' That girl loved books. Sap too. They sho' din't git that from me." Mary's chuckle pushed the cloud of sorrow on, turning the gray in her voice to yellow again and Deborah relaxed. "Yep, I guess there mighta' been some good from Shandra's passin.' Sap say he home for good. I shore hope so. Did you meet him at the service? Sap, my baby?"

"Briefly. There were so many people around. We didn't get a chance to talk long." A mental picture of a slender, short, handsome man filled her mind. He'd looked only slightly like Shandra. More like Mary, even though their skin colors didn't match. Mary was a deep, dark chocolate brown; Sap was caramel in color and Shandra had been in between. Deborah remembered, too, that even though he was younger than Shandra, he had more gray in his hair than either her or his mother—a by-product of the hard life of drugs and alcohol, according to the whispers at the funeral.

"No, I bet not. You in town?"

Deborah followed the quick, unexpected change in topic; Shandra had trained her well in the talking ways of Partway folks. "No, I'm in Dallas. Working on the family tree."

"Oh, good, that's good. Shandra was so excited 'bout that. When she wasn't goin' on 'bout these boys or some book or 'nother she was goin' on 'bout that tree." Mary mimicked her daughter's voice: "Deborah doin' this and Deborah doin' that." She chuckled again, adding, "Girl, I got so sick of hearin' your name."

This time, Mary laughed full out and it reminded Deborah of the tinkling of wind chimes. She couldn't stop her own smile from popping out and from thinking: like mother, like daughter. When God created both, he had deposited in them an earthy sense of humor, a fever for living and a boldness for loving family. Choice qualities that came out of the mother now.

Mary's laugh faded. "I'm just messin' wit' ya'. You made my daughter happy. Gave her companionship and somethin' else to look forward to. I thank you for that."

Those appreciative words formed a vice around Deborah's heart, creating a tightness that squeezed out tears. Silent tears of fullness, of warmth, of love.

Shaking her head no, as if Mary could see the denial, Deborah reversed the thanks. It was she who owed Shandra thanks. The young woman had provided over-reaching, over-abundant support for the project. There was no doubt that if not for Shandra, the Partway and Dallas Fullers would still be unlinked, with the Dallas Fullers living their lives only hazily aware of the Partway connection. Because of Shandra's welcome, because Shandra had given of herself, all of the Dallas Fullers now eagerly awaited a break in their schedules so they could cross the bridge to home.

On the precipice of losing complete control, Deborah brushed away the tears and sought to gain enough emotional traction to complete her task. Before she could do so, Mary asked, "So what? You get stuck on that tree?" The woman had more resolve than Deborah could seem to muster.

Sitting up ramrod straight, clearing her throat of emotions, Deborah challenged herself. If Mary wouldn't cry about losing Shandra, neither would she. If Mary, the mother, wouldn't dwell on the loss, then what right had she? The challenge was enough to help Deborah move on. She cleared her throat again and said in a shaky voice that strengthened with each word. "Not stuck, no. I'm actually finished with our family tree." She reported this with more brilliance in her voice than she thought possible. "I'll bring it to Partway, hopefully next week, so you can look at it. I'm pretty proud of it."

"I bet you are. Cain't wait to see it."

Getting to the real business of the call, Deborah plunged ahead, "I'm calling to see if you can clarify something I heard—"

"Mom, I'm home. What's to eat?" Distant but discernible shouts interrupted Deborah's question. The shouts from her teenage daughter reminded Deborah of her family's absentee dinner.

Her thoughts about the Fuller's Curse thinned as her mind switched to mother mode. Rising, she tucked the cordless between her shoulder and ear, grabbed her notebook and pen and finished asking as she entered her sterile, underutilized kitchen, "…at, well…from Billy and Clarice."

"Oh, those two…" Mary pooh-poohed the pair. "I saw they had you cornered at the interment. What they shoutin' in your ear? What lies they passin' on?"

Before Deborah could respond, Hope's escalated voice again reached her. "Mom, I'm home. Where are you?"

This time, the girl's voice sounded closer and sure enough, within seconds the girl herself appeared. Deborah immediately put a silencing finger to her lips and pointed at the phone.

In her own teenage world, focused on her own teenage needs and wants, Hope ignored her mother's sign language and demanded, "What's to eat? I'm starving." Wearing the standard-issue medical smock and non-standard blue jeans—the uniform of her father's office—Hope flung her purse on the counter and headed for the refrigerator. Yanking it open, she repeated, "What's to eat? I don't smell anything."

"Mary, I'm sorry. One second, please." Frowning crossly at her daughter, irritation lining her voice, Deborah disciplined lightly. "Hope, you see I'm on the phone. Be quiet." It was only a second or two lapse in attention, but an apology was needed, nonetheless, and Deborah extended it. "Sorry Mary, you know how rude kids can be."

"You don't have to tell me. I raised two, fixin' to raise two more."

As a compromise between meeting her family's needs and working on the project that had breathed life into her days, Deborah multi-tasked, something she normally hated doing because it usually meant one or the other thing didn't get done right. Oh well, it couldn't be helped. With all the phone calls, the day had gotten away from her. So, while turning on the oven and retrieving bakeware, she also gave Mary her attention. "I feel silly for even asking you about this, but they mentioned a curse and—"

"Girl, no they didn't bring that up! I swear to God, they ain't gonna be satisfied 'til sum'thin' bad happens to 'em. Jeez-us!"

Deborah smiled at Mary's reply. She was as animated as her daughter had been.

§

In their small universe of three, the one person who was not smiling or animated was Hope. Having snagged a soda from the fridge, she had been walking to the pantry, intent on making an appetizer of Lay's and Coke when she heard "curse." She stopped and tuned in to her mother's end of the conversation.

§

"So, it's black magic, a fable?" Deborah asked as she transferred the chicken to a baking dish and slipped it in the oven. She returned to the island in the center of their kitchen where her notebook and pen lay. The entire time she ignored her daughter, even forgot the girl's presence.

On the Partway end of the line, Mary explained dismissively, "It just a story...from a long time ago. Nobody pays it much mind, 'cept them two."

"That figures." Deborah turned to the page where she and Ester had written a few questions on the subject. She skimmed down the questions until she found the one pertaining to believers—*'Who believes this curse?' 'Is there a following?'* On the blank line under the question, she wrote the answer—*'Billy and Clarice. Period.'* With that question answered, she returned to the top of the page and started with the first one.

"So what is the story? What is the curse?"

"S'posed to be that randomly in the Fuller family, a child is born with a black heart. The child appears normal, but the black heart makes the child kill. When that child dies or is killed, the black heart moves to another Fuller child and the killing starts all over again."

Even before Mary had finished the telling, Deborah had stalled in her recording, knocked still by the words "kill" and "child," which took her right back to Shandra's death. How many times was she going to flay them with reminders of a life cut short? How many more mistakes of rubbing death, even unintentional, into Mary's face? Deborah felt low, awful, and she couldn't offer a sincere apology quick enough. "Oh Mary, I'm so sorry. If I'd have known it was so horrible I would not have asked you. I'm so sorry for bringing it up."

"Oh girl, please." Even though Deborah had not used the exact words, Mary seemed to know the reason for the apology and judging by her words considered it a non-issue. Her voice remained light when she said, "Like I said, it just a story. Old-timers used it to keep the kids in line." Adopting a false, admonishing voice, she quoted, *"Kids, if you don't straighten up, the BlackHeart gonna gitcha."* She laughed at the foolishness of it and continued chuckling when she said, "Thanks for remindin' me 'bout it, though. I might have to use it on these boys."

Deborah smiled and relaxed at Mary's forgiving spirit. She still felt discomfort about the subject. Not only because of its inherent reminders of death, but also because faults and fallacies sprang up at combining the words "black" and "heart." No, Deborah had not taken the great number of medical classes Samuel had, but she'd taken plenty and knew it was impossible for a heart to be black in color. Not to mention the impossibility of passing on a condition that didn't exist in the first place. And the last problem, killing and getting away with it? Sheer lunacy. No, the story was too far-fetched to waste paper and ink on, but no wonder Billy and Clarice believed it. This type of fiction fit right in with their characters.

Deborah thought to end the conversation right there, not even ask the remaining few questions. But Ester presented a problem. Her best friend—whether at work, home or a personal project between friends—demanded thoroughness and a strict application of analysis. Ester would not let Deborah off the investigative hook until every question had been turned over, examined and satisfied. So putting her prejudice aside, Deborah read the next question, "Do you know about the origins of the story? How it came to be?"

"Shoot, naw, it been 'round longer'n I have. But you can check with Governor. He much older than me and know about it just like every other Fuller in Partway."

Deborah skipped down a few lines, wrote "Governor Fuller" on a line by itself and underlined the name, as well. Then, more than a few lines down, she wrote "Mattie Fuller" and underlined her name, too... just in case. On to the next question.

"Do you know if there's anything written pertaining to this curse? Any type of documentation?"

"Not that I know of, but really, Deborah, you takin' this too serious." In a less patient voice she said, "I don't care what Bullheaded Billy or Crazy Clarice said, ain't no realness to it. Don't waste your time, honey."

Deborah couldn't agree more, but Ester...Shaking her head, Deborah looked down the page. Only one more question, but before she could voice it, Mary had one for her. "I saw Aunt Mattie talkin' to you at the funeral. What did that mean ole bat want?"

Deborah's eyebrows lifted in surprise and curiosity. Now, here was a difference between mother and daughter. Shandra had had nothing but respect for everyone—except Billy and Clarice, of course—including their strange old aunt, and yet Mary's reference to Mattie was anything but respectful. Sensing a backstory that ached to be told, Deborah made a note on a side margin, planning to return to that comment later. For now, she squelched curiosity to focus on answering Mary's question.

Twice now, Fullers had asked Deborah about Aunt Mattie's confusing dialogue and twice now, Deborah stumbled around for an answer. She couldn't tell Mary what Aunt Mattie truly said because the old woman hadn't made sense at the time and now, almost three weeks later, her words still didn't make sense. And even though Mary deserved a detailed answer, Deborah had no choice but to recycle the words she'd shared with Billy and Clarice—words which had set her to this ridiculous task of studying death and curses by default. "I'm not really sure. She spoke in riddles."

"Humph! I bet she did, the mean ole coot. She was just tryin' to upset me even more. Been waitin' all these years to get back at me. What a hateful ole woman!"

Now, Deborah was sure of a *real* story. She held on, waiting to see if Mary would volunteer more.

"When I—" A loud thump, followed by a deathly howl ended the telling before it could start.

"Mary! What happened?" Deborah shouted over the clattering of the phone as it apparently dangled from its cord and banged against something hard and immovable.

One of the boys, Deborah guessed, *but which one and what happened?* Her hand gripped the receiver hard as she strained to listen for words between the cries and screams. Only a few minutes passed, never to be recaptured, but in that space, many unpleasant scenarios paraded through Deborah's head. Finally, when her mind switched to help mode—what could she do a hundred and forty miles away?—the wild cries diminished to a boisterous cry, lower in volume and intensity, yet still severe.

Moments later, the phone's banging stopped and the cries—now civilized—roared in Deborah's ears.

"Sorry, Deborah..." Her voice somewhat shaky, yet still in grandmotherly control, Mary explained hurriedly, "...I gotta go. These boys tryin' to kill each other. Next time you in town, stop by."

"I will. Tha—"

The dial tone sliced Deborah's gratitude, indicating Mary was off comforting the wounded and righting the wrongs in her house.

"What was that all about?" Hope demanded to know as soon as Deborah hit the END button.

"I don't know. It sounded like one of the boys was injured," Deborah answered absently.

"The Fuller's curse," Hope stated in a brutal tone, her eyes just as savage. "What did she say about that?" While Hope's mother had talked to Mary, the BlackHeart had forced Itself to remain as normal and detached as possible, to stay in teenage mode, which was sometimes hard to do. Now that Hope's mother was free to share, the woman acted as dumb as a dunce, angering the BlackHeart and making it that much harder to play out the teen role.

"Ohhhh, that," Deborah returned the phone to its base, kissed her daughter on the forehead and returned to the interior of the kitchen to finish dinner. "Your Aunt Ester asked me to research Billy and Clarice's claim about the Fuller's curse." From her station at the island, Deborah threw a frown at Hope who sat at the bar. "You're not spoiling your appetite, are you?" Her eyes pinpointed the chips and soda in front of her daughter.

The BlackHeart's anger came to a full boil. *This woman can be so stupid. With all the evidence in front of her, she still doesn't get it. She still doesn't understand that important, eternal matters hang in the balance. And those matters far outweigh the issue of a damn snack.* Hateful curse words pushed to be free and her hands twitched to wrap around Deborah's neck until she gave up life, but the BlackHeart locked down Its intense desires. Within seconds, she was right again, or as right as a cursed child could be. She even managed to control her breathing as she stared at her mother's side profile, feeling both love and hate for the woman, feeling that conflicting pain humming to a start inside her. "What did Mary say about the curse?"

"Not a lot. Not a lot that makes for a good comparative study, anyway," Deborah replied while transferring the packaged potato salad to a casserole dish.

"Your words or hers?"

"It ought to be anybody's who's heard the story." Deborah finally turned to face her daughter. "A child born with a black heart that causes it to kill." Deborah scoffed, "Ridiculous." She returned to dinner preparations, adding a final commentary, "Impossible."

This time, when anger devoured Hope, the BlackHeart took over. *She dares to dismiss me?* It yelled in Hope's head. *She dares to mock and belittle? I could end her life right here, right now. A gas leak. A slip and fall. Electrocution. And I wouldn't even be killing the best. I've inhabited adults and children who were far better vessels than she, and yet* she *dismisses me.* Its anger quadrupled, causing the young girl's eyes to turn from brown to black, the palms of her hands to turn charcoal, the blood pumping wildly within—stark black. In this dark emotional state, the BlackHeart aimed to hurt, to cut deep, and at times, to kill. Its next move depended on Deborah or rather her answer to: "You make fun of a story that others believe in, that others know to be true?"

Still clueless as to what she'd birthed, Deborah turned her back to the BlackHeart and shoved the potato salad into the oven with the chicken, taking the time to cover the chicken before shutting the oven door. "It's not true. It'll never be true. And I'll tell you why." Deborah threw her oven mitts on the counter and then reached into a cabinet for a serving bowl. "Black magic, voo-doo, curses and the like are all rooted in fear. They play upon some people's need to sidestep personal responsibility or the need to pacify greed or other selfish motives. I don't know yet what prompted this Fuller's Curse story, but I'll bet when Aunt Ester and I get to the bottom, it'll be some innocuous detail that grew out of proportion."

Deborah moved to the fridge, not aware that her daughter had taken on a darker than normal hue. That her eyes glowed black and a vague haze surrounded the girl. She stuck her head in the box and missed the BlackHeart's conciliatory look. The woman's answer had tripped on itself. On one hand, she called the BlackHeart's story false; on the other, she planned to research it. The contradiction saved her—for now. But the BlackHeart also admitted that what saved her was the BlackHeart's own need. It needed Deborah. At least until It secured the Truth and destroyed it. She might prove useful in securing or relaying information, as a shield, or possibly even in recovering the Truth from Aunt Mattie. So, It retired Its anger and folded Itself back, allowing Hope's teenage personality and looks to emerge. The teen wasted no time in searching her purse for her cell phone and iPod. Thus occupied, she didn't see her mother approach, but she felt her coming and knew what Deborah planned to preach about: Dr. Beeker.

She brought out the electronic devices at the same time that Deborah started in. "Hope, I was very sorry to get a call today from Lesley in Dr. Beeker's office. Why didn't you keep your appointment today?"

Skilled at role-playing, Hope lowered her thick, dark lashes, hiding the conflict between truth and falsehood from her mother. "She can't help me." The truth was neither Dr. Beeker nor any other psychiatrist in Dallas could help her. The lie was that Hope had never planned to keep the appointment.

Deborah rounded the bar, and as if she couldn't live another second without touching her daughter she pulled Hope into her arms, rocking, caressing her. "Sure she can. Wasn't it helpful last Monday when you went? Didn't she help you come to grips with Anna's and Curtis' death? She helped you then, and she'll help you now, if you let her."

The BlackHeart tolerated being in Hope's mother's arms. Sometimes It even appreciated it, but now was not one of those times. Now, the pain of being in a loving family was gnawing at her. Soon, it would overshadow all else and demand release. Then, another Fuller would have to die. With her mind racing ahead, she unintentionally said the words out loud. "The pain."

Her mother misunderstood. "I know it hurts, Hope. Lord knows I do. Do you know how many times I've replayed that scene in my head? Do you know how many times a day I beat myself up for not being more forceful with my decision?"

The BlackHeart heard the catch in Hope's mother's voice and knew she was close to tears. It supposed It needed to conjure some as well; It did.

"Hope, you just…we all went through a tragedy. But you, more than anyone, because it was your idea to chase that bird, and you were there when Shandra fell. Even with Mary's forgiveness and knowing the situation was out of your control, I know you're carrying guilt and punishing yourself because I am, too."

Deborah pulled back and the BlackHeart could see Hope's mother's eyes, like Its own, were glossy from unleashed tears. It accepted Deborah's stroking and maintained deep, bonding eye contact.

"We love you, Hope and want the best for you. You'll be going off to college in six weeks, and your father and I want you emotionally and mentally ready, understand?"

By no means, no way was the BlackHeart dumb. It heard the unspoken threat in Deborah's words and said, "Come right out and say it, Mom." It wanted to hear it. It wanted Deborah to offer the lifeline It'd been trying to orchestrate on Its own.

Deborah sighed painfully. "Your father and I discussed it and decided if we don't feel you're solid by the time freshman orientation rolls around, you won't be going to Spelman. You'll stay here and attend a local college."

The BlackHeart, through Hope, excelled at manipulation and deceit. But the young girl played her role well, too. "What?!" she exclaimed, stepping away from her mother's loving touches.

On the outside she appeared outraged and indignant, but on the inside It celebrated. It had never been the BlackHeart's idea or intent to attend college so far from family. When the pain erupted into the kill urge, It needed to be around family to satisfy It. More importantly, how could It steal and destroy the Truth with it in Texas and the BlackHeart in Georgia? Hope's parents had been the ones pushing Spelman; It'd simply gone along until an opportunity could be twisted to suit Its plans—and here it was.

"It's for your own good, Hope." Deborah stepped forward, holding out her hand.

From years of playing out the mother-daughter scenario, the BlackHeart knew what the extended palm up meant: punishment for missing today's appointment with the psychiatrist. Deborah expected Hope to give up her car keys. Because her mother would expect her to, Hope whined and complained, begged and wheedled, promised to do better, but it was all an act. Just like Spelman had been an act.

When both had had enough of Hope's performance, Hope pulled out her keys and smashed them on the bar counter. Pivoting wildly, she stormed up the back stairs to her blood red and yellow room, smiling the entire way. When the BlackHeart reached Hope's room, It slammed the door behind It and then burst into laughter.

Later that night, in the early hours of morning really, when most good people are asleep, Hope softly opened the door to her parent's bedroom. Peeking her head in first to make sure they were asleep, she carefully slid the rest of her thin body through the narrow opening. Not on tiptoe but very quietly, she cut a direct path to her mother's side of the king-size bed. Deborah's face was uncovered, and Hope realized again how very pretty her mother was. Pretty and loving and good-hearted, like that damn Shandra had been.

The BlackHeart didn't care for good-hearts, wouldn't give a rat's ass for loving people. Those kinds of Fullers were the worst. They were the ones who stood the best chance of spoiling everything by saving the family—and if that happened, It'd fizzle away…become extinct…a relic of the past…a memory. It wouldn't allow that, not while It served a purpose on this earth, not while It reigned as a child of Lucifer.

The light from the midnight moon wasn't bright enough, so the BlackHeart switched on the bedside lamp. It knew the light wouldn't wake either husband or wife, father or mother. It'd done this before…just watched them breathe.

When Deborah exhaled, Samuel inhaled, as if they could share only one breath between them. This action fascinated the BlackHeart, reminding It of the frailty of human life and making It wonder… Once Deborah exhaled her very last breath, the breath that would start her otherworld journey, did that mean that Samuel would inhale his last breath? And when Samuel exhaled his last breath, did that mean another inhaled their last? The question of breath dependency drove the BlackHeart mad, making It glad It was not wholly human.

Tiring of the breath exchange and its confounding riddle, It lightly walked Its fingers over Hope's mother's face in a gentle caress, tracing the line of her nose, circling the pulse that beat at her temple, lining the fullness of her lips, curving her jaw.

Inside Hope, love simmered, but hate boiled stronger, and the BlackHeart knew that soon the time for a showdown between blood relatives would ensue.

It wouldn't be long—the waiting or the battle.

"I love you, Mom. As much as I can, I love you."

She stooped low and kissed Deborah's smooth forehead. Then, with one quick snap, the light went off and the BlackHeart retreated to Hope's room to rest—but mostly to plan how to acquire and destroy the Truth.

This can't be right! It just can't be. The thought went round and round in Deborah's head. *No, this is not right.* Round and around and around it went; denial danced a complicated jig.

She looked down at the evidence of Ester's recently completed work—charts, clearly depicting her family's dysfunction. Deborah stared at them, her thoughts simple and repetitive. *This is just not right.*

"I know how you feel," said Ester. "I thought the same thing when I first reviewed the results, so I double and triple checked myself. Same outcome."

"I just…I can't believe—" Part confusion, part appreciation for Ester's hard work, but mostly disbelief had unsettled Deborah. In a querulous, high pitch she questioned, "We're this far off the norm?"

Ester shrugged. "Facts are facts. I did everything by the book." The statistician explained in her workday, facts-only voice, "Using the data you provided from your family's death records and the data from the insurance board, I ran several comparisons. This is what the data told me." She crooked her head at the charts in Deborah's hand. "I even re-ran the data from the insurance board and verified their formulas to ensure the baseline was reliable. No problems there. Then, I ran a variety of scenarios to validate my results. Everything checked out." Ester shrugged again, her shrug telling Deborah to get over it and accept what was before her. "The results are solid. Your family is way off, playing in a field all by themselves."

Deborah fisted a hand, rested her chin on it and studied the chart with a Bell-shaped curve. Her troubled eyes moved over the pinprick data points, then scanned the summary at the bottom which bulleted Ester's process and findings. Unlike the first three lookovers, this the fourth time, Deborah slowed way down, ingesting every word, every number, studying Ester's methodology. When Deborah's mind processed to a stop, she nodded her head, conceding to Ester's expert work.

"This just isn't what I expected." Her words weren't soft enough to register as a murmur. Neither were they hard enough to tip the scales as a whisper.

Regardless of the sound decibel, the wallpaper in the King's upstairs study caught the words and delivered them to Ester.

"Believe it. Y'all's numbers are horrible. Horrible!" She scolded Deborah as if *she* were the sole cause of the Fuller's abnormal results. "They greatly skewed my charts. I had to do some finagling just to get your dot on the control chart. Regardless, the data clearly shows your family is way above the norm in volume of deaths—especially in accidental deaths."

A protracted, disturbed sigh seeped out of Deborah. "Yeah, it appears so." She continued shifting through the charts, staring at the summaries as if staring would fade the damning evidence just as the continual rising of the sun fades life.

Impatient with Deborah's long, cracked face, Ester reminded her friend of the initial goal. "Look, Deborah, I know this isn't what you expected, but you wanted to prove Billy and Clarice wrong, didn't you? You wanted to prove to them with indisputable evidence that Fuller deaths are not caused by spells and curses and all that crazy, superstitious nonsense. This clearly shows accidents as the most frequent form of death for the Fuller family. Tragic, violent accidents, but accidents none-the-less. And let's not forget that a number of those accidents have police and other investigative reports to *prove* they were accidents. And the rest of the categories are explainable—disease, natural causes and some lynchings during the good ole Reconstruction era..." she said, the latter delivered with a heavy spread of indignation on a slice of white bread hatred. "...so, even with the extremely high number of deaths compared to other families, every death can be logically explained and categorized. There's no room for Billy and Clarice's nonsense."

Being reminded that Billy and Clarice were wrong, that this data— disappointing as it was—might make them turn from the absurd and unite with the rest of the family in sanity, perked Deborah up a bit, not much, but enough for denial to dance out of the way, allowing acceptance to waltz in. She even managed a tiny, mocking smile. "Well, when you put it like that."

"Figured you'd see it my way."

Deborah eyed the letter size manila folder resting under Ester's elbows. Her inbred need for discovery peaked. She pointed and reached for the folder. "What's that?" Twisting her face warily, her hand halted midway in the grasping. "Do I want to know?"

Ester pushed the folder between them, opening it to reveal more sheets with more lines, graphs, numbers; data made understandable. "For kicks, I examined a few categories. You know, peeled back a few layers. This one is a chart on variations within each category of death. This one here is on deaths within each of the eight major family lines. And this final one is a graph on y'all's life span. Also, not normal." Ester pointed at jagged lines on a sheet of paper that rested between them and repeated, "Again, not normal." Her reprimanding look condemned Deborah for the head-shaking results; another Fuller shortcoming brought to life with numbers. "The Fuller life span is patterned completely different from other 'like' families. Y'all either live a long, long time or die in your prime." Ester leaned closer to Deborah. "Remember that graveside deal you went to? When was it? ...about a month ago?"

Yeah, it had been about a month; Deborah couldn't believe it. Shandra had been gone that long. It seemed longer. Her mind was about to settle in and consider this fact further when the statistician's blunt voice detoured her thoughts.

"Do you remember the ages represented?"

Freed to go there, the ex-scientist stared beyond Ester, beyond the papered walls of this room. Her mind travelled south, from city to countryside to resurrect that day. Hot and sunny. Black Hill attired with aged trees, iron gates, grassy pathways, granite headstones and Fullers galore. But age?

"There should have been a lot of kids and old folks, but considerably fewer folks in the twenty to fifty age range." Ester supplied, hoping to boost Deborah's memory.

She stretched her mind, trying to fit her family into neat, sensible age groups. Uncle Bob, Aunt Sallie Su, Paw-Finn, Uncle Roy. They had been some of the first ones Shandra had introduced her to, but they fell in the just-retired or near-retirement age range, possibly older. Then, there'd been Matilda, Conroy, Aven and Thomas. They'd all had grown kids with kids. *Does that make them older than me?* Deborah wondered. She sure couldn't judge by their tightly pulled faces, their satisfied smiles and upright bodies. Now, the elders...the elders she knew. They held old age in their cloudy eyes, wintertime bodies and historical minds. Aunt Martha, Mr. Veston and of course, Governor.

But that was only a few and there had been many—too many to categorize and honestly, age—it had been too insignificant a detail to hold in her mind. Substantial events had occurred *that* day that occupied her mind: reconnecting with *that* side of the family; filling notebook page after page of family names and history; and of course, *the incident*...the fall and death of a Fuller. A testimony to Ester's findings. The mental photograph of that death now dominated her bruised and battered mind. She shook her head to move it aside, along with Ester's question. "I don't recall. I know I spoke to a lot of elders. I needed to for the family tree, but a lot of folks were off in different parts of the cemetery. I didn't meet or see everyone and then after Shandra's...well, things just...blurred."

As if Death brushed against her, Deborah felt suddenly cold. Her arms crossed at the chest and she rubbed them until the raised bumps went away. Then, all at once, that previous debilitating darkness came upon her. It sat down, forcing her soul into submission; sitting back, it blocked her spirit; crossing its legs, it muted the protests of her heart.

She'd encountered darkness before. It had made its first visit during her tenure at The Lab when work had depleted her. And it had never really left, choosing to prolong its visit after Rachel died of SIDS and after Anna's and Curtis' deaths. But with the help of Dr. Beeker and handy doses of coping pills from Samuel, she thought she'd kicked darkness out of her life once and for all. Occasionally, however, it made brief, superficial visits, such as when a familiar body type passed her vision, bringing to mind a deceased loved one. When a similar voice called out as she shopped, darkness rose, bringing with it a fitting memory of one of her deceased loves. Now it came because it felt her weakness; a weakness brought on by death charts and the catastrophic memory of that horrible day.

Right then, Deborah could have stopped being, subordinated as she was by the power of darkness. But darkness had failed to completely subdue her mind, and now it presented a way out—counseling. An appointment with Dr. Beeker, the petite, natural-hair wearing, cross necklace-wearing psychiatrist would, like the servant Joshua, lead her from the enslaving press of darkness to the Promised Land. Deborah greedily latched on to the idea and quickly expanded it to secure back-to-back appointments for her and Hope. That would intimidate the girl into keeping her appointments and free them both. Deborah smiled, loving the idea and the thought of her soul, spirit, heart being freed.

Renewing her focus on Ester, she heard her friend say, "Well, we really don't need your anecdotal observations. Look at this chart." Ester flipped through several more sheets until she found one she liked and pulled it forward. "It shows two things: the highest volume of deaths occurs within the eighteen to fifty year range and within that age range, accidental death is the leading cause. See here…" Using a mechanical pencil as a pointer, Ester continued, forgetful of the humanity behind the numbers. "...the age range starts escalating near the twenty-year old mark, with a few exceptions. Curtis at eighteen, some other kid at fifteen, then..." She sketched an asterisk to highlight the ending range. "...accidental deaths start falling off around the fifty-year mark, with a few exceptions here and there. Definitely a relationship." Ester looked up from the graph smiling, loving how numbers made everything so simple until she saw Deborah's grave face. "What? I'm not clear?"

"Ester, you're telling me I'm going to die within two years or live to be as old as Aunt Mattie."

Both women stared at each other as the full impact of Ester's study hit home.

Last Saturday, six days ago, Deborah had been ignorant about her family's terrible history, completely unaware of the linkage between death, age and accidents. But a simple chart had changed that, absolutely wiped out the ignorant life she'd been living and now, this knowledge had her living in fear. And not just scared for herself, but also for her sister, Hannah, who fit the "Age and Cause of Death" chart, as Ester had labeled it. Also for her one remaining nephew, Shawn, who had three more years before Accidental Death began to stalk him. Most of her fear, however, she reserved for her daughter who had entered the lower end of the Accidental Death age range with her eighteenth birthday last October.

After being fully informed of this Fuller anomaly, Deborah had thought irrationally to protect those she loved by collecting every one of them and restricting them to safe confines. But where was that? Not a house. Not work or school. Not the streets. That was the thing with accidents; they were unpredictable. Out of the blue, a city bus rams and crushes one's car—death. A misplaced step off the curb, head meets pavement—death. A fall out of bed, land wrong, break neck—death.

Anywhere. Any time. Any place.

By the time Deborah made her way to the impossible conclusion of her irrational thought of hiding her loved ones from Accidental Death, Ester had developed an out. "Let's delve into these accidental deaths. Starting with the ones in Partway, since the majority of accidental deaths occurred there. Some of these might be improperly classified. It might not be as bad as it looks," she'd suggested.

That had somewhat relieved Deborah, had allowed her to staunch the flow of fear to get to this point—this point being parked in front of the Partway municipal office on a Friday morning with plans to search out records. More specifically, records from the morgue's library which had temporarily moved from the county seat to Partway due to a burst water pipe and subsequent construction at the permanent location. Their plan involved severing the connection between Fuller deaths and accidents in the hope of allowing Deborah to return to ignorant living.

As she and Ester gathered soft side briefcases and their purses from the back seat, then climbed out of Deborah's SUV, Deborah thought about the game plan Ester had outlined. First, pick through the medical files and interview appropriate personnel during business hours. Second, talk to Governor, as Mary had suggested and third, talk to Aunt Mattie, which Mary had not suggested, to better understand the story of the curse. Coming to grips with the "off-the-charts" accidental deaths of Fullers between eighteen and fifty was heavy enough. So, the pair of investigators thought to eliminate the burden of the curse (and set Billy and Clarice on the same sanity road as the rest of the family), freeing them to focus on the topic that disturbed them both greatly. This subject, too, they planned to ask Governor and Aunt Mattie about. Surely, the elders knew of any accidental deaths of which they might be able to speak on, or at least inform the researchers of any family members or family records, as yet unsheathed, that could be used to disassociate Fullers, age and accidents. Deborah prayed this would be the case.

The final step, which wasn't part of the actual investigation, involved a visit with Mary Fuller to share the family tree. She would be the first family member to see the complete tree. Deborah thought this fitting, considering her daughter had been essential to its completion.

Given all they planned to accomplish, the day loomed long and full, and because of that and any other unplanned delays, they had packed overnight bags and reserved a room at a local inn. If they had to spend the entire weekend in Partway in order to erase the bad news charts, then that's what they would do.

As they approached the wide, steep stairs of the four-story red brick building, Deborah looked over at her friend, feeling herself going soft and vulnerable on the inside. She spoke sincerely, with tears discoloring the pretty brown of her eyes, "Ester, if I haven't already said so, thank you. You didn't have to take off work today, and you certainly didn't have to devote the last few weekends to *my* project. I appreciate you so much for going through this with me. You're giving me strength."

Deborah thought she saw a shimmer in Ester's eyes but Ester bowed her head, blocking Deborah's view. Deborah smiled. What Ester's ex-husbands didn't stick around long enough to find out was that beneath that rough, callous exterior resided a caring, loving and loyal person. And while Ester rarely used tender or tactful language, her words were always honest, and she always gave more than required. Being a friend, lover or husband to Ester was like anything else—if you invest the time, you get the payoff, eventually.

As she always did when Deborah paid her a compliment, Ester detoured the conversation, "I think we should start with those two deaths where the ME listed the words 'black' and 'heart' on the autopsies. I'm sure it's a mistake, but it occurred to me that some Fuller from way back when might have seen those words on the report, didn't know the doctor had made a mistake, took that incorrect information and got the story of the curse rolling. That's the only logical explanation for how the story could have started."

"Oh, Ester," Deborah exclaimed, stopping suddenly. "You're absolutely right. That's got to be it." Deborah acknowledged the tingle that announced she was on the right path of discovery. Smiling broader now, she began moving again and soon reached for the handle on the door. She pulled the heavy glass door open for her friend. "I love you, Ester."

That stopped Ester cold under the threshold. She turned partially to Deborah, and a teary film softened her eyes as she struggled to say, "I love you, too."

She turned forward quickly and marched into the air-conditioned building. Deborah followed, pausing to ensure the door closed solidly behind them. When she happened to glance outside, a spot of red caught her attention. While doing a double take, she turned fully to the door and pressed her forehead against the glass, squinting. "Is that Hope?"

A Mustang with the same classic body shape as her daughter's car idled at the traffic light two blocks away.

"Can't be," she reasoned, "Hope's at work." Even knowing that to be a fact, Deborah pushed through the door, hurrying outside to get a better look. Unfortunately, with the distance and the intensity of the sun's rays, which caused her to squint harder, she could not be sure, and then the light changed. The car sped through the intersection and within seconds disappeared, or rather was blocked from Deborah's view by the two and three-story downtown office buildings.

"What are you doing out here?" Ester demanded.

"I thought I saw Hope's car," Deborah answered while searching the landscape and fumbling around in her purse for her cell phone.

"What would Hope be doing here? If it was an emergency, she would have called. Or someone would have."

Ester put into words Deborah's fear—that there had been an emergency, that accidental death had claimed another Fuller. Either an immediate family member or an extended one. Ester's charts were not generous enough to predict a name, only an age and a wide age range at that. Already bowled over by fear and uncertainty, Deborah took on even more.

Finally, her fingers stumbled upon her phone, and she yanked it out. She punched the right sequence for Hope's number and listened desperately as the rings began. It seemed her heart couldn't decide if it wanted to thump, race or be still. So it did all three while she worried if Hope were in Partway. If, indeed, that had been Hope, the question was *who*. Hannah and Hope were the only two who fit the age profile in their immediate family. Samuel was not a Fuller and therefore exempt. Her parents were too old, closing in quickly on seventy, and Shawn was too young, although there had been some exceptions on both ends of the age range. It had to be Hannah. Unless death had claimed a Fuller from the extended family. Perhaps one here in Partway or in Dallas or some other part of the country where Fullers had migrated. There were plenty of Fullers in that age range for accidental death to choose from.

"Damn this study of death," Deborah cursed under her breath. She wished she had never gotten involved with Billy and Clarice and their stupid conversation at the funeral. If only she had walked away, she would be living happy and innocent. She certainly wouldn't be here, scared to death and trembling on the steps of a one hundred and fifty-year old building in a town south of where she should really be. She shook herself out of fear long enough to listen as Hope's voice invited callers to leave a message. She bowed her head, waiting impatiently for the beep. "Hope, it's Mom. Call me as soon as you get this message. Love you."

Disconnecting, frustrated, she turned to Ester who stood beside her and was speaking into her own phone. "…for Deborah. She's… we're in Partway today and Hannah, Deborah just wanted to know if you need anything from here." Ester shrugged her shoulders as if to say that was the best excuse she could devise, given the circumstances.

Deborah smiled gratefully at Ester. So, it wasn't Hannah. And maybe not Hope. Time to check on her parents and then, well, she didn't know. She supposed she would just have to wait and see what news presented itself.

While Ester wrapped up her call with Hannah, Deborah dialed her parent's home number. Her father hated a ringing phone and picked up on the first ring, sounding gruff, just like Samuel when he hadn't had enough sleep. Deborah had never been so glad to hear her father's unfriendly hello. She tried a smile and failed.

"Hello Dad, are you and Mom okay?" A few seconds passed and then Deborah nodded her head at Ester, signifying all was good. "I was calling to tell you I'm in Partway today. Maybe the whole weekend. Just wanted you to know, in case you need me."

Again, more lost time while her father spoke and then, "Okay, I will. Um…have you heard from Hope today?" Deborah's shoulders slumped and her frown deepened, telling the world she didn't like her father's answer. "Okay, I gotta go. Love you."

As soon as she disconnected, Ester handed her cell phone to Deborah while saying, "It's ringing at Samuel's office."

When Loren, Samuel's long-tenured receptionist answered, Deborah skipped her usual procedure of asking about the woman's family. Instead, she abruptly asked for Hope.

"Oh, sure Deborah, let me get her for you."

Deborah closed her eyes and mouthed, "Thank God." Relief, sweet relief coursed through her, overtaking the earlier fear and worry that had prevailed. She smiled, feeling so good. Everyone was okay, alive and accounted for. She felt better than good; she felt great.

Seconds later, Loren returned with, "Sorry, Deborah. I guess she went downstairs or to the restroom. Would you like to leave her a voicemail?"

Now that Deborah got what she wanted, she could afford to be her usual gracious self. "No, Loren. Thanks, though and have a great weekend." Deborah pushed END and impulsively, excitedly hugged her friend. Her smile extended long and wide, as if she'd won the Nobel Prize in Medicine.

When she pulled back, handing Ester her phone, Ester voiced exactly the words circling in Deborah's mind. "Deborah, we can't go through this every time we see a red car or hear about a death or someone takes too long getting home. Let's get in there and dismantle this thing before *it* kills *both* of us."

"I'm with you," Deborah said, thinking relief was a lovely thing, but she never wanted to feel that type of relief again. Like Ester said, it was time to dissolve this dark cloud of death that seemed to favor her family.

Tucking her cell phone away, she rushed into the building behind Ester. That day, Deborah and Ester researched like they'd never researched before.

Loren had lied. Not intentionally.

Along with all the other employees, Hope had reported to work on time. Actually, she'd been early since it was her Friday to bring the bagels and cheese. She'd stayed exactly one hour, then feigning sick had told her father she was going home. He hadn't asked too many questions since he was aware, through her mother, of her difficult menstrual cycles and then she was gone, on her way to Partway still dressed in the uniform of her father's medical office.

That *was* Hope's car Deborah had seen at the intersection of Main and Broad. That *had been* Hope speeding through downtown, oblivious to the posted thirty-mile-per-hour speed limit. A way to acquire the Truth had finally come to the BlackHeart in the moonlight hours and anxious to implement Its plan, It'd sped not only through Partway, but also all the way from Dallas.

Once It made it past the traffic lights of downtown Partway, the BlackHeart turned eastward, traveled eleven miles and then hung a left at Pritchard's Red Barn, which was not a barn at all but a one-story square convenience store which made its money from selling bait and fireworks. Another left at Post Oak Road and a right into the town's cemetery, and It was where It wanted to be.

The BlackHeart slowed down then, being respectful of the bodies and spirits that inhabited the place. Not that it would matter if It ran either body or spirit over. It laughed at the thought, a full-bodied laugh that made It wipe tears from Its eyes. While following the gravel path toward the back acreage, Its demeanor became sober as the beauty of the place absorbed It— the angel statues carved of stone so white they looked almost transparent, the granite benches angled just so, the groomed hedges and trees that wore a hunter green color year round, thanks to Governor's care and the scrolled ornaments scattered here and there. *Such a difference between this cemetery and Black Hill*, It thought.

About halfway to the back property line, the BlackHeart pulled off the drive and parked on the stately lawn. It exited the car, surveying the grounds.

Governor really does good work. Not a weed to be seen. Uniform too, as if he used a razor and measuring tape to clip every blade. It stood a second longer, appreciating the view. Then, attracted by the call and response of two blackbirds, It shaded Its eyes and watched as the birds circled and dipped, swerved and dived. They seemed to be having such fun, It thought about transforming into one and joining in their games, but It dismissed the idea almost as soon as it formed. It was much more fun being human, more hell It could raise that way. The BlackHeart chuckled at the thought, but abruptly snipped it. It'd delayed enough; It had important work to do.

Turning within herself, Hope decreased as the BlackHeart increased. The balancing act took less than a second and once complete, It wasted no time reaching out and feeling him—Governor, the next keeper of the family secret. He worked diligently in the "back forty" as the old timers used to say. It liked that. Back there, there were no extra eyes. No busybodies. No witnesses.

Of course, Governor felt It too. It watched as he straightened up. Then, in slow, awkward movements, he rose from kneeling to standing; the headstone he'd been setting back to its rightful position forgotten. He turned in Its direction, and when their eyes met over the distance It smiled at him. As quick as a flash, the smile collapsed and with Evil darkening Hope's eyes, skin, and blood, It reached out in spirit form and wrapped Itself around him.

It was different this time. Not like at Black Hill when It had viciously attacked him, when it had showed off Its strength so he would know just what he had to look forward to. This time, the BlackHeart touched him as Cora Jean would have—softly, seductively. Within seconds, It felt his response. It felt the tingle within him, which blossomed into a warm, liquid feeling. It saw him smile and hug himself and seconds later, It felt his heart opening. That's when the BlackHeart knew It had him.

They had weaknesses, these favored creations of God. Charles Fuller's had been his devotion to ego. Mattie Fuller's, her immediate family, all dead and gone. Cora Jean was Governor's. He loved that woman while she lived and even now in death. The good thing about weaknesses were that they could be used like a weapon. The bad thing about weaknesses were that the use of them sometimes backfired, as had been the case with Mattie recently. Still, the recent loss to Mattie didn't stop the BlackHeart from exploiting Governor's weakness. It had a better chance with Governor. The old man was inexperienced, still growing into his role as Record Keeper, Truth Bearer, or whatever term the others used to describe themselves—and that made him vulnerable. That meant he could be turned and used to obtain the Truth. It might work. It might not. That depended on his strength and commitment; that depended on Its cunning.

Right now, at this very moment, It was winning. Caught up in loving memories, Governor had not thought to shield himself by going inward, nor had he accessed his words of assurance, nor had he reached out to Mattie. All he felt were good, warm feelings coursing through him as he bathed in the thoughts of Cora Jean that the BlackHeart had instigated. Just when Governor stopped hugging himself and reached out his long arms to take an absent Cora Jean into them, the BlackHeart withdrew from him, gently taking the loving memories with It. Looking as if he'd been left with an empty ache, Governor glanced around, searching with dazed eyes for a person who no longer existed. He took a few steps, seemed unstable and confused, as if he'd lost north from south, east from west. With his arms dangling at his side and his head beginning to droop, he appeared crazy. It would take some time for him to come fully to himself and realize he'd had one hell of a hallucination. During that time, as he righted his world, the BlackHeart entered Its car, started the motor and drove off.

It was not done with seducing Governor.

Even though the time approached for Friday night fun, Deborah and Ester kept working their game plan with no consideration for amusement. What drove them to ignore the usual social norm was their failure—thus far—to make the chart change its depiction of Fullers, age, and accidental deaths in spite of their aggressive and thorough probing.

The research had started off promising that morning. They'd been welcomed by the small staff of two in the morgue's office, and after Ester had thrust her business card in their faces—Director of Statistics, Analytics and Methodology, Southern Region Science Institute, Dallas, Texas—and shaded the truth, they'd been given an all-access pass. For more than five hours they'd pulled files, starting with the most recent accidental deaths. They'd read the files from cover to cover and made calls to the DA's office, private citizens, retired and active coroners, as well as retired and active doctors for additional information when needed. With only a handful of files in various stages of research, they realized two things: it would take weeks to go through every accidental death file on the Fuller family, those that occurred in Partway, *and* some of the people involved in investigating, reporting or examining the deaths were, themselves, dead.

By mid-afternoon, with less than a handful of deaths fully examined and having found nothing to remove or move the data points on the chart, they decided to break and change topics. After a quick pass through a drive-thru for food, they arrived at Mattie's house, prepared to discuss the curse. Mattie's property had been eerily quiet and still. Looking around carefully, they approached the rickety porch steps. Then, they pounded on the locked screen door. No answer. Desperate, they circled the house, springing up and down to sneak peeks in windows to see if Mattie was simply ignoring them or, indeed, was not home. Unfortunately, being average in height, neither got a long enough look to decide which. Disappointed but determined, they re-entered the SUV and within minutes pulled up to the rusty iron gates of Black Hill. Giving Ester the same tour Mattie had given her, Deborah's hope to find Mattie there died. No Mattie. Not even impressions on the grass of her small body.

After leaving Black Hill, they'd driven along several weary roads to Governor's house. Following the same MO as at Mattie's, knocking, pounding and circling his white wood frame house, they met with the same result. No Governor. And again, the same at his job—no Governor.

"Partway is not *that* big," Ester stated in disgust when they'd turned left onto the road that led to Post Oak Road and town. "Where could two old people be?"

Where, indeed? Deborah wondered while answering Ester with a shrug. Deborah hadn't a clue, but both of them being absent bothered her.

Following the roads to downtown Partway, they returned to the morgue and re-settled themselves at the only clutter-free table in the morgue's library. There they stayed until close, slowly picking their way through one accidental death after another.

Upon leaving the municipal office, they conducted another city-to-rural-to-unincorporated tour of Partway in search of Mattie and Governor. Still, the elders evaded them. Giving up for the time being, they backtracked to inner Partway.

Residential neighborhoods of one and two-story homes fanned out from the downtown square and in some cases edged the buildings, alleys and streets of downtown. Schools, churches and gas stations claimed a few corner lots in these neighborhoods, and Beacon Street, where Deborah and Ester were headed, had the only housing project in the town of 5,000-plus people. Turning off Beacon onto Clement and motoring a few blocks south, they arrived at Mary Fuller's house.

When Deborah and Ester had been unsuccessful in raising either of the elders, Deborah had called Mary and asked if they could stop by for that promised visit. Mary's squeal, so like her daughter's, and her vocalized, "You'd better," had made Deborah smile. Something she appreciated after the frustrating day she and Ester had had. Now, twenty minutes after the call, Deborah parked on the street in front of Mary's house, wondering if this was a good thing to do or not.

Sure, Mary had sounded enthusiastic and excited about their visit and the family tree, but Deborah worried that it might sadden Mary. Shandra, who had contributed so much to its development, would never see the completed family tree, and it was that point that raised doubt in Deborah. Would seeing the tree add to Mary's grief? Would it add pain to suffering? Deborah sat back in her seat, deliberating, and decided it was too late for doubts and worry. They were here. The tree was here, and there was Mary, waving at them from her open front door.

Deborah returned the wave and after bolstering her emotions, she cut the motor, gathered her purse and briefcase and climbed out of the SUV with only one remaining concern—Ester. Her dear friend took defeat hard, and with every strikeout today Ester's mood had darkened. It now radiated at a deep, black-blue. Feeling like she needed to remind Ester of the social nature of this visit, she did, floating a whisper to Ester. "Remember, Ester, this is *not* an official visit. I just want to see how she and the boys are doing and show her the tree."

In a tight, low voice, Ester pushed back, "But she might know—"

"No, Ester, please," Deborah cut her off with a fierce reply and an even fiercer look.

There was no more time for cajoling, begging or threatening. They'd traveled the lily pad stone path that led from the sidewalk to the front porch and had reached the porch steps and Mary's hearing.

"Hello, there." Mary greeted them, still waving and smiling like nobody's business, looking like summer with a personality. The grieving mother wore a white swing dress with a huge sunflower on front and matching sunflower flip-flops. A questionable outfit on some, but Mary's wire-thin body and chocolate-toned skin carried it without judgment.

"Y'all come on in here now. Come up outta that heat."

She held open the screen door as wide as it would open and with her free arm, hugged Deborah tightly. She repeated the gesture with Ester, pulling her close, even though she didn't know Ester from Queen Victoria. That was just her way.

"So glad to see y'all. And can't wait to see this tree," she said as she closed and locked the outer and inner door. "Come on back where it's cooler." With light steps, she led them down a long hallway, chatting the entire time. "Yes, Lord, I sure was glad to get your call. Didn't have a thing planned to entertain myself tonight. So, I decided to cook this big ole dinner. Hadn't done that since...shoot, I can't even tell you when."

Every few steps, Mary glanced backward to make sure her guests were still with her. "Sap took the boys off to a baseball tournament in Waco. Won't be back 'til Sunday. Thought I'd go out and celebrate my freedom, but when I went in that fridge and seen them greens sittin' there pretty as you please, I decided I'd rather eat me a good meal. Since the boys moved in, they been wearin' me out on McDonald's."

Mary walked as fast as she talked and Deborah barely had time to register the rooms they zoomed by. Already, they'd passed a formal sitting room on the right and a short hallway on the left, from which sprouted three doors. Straight ahead, where Mary seemed to be headed, Deborah saw a family room. This, she surmised from the casual furniture and the toys spread willy-nilly. To her surprise, however, Mary actually disappeared through an opening on the right several feet before they reached the family room.

Following blindly, Deborah walked through the same opening and faced a large room cordoned off into distinct areas. The bulk of the room had been reserved for the kitchen. It had walls the color of the yellow sunflower on Mary's dress and cabinets that matched the white of her flip-flops. Sunflowers were everywhere…as appliqués on the small appliances, on the wall calendar, the decorative plates and towels, in planters and, well—everywhere. The wall coloring continued into the next space, which was a dining area outfitted with a table, four chairs, a buffet, and a baker's rack. The sunflower theme carried over here, too, but in less abundance. The remaining space, a utility closet really, housed a full-size washer and dryer and yes, the walls were yellow and someone had stuck sunflower magnets on the energy-efficient, water-conserving appliances.

Deborah smiled. Although the sunflower theme had been overdone by her standards, the rooms did radiate a welcome that could not be mistaken for anything else. Deborah thought it the perfect environment for a young Shandra, and now her sons, to thrive and flourish.

"Sit, sit," Mary waved a hand toward the bar stools as she continued to the double wide refrigerator. "What y'all drinking? I got everything. Tea, water, lemonade. Me, personally," she turned away from the fridge to grin wickedly at her guests, "I got the Grey Goose on ice, but if y'all are church-goers, I also got beer and wine." She chuckled and quickly continued, "Or, I make a mean Cosmopolitan. Got the recipe from Oprah's magazine."

Deborah's smile grew wider, and she noticed that even Ester's funk seemed less funky. Ester ordered a beer. Deborah, a glass of white wine. She tried to ignore the rumblings in her stomach that had started the second she entered Mary's kitchen. Their hostess had not been teasing about that big ole dinner. From her seat at the bar, Deborah could see fires flaming under several pots on the stove, and the oven's heating element hummed, telling Deborah something good cooked within. Mary was not only going to enjoy a big meal, but a delicious one, too, if the appealing smells were any indication.

"My mama really did beat some manners into me," Mary continued the conversation as she poured drinks into glasses already chilled. "I'm Mary Fuller. You have to be Ester." She paused in her hostessing duties to smile and nod at Ester.

Deborah's reaction was instant. "Oh Mary, Ester, I am sorry. I'm the one who's derelict in my manners. I wasn't thinking." She gushed, feeling her face grow warm.

Mary waved the apology away. "You know I ain't one to stand on that hoity-toity stuff. I just figured I wouldn't want nobody callin' me outta my name, so I better make sure she's who I think she is."

Grateful for the pass, Deborah acknowledged that at least she'd used decent manners when she'd called earlier and shared with Mary that she wasn't alone and that her friend Ester rode with her.

Mary brought their drinks and Ester, while accepting her cold glass of beer, remarked, "Your house is larger than it looks from outside."

Their hostess beamed as she replied proudly, "Soldier benefits." Turning, she retreated to the stove to stir her pots. "My husband was Army. Bought this house and a few years later got hisself killed. I couldn't stand to leave this place, so as the kids grew, I added on."

Hearing Mary's explanation brought to mind a secret Shandra had shared during one of their work sessions at the library. All the Fullers in Partway speculated about how Mary got her money. A few thought it came from death benefits, courtesy of the U. S. government. A few tagged it to wise investments. But most subscribed to the "business dealings with her criminal ex-boyfriend" theory, even though the timeline wasn't right, and even though the IRS never came calling, even when tips had been called in repeatedly to them. None of those assumptions were correct, but the closest was the wise investment theory.

Many, many years ago, when her children were still unfertilized eggs, Mary had traveled to Las Vegas on a solo trip for work. Lady Luck, as if knowing her husband would be stolen from her and a daughter too, had rewarded her with not one, but two big payouts—$400,000 at a Las Vegas casino and $50,000 at Stateline. After paying the IRS their healthy cut, she'd taken the rest, dumped it with the first financial planner who'd passed the ethics test, and her winnings had multiplied at a steady rate ever since.

The winnings had allowed Shandra to obtain her bachelor's and master's degrees without incurring any education debt. It had also afforded Mary the means to buy Shandra and Dexter—Shandra's ex and the father of her two boys—a house as a wedding present and five years later to buy out Dexter when he split for what he thought were greener pastures. Having access to Mary's money had not worked out as well for Sap, who used her resources for alcohol and illegal substances, which served to cut his dreams short and stunt his potential.

Shrewdly, Mary had told no one, not even her husband, about the money or how she'd acquired it. She'd only shared the story with Shandra after she had put her wedding-present-house on the market during the divorce proceedings because she didn't want Mary to have to pay for her poor decision in selecting a mate.

Smiling into her glass of wine, Deborah recalled that at the funeral, or perhaps it had been the graveside cleaning, some of the family members had whispered about Mary, behind her back, of course. They'd said things like: "Mary didn't have a specialized skill or degree that produced the type of money she had in the bank," and "She'd never had a sugar daddy, and that criminal ex-boyfriend of hers had been history for a while, but still she got money." It drove the Partway Fullers crazy. Kept them up at night wondering how a secretary lived in a mortgage-free house, drove a top-of-the-line, paid-for truck, dropped huge checks in the offering plate on the Sundays she made it to church, and had never had a to-do with the law—other than bailing her son or boyfriends out of jail. How did she do it? They scratched their heads.

Mary's high, light voice tugged at Deborah, inviting her back into the present conversation. "I hope y'all're hungry. There's too much here for just little ole me."

Their sunshine hostess now flitted about the kitchen, pulling down mixing bowls, selecting ingredients and popping in and out of the refrigerator.

Deborah's stomach chose to respond to Mary's dinner invitation with a loud and painful growl. Hers wasn't the only one. Ester's stomach sounded off, too and Deborah spoke, answering for them both. "If you're sure it's no bother, we'd love to stay for dinner. Thanks for the invitation."

"Oh, don't thank me. Shoot, you family. You too, Ester." Mary charged on, ignoring any type of smooth transition. "My silly boyfriend got a charge throwed at him and I'be damned if I'ma take my money and bail his sorry tail out again. He gonna haft to sit this one out." Mary took a break from words to hold her head back and tip her glass up, slurping all the way to the end of the drink. She smiled and held up her glass. "Y'all ready for another?"

They shook their heads, and Mary zoomed on. "Gone help yo'self when you are. Five minutes here, and you ain't company no mo'."

Deborah laughed. Even Ester chuckled, and Deborah assumed the beer was working its magic on her, mellowing her out, softening that hard core.

"Yeah," Mary continued while mixing another drink for herself. "Almost broke down and went and got him so I wouldn't be alone." She paused briefly, staring into her glass, and Deborah knew that her mind had switched to Shandra. Her next words confirmed it. "I don't like to be alone. Gives you too much time to think. Know what I mean?"

Deborah knew. It would be a simple thing to resurrect what Mary was feeling and thinking, because she'd been there. But she couldn't go there again, for to do so meant she might not return fully sane. So, she pulled the shades on those memories, plugged the associated feelings and desperately clung to the face, hopes and dreams of her remaining child.

Giving her near best, Deborah replied softly, "I do, Mary, and I'm sorry."

Their eyes met, and they recognized the pain in each other's eyes and in that moment, they bonded more deeply in their shared experience.

Mary attempted a smile, but failed. She lingered a moment longer at the dark door of death and then bulldozed her way through the pain to again introduce light and levity to her home. "Enough of that," she exclaimed as she plunked her drink down to wipe the tears that floated in her eyes. She managed a full smile this time and pointed at Deborah. "You came with a tree. Why don't you dig it out? I cain't wait 'til after dinner to see it."

"Sure," Deborah croaked. In spite of her intent to avoid the emotions associated with death, they still clawed at her, making her throat tight and her eyes fill with tears. She did a good job of controlling the tears by focusing on Mary's request, which led her to the earlier doubt she'd had in the car. Was this the right thing to do? Show Mary the tree? A project that had been so important to Shandra? Mary was struggling and would continue to struggle for as long as she drew breaths.

Still undecided, Deborah slid off her stool, picked her briefcase off the floor and set it on her bar stool. She hesitated, wondering what to do. Ester's under-her-breath mumble, "We're missing an opportunity here," helped Deborah decide.

After casting Ester a direct, meaningful look that threatened harm if she referenced the accidental death chart, she pulled out several folders, looking for the one that contained the working copy of the family tree. Better to show Mary the tree, she thought, than to hit her with a double blow—the tree and Ester's chart. While Mary threw cornbread together, dashed it in a pan and then the oven, Deborah pulled out her copy and unfolded it. She had hired a graphic designer—and paid extra for a rush job—to lay it out portrait style and had paid a printer—extra money for a twenty-four-hour turnaround—to print it on vintage sepia paper. The result was a large four foot-by-four foot attractive document that could easily pass as wall art.

To ensure that her earlier message to Ester stuck, she shot her another dark look as Mary approached the counter.

"Another few minutes, and we can eat," Mary announced, drying her hands on a sunflower dish towel. She reached the counter and went still for several long moments as she stared at the document. Then, "Oh, my…" slipped past her lips and tears plopped on the tree before she could stop their descent. Hurriedly, she wiped them away and then let her fingers linger on names—Fullers, just like her. "Deborah, this is really sumthin.' I didn't know how our family would look on paper." Deborah flinched at Mary's unwitting, double-sided comment. *If only she knew,* her mind taunted, thinking about Ester's charts. Apparently, Ester's mind worked the same as Deborah's because Deborah felt Ester's willful eyes on her and felt Ester's urgent nudge against her thigh. She knew what the statistician wanted. Since Mary was the only Fuller they'd found at home today, Ester wanted answers or at a minimum, information.

But Deborah was just as determined to *not* point out how Shandra's death validated Ester's charts. So, neglecting Ester's wishes, Deborah cut in on Mary's perusal and started her at the genesis of her family line—not the same family line as Deborah's—that ended thus far with Shandra's boys. The walk through time didn't take long, about forty minutes, with Mary asking few questions. At the conclusion, Deborah marveled at Mary's strength. Several times, Mary had fingered the spot where Shandra's name and corresponding birth and death dates were recorded. Several times, she had smeared tears on the paper—once at her deceased mother's name and again at her deceased grandfather's—and had apologized needlessly. A couple of times, Mary whooped in pride, pointing out the one Fuller who had served in the state legislature and another who had been a pro ball player. And there had been a few times she had Deborah and Ester laughing at stories about this cousin and that one. Witnessing her bounce-back ability, Deborah felt at peace knowing she'd done right in showing her their family tree.

While Mary lingered over the tree, Deborah excused herself to pour another glass of wine for herself and fetch another beer for Ester.

"I wish Shandra was here to see this."

Deborah tensed, listening for a catch in Mary's voice, but it was a needless action because there was nothing there except pleasure.

"She was always talkin' 'bout that tree. Had wanted to do it herself, had even started, but with two boys—"

At the sudden stop, Deborah tensed again, and this time she had a right to do so. Mary had snagged on one of those unexpected moments when the reality of her life hit her. Rushing back to the bar, Deborah set their drinks down and hugged Mary's shoulders, caressed her back, soothing, calming the grieving mother as best she could. Minutes later, the moment passed and the Mary of light and joy rebounded, wiping her face with fabric flowers and finishing her thoughts.

"Yeah, she loved our crazy family even though some didn't deserve it. Seein' that…" Mary nodded at the tree, "…our family, all nice and neat on that paper would have made her day. You know, it didn't take much to please her." She chuckled, soaking up residual tears and then fanning herself with the same dish towel. "This is wonderful, Deborah, just wonderful."

Then, without warning, she wrapped her scrawny arms around Deborah's neck, hugging her hard and long. Deborah gladly accepted the embrace, melted into it, loving the feel of shared comfort.

When she pulled back, Mary was her everyday self again. "I wanna get a copy of this to share with the boys. They need to know their history, and they need to know how important this was to their mama."

"Of course," Deborah's voice cracked, so she left it at that. Really, she could have gone on to tell Mary that she'd had the printing company reproduce twenty-five copies and she'd brought half that many with her to Partway with plans to present four copies, one each to Aunt Mattie, Governor, Mary and Sap. Deborah didn't share any of this. She quietly folded the tree and replaced it in its folder. She pulled out two trees, rolled like posters and cased in a plastic sleeve, and left them in a corner on the counter out of the way.

Clearing her throat, Deborah spoke to Mary's back; their hostess had returned to kitchen duty. "I'm leaving copies here, Mary. One for you and one for Sap. You can frame them, if you want, but I plan to update the tree every year after the graveside service, and I've still got work to do with the Fullers prior to Charles."

That is, if Accidental Death doesn't claim me, she thought. Oddly, her mind didn't stay on that topic. It skipped to wondering about Aunt Mattie's and Governor's whereabouts. She desperately needed to speak with them.

"That's great, Deborah," Mary said removing plates, utensils, and glasses from her cabinets. "That's what all those papers are? You got more to add, already?"

In the act of returning her case to the floor, Deborah slowed to compose a viable response. One that didn't expose Mary, who fell outside of the age range, to the ugly truth; that truth being that her son needed to live carefully and one day, her grandsons too.

As if sensing Deborah's struggle to come up with a meaningful, yet meaningless response, Mary continued, "I thought Shandra said sumthin' 'bout you lookin' into some conflictin' dates for some deaths. I told Shandra I wouldn't be surprised if you came up with a couple of dates for Cynthia and Tate. I don't think the police ever got those right. Boy, that was a mess and others, too, from further back. You find anything on that?" And still, Mary went forth as if she'd received answers. "And hey, did you ever get hold of Gov'nor 'bout that silly curse?"

"Actually…" Ester jumped in, seeing an opportunity to finally get answers. "…we missed both Mattie and Governor today. We stopped by both houses and both cemeteries twice. Do you know where they could be?"

Mary continued setting the table as she reported. "Ain't but a few places Aunt Mattie gonna be. If she wasn't at home or Black Hill, she was prob'ly at the grocery store buyin' up every can of Alpo on the shelves. And Gov'nor, he might be gone to go pick up a body. He does that sometimes."

Ester continued, unable to stop herself from forcing logic and sense into a disorderly world. "Deborah and I suspect the story of the curse is the result of two incorrect medical reports. Unfortunately, the doctors who wrote the reports are dead; it's been that long ago, but I'd bet my life on their mistake being the origin of the story."

"Well, it don't take much, do it? 'specially with our fam'ly. Give 'em an acre and they'll take a whole county. Give 'em a county and they'll take the whole state." Mary laughed, shaking her head, changing the subject. "You can wash your hands at the sink, if you want. Then, come on over and have a seat."

While the two guests did just that, Mary prattled on while dishing food onto serving platters. "'Course I 'magine it's hard to get to any kind of truth with Aunt Mattie hoggin' the fam'ly Bible. Plus, she's as close-mouthed and orn'ry as they come. I'm sure she knows more than she tells."

"Mattie told Deborah she didn't have any family records or documents of any kind," Ester stated in her stern doctor voice.

Mary harrumphed and then confessed in a throw-away manner, "Who knows? Aunt Mattie don't let nobody but Gov'nor inside her house. And the only thing she carry outside is herself and Alpo. And..." Mary set steaming platters of food on the table and returned to the kitchen for more. "...you don't want her talkin' to you 'cause that's gonna be a cussin' out." She turned to Deborah with a question on her face. "You 'member that day we was talkin' and I had to get off the phone, 'cause them fool boys thought they was Spider Man?"

Deborah nodded. Of course, she remembered! She'd been paralyzed, waiting on the outcome.

"'Member I told you Aunt Mattie been waitin' all these years to get back at me?"

Deborah nodded. That had been the most enticing setup to a story, ever.

"Well, I was fixin' to tell you 'bout the set-to I'd had with Aunt Mattie when I was a little girl."

Deborah and Ester shared a look and then leaned forward in their chairs as Mary set the last of the food on the table and took her seat. They could tell by the shine in her eyes and her sly smile that whatever followed was going to be good.

"I was quite a handful when I was young…smokin', skippin' schoo', puttin' the sheriff's car on flat, burnin' the cotton fields so I wouldn't haft to pick it. You know, little kid stuff. Well, one day, I musta been 'round twelve or thirteen, Chunky, one of our cousins, put me up to this dare. He dared me to go inside Aunt Mattie's house and bring him the fam'ly Bible. All the old Fullers really wanted this Bible. I used to hear 'em say it was a link to the past, had the fam'ly history in it and names, too. You know, like your tree."

Deborah nodded.

Mary talked on. "He thought I was stupid and didn't know none of this. But I knew, and *I* knew what he really wanted was to give the Bible to his mama, but he was too chicken-shit to break into her house and git it himself. Well, I ain't one to back down from no dare, whatever the reason. So I skip schoo' one mornin' and watch as Aunt Mattie feeds them mangy dogs. Then, she cuts across the back woods to Black Hill. She always goes there; ever'body knows that. I wait 'til I think she's good and gone and break in her place. See this—" Mary stood, lifted the hem of her dress and pointed to a jagged line just inside her right knee.

Deborah and Ester stretched their necks, staring at it. Not a straight line at all, the line crooked half a palm's length, and decades later, it still looked angry. "I did that crawlin' up under the house to let myself in by the floor trap. Anyways, I found it. In the livin' room on some old desk. I looked at it, flipped through it, and I 'member thinkin': *'Is this what ever'body wants? Shoot, they can have it!'*" Mary chuckled at a twelve or thirteen year old's reasoning. "Now, don't get me wrong, it was beautiful. The only Bible I'd ever seen with colored pictures on the inside. 'member, this was way before color started sproutin' ever'where, includin' people's hair—Hold on," Mary bookmarked her storytelling, "I gotta get the tea and then we can eat. I'ma need to finish this story with some food in my belly."

This task she completed right away and soon, they were stacking their plates with homemade smothered chicken, greens, macaroni and cheese, carrots, cornbread and, of course, the staple on every Southern table, sweet tea. Deborah just barely resisted the urge to dig in caveman-style.

Mary murmured a simple "God bless" for grace and told her guests, "Dig in and eat 'til you bust."

She picked up her story while filling glasses. "Now, I'd seen plenty of black Bibles and small ones, like at church, but not one this big or white—with gold letters on the cover and gold edges. It was beautiful, and I don't mind tellin' you I decided I was gonna steal it alright, but I was gonna give it to *my* mama, and Chunky could just go to hell."

She chewed, swallowed and then continued, "I got it out the house, which wasn't easy, since I was tryin' not to get it dirty."

Deborah and Ester nodded their understanding, engrossed in the telling.

"Anyways, I did it. Made it all the way to the fence—you know that corner fence that separates Aunt Mattie's property from the FM road?"

Even though it seemed like all of Mattie's property was fenced either naturally by trees, brush and the creek or unnaturally by wire or cattle gates, Deborah knew exactly which corner and fence Mary referenced; Ester did not. At Ester's negative head shake, Mary deemed the detail unimportant and continued sketching in more of the story. "I 'member that Bible was so heavy my hands was numbin' up on me. I had to put that thing down, and I set it under one of them oaks by the fence. Then, I slid between the wires and down the ditch to wet the bottom end of my shirt in the creek. I knew if Mama saw that blood she'd flip out. She wouldn't care as much about the torn jeans, shoot, that happened all the time. But blood, I had to clean that up. And it was hard, 'cause my leg was really smartin'. 'Course the pain dulled to nothin' when I thought about how I had my mama a good gift, *and* I'd beaten Chunky. I couldn't wait to mess with him."

Mary took another break in storytelling so she could start the coffee brewing. When she returned to the table, she explained, "Cain't eat pound cake without coffee." Picking up her fork, she continued. "Well, when I fine'ly got myself cleaned up, I went back to the Bible, and it was gone. I couldn't believe it. I looked from one tree to the next thinkin' *'I ain't crazy; I know I left it here.'* I mean, it hadn't been but a few minutes. I stood there for the longest, tryin' to figure it out, and fine'ly it came to me. Aunt Mattie! She must have cut her visit short, saw me leavin' her house and followed me. Had to be Aunt Mattie, 'cause only one other person knew what I was up to that mornin,' and it couldn't be him, 'cause he wouldn't dare skip schoo' with his Daddy bein' a teacher and all. Besides, Chunky had enuff sense not to steal from me."

Mary chewed, swallowed and told some more. "I was mad'r'n hell. Here I done missed a half day of schoo', cut myself, lost my Mama's gift and a dare. Oh, no! I wasn't havin' that. I started out for Aunt Mattie's, and when I got there, I bammed on her screen door, yellin' for her to come out and bring that Bible. She came alright, holdin' that Bible in front of her. I couldn't believe the old biddy was bold enuff to put it right in my face. But I tell you what..." A short pause so Mary could chew, swallow, wipe. "...she got my respect that day. That woman is badder than me. 'Fore I could even start whinin' or threatenin' or doin' whatever I needed to do to git that book back, she stepped out on her porch and pointed a big ole rusty butcher knife in my face right here, up under my eye, like she was gonna cut it out."

A clatter of silver against everyday china broke Deborah's concentration and made her jump. She looked across the table and saw Ester reaching down to retrieve her fork from the floor.

"Sorry," Ester apologized, "I wasn't expecting that."

"Shoot, neither was I." Their hostess rose and soon returned with a clean fork. "Scared the pee out of me. She didn't get a chance to cut me, though. I ran my butt off. I swear, I ain't never run so fast or so hard or so long in my life. I know she was behind me for a short ways, cussin' and fussin' a mile to a minute, but all I 'member hearin' was 'I'ma kill you if you cross my sight, ever.'"

"Well..." Mary sat back in her chair, chuckling and wiping her mouth at the same time. "She didn't haft to worry about seein' this black soul, ever. I hid for weeks. Schoo' and home. Schoo' and home, that's all I went, I was so scared." Mary laughed outright now, shaking her head and fork, thinking about that memorable moment of childhood. "Yeah, my, my, my. I can laugh now, but I wasn't laughin' then. Shoot, that Aunt Mattie is crazy. Threatenin' to cut a child over a Bible. Now, ain't that sumthin'."

A napkin dropped beside her plate signified the end of her meal and her story. "Y'all both coffee drinkers?" she asked, rising. "Me, I drink it all day, 'cept summer, only mor'nins and eve'nins, then."

While Mary cut huge chunks of cake and poured three cups of coffee, Deborah dissected Mary's story, considering any statement that might serve them in undoing Ester's charts or the curse. On the surface, the story proved that Mattie hated thieves—or really loved her Bible—and that Mary was indeed "quite a handful." But dig a level deeper and Deborah acknowledged the existence of family data that she had yet to peruse. Of course, the incident happened decades ago and today, there was no proof that Aunt Mattie still had the Bible. But if she did, Deborah just had to see it, and if the only way to see it was to park outside Mattie's house before daybreak and wait all day for her, then that's what she and Ester would do.

Deborah set that resolution aside to join the ongoing conversation.

Ester was in mid-sentence asking Mary, "...looked through, do you recall seeing any written records? Maybe some loose papers or notes in the margin?"

It didn't take a Ph. D. to figure out Ester had zoomed in on the Bible as a possible source of data just as Deborah had. Still, because of Mary's delicate position, Deborah had no intention of asking her any follow-up questions, and she thought she had made it clear to Ester to steer away from the subject of accidental deaths. Deborah reevaluated Ester's question and supposed it could apply to dismantling the curse as well and because of that, she refrained from jumping in and redirecting the flow. She would wait and see how the dialogue progressed.

"Could have been; I wasn't lookin' that hard. The only thing I 'member was the fam'ly tree at the front. It was a pretty color drawin' of a tree with blank spaces in the branches to write names and dates. But wasn't a name on it. Not one. Or dates, either. I guess Aunt Mattie wasn't into recording. I bet the old folks didn't know that."

"Did you and Mattie ever talk about the incident afterwards or, more specifically, the Bible?" Ester probed deeper.

Incredulity bloomed on Mary's face. "Girl, please! When we fine'ly ran into each other months and months later, I 'bout jumped out of my skin. I could hardly look at her. But Aunt Mattie, she looked right at me as if she was tryin' to blot my soul. She stared at me the 'hole time Mama shopped. I was so glad when she fine'ly finished and we left the store. Shoot, that ole' woman could a had that knife in her pocket. It wouldn't surprise me if she did."

Ester looked over at Deborah, both reading the other to know they had to speak to the elders tomorrow. If they wanted to save the Fullers, free them from the accidental death chart, they had to interview Mattie and Governor. They had to discover some material information and, it was quite possible, Mattie's family Bible or the knowledge in her or Governor's head might be the very thing they needed.

"Yep, that's our Aunt Mattie for you," Mary remarked, smiling. "Ain't no tellin' what else she got, but I know she got that Bible. And even if she don't have it no mo' or she's no better at keepin' it updated, she been livin' forever and knows ever'thin' 'bout this fam'ly. How? I don't know, since she stays in her house or lays around Black Hill all day. But I tell you what..." Mary stood up and began collecting dirty plates, cutlery, glasses. "...anybody wanna know anything 'bout a Fuller, past or present, I bet you can ask Aunt Mattie, and she'll know. Now…" Mary crooked an eyebrow. "…whether she tells or not's another thing. But you, Deborah, you seem to have the magic touch. She talks to you. I guess you made a friend of her with this fam'ly tree."

That didn't make Deborah smile, laugh or sigh. Mary's comment made her all the more desperate to get to Aunt Mattie and discover any information that would unlink one, twelve, thirty accidental deaths and therefore change the charts to their favor. Mattie had to give them something, anything to save them!

As the ladies all pitched in to clear the table and clean the kitchen, Mary learned that Deborah and Ester planned to spend the night in Partway and try the elders again at first light. She insisted—no—demanded that they forgo their hotel plans and stay with her. She closed her ears to their arguments and thus, Deborah found herself outside collecting their overnight bags while Ester finished the dishes and Mary changed bed sheets and towels.

A few hours later, after chatting, well, after Mary told more stories, Ester ate more cake, and Deborah drank more wine, they called it bedtime. When the big hand struck midnight, all three were in separate bedrooms, dead asleep.

Not the BlackHeart.

When the midnight hour struck, It was sitting in Hope's car, parked in Governor's driveway as if It were wanted company, as if It had been invited by Governor to visit, not only now, but intermittently all day.

Earlier at the cemetery, after Governor had returned to reason, he'd resumed his work duties, at one point leaving the site of the dead and buried to travel into town to pick up supplies. The BlackHeart had followed him boldly and had parked conspicuously, waiting patiently while Governor loaded his truck before instigating more pleasant, loving thoughts of Cora Jean. Governor had responded as he had earlier, opening himself to the happy, feel-good memories, forgetting the outside world to sink into that powerful, sweet love that caressed his core. When the BlackHeart had finished toying with him for the second time, Governor came to as before. It could see he was feeling sluggish and bemused, with the added feeling of satisfaction. Apparently curious, he looked over himself and saw that he'd squirted semen all over his crotch. Then, looking around as if in embarrassment and seeing no witnesses, not even Hope, he'd hurried home, cleaned up and returned to work.

Hours later, he'd gotten a phone request from the Veterans Administration Hospital in Dallas to pick up a veteran who'd requested burial in his hometown of Partway. Governor had climbed in the hearse and driven off, missing Deborah and Ester by minutes. He'd whistled and smiled all the way to Dallas.

Yet again, uninvited, the BlackHeart trailed Governor to Dallas, sometimes passing him, waving as It cruised on by. Sometimes It lagged behind, but It consistently straddled that thin line that separated pleasure from anger. It could not afford another Mattie incident where It almost had her and the prize only to lose both by not balancing.

Where I-20 and I-35 intersect in Dallas, the BlackHeart waved bye-bye to Governor and turned instead toward DeSoto for home. There, to leave a brief note full of lies for Samuel about where It planned to spend the night. Successful in that minor task, the BlackHeart locked the house and considered picking up again with Governor at the VA to tease and play with him on the return trip to Partway. But curiosity about Deborah's and Ester's progress on their paltry study of death had a stronger pull. It knew how ferocious Ester could be when it came to making sense of facts and figures, and Deborah was almost as bad. So turning southward, It ate up the miles to Partway in record time and once there, allowed Its vibrations to lead It to Mary Fuller's house.

True enough, Deborah was there, her huge Suburban taking up plenty of space in front of Mary's house. Parking boldly behind it, the BlackHeart got out and, because only one streetlight worked on this block, It sensed Its way to the front of the SUV to touch the hood. It was lukewarm, telling the BlackHeart that Deborah had been there for a while. Turning to face the house, the BlackHeart saw no signs of activity. No lights streaming out of windows; no movement of the curtains; no noise. It seemed devoid of any humanity, but the BlackHeart knew differently. It knew Deborah sat in there with the other two, receiving little to no help from Mary.

Sometimes, the BlackHeart thought about leaving the Fullers of Its own accord. Mary and the rest of the Fullers had butchered, forgotten, or maligned the facts so that Its continued control over them was hardly sport anymore. The Fullers, with their feeble human minds, simply could not hold large vats of information or grasp the full power of the spirit, leaving them incapable of passing on the true essence of the BlackHeart. To add insult to injury, the small number of Fullers—Billy, Clarice, and Mattie—who got the story right and knew to fear the BlackHeart were the laughing fools of the family. The BlackHeart shook in disgust. If not for Mattie and her kind keeping it interesting and if not for the compelling goal of destroying the Truth for eternal glory, It would have withdrawn from the family, sure enough.

Frustrated, It climbed back into Hope's car and through Its internal tuning learned that Deborah and Ester had gotten nothing for their troubles today. Nothing that would disclose the BlackHeart or Its intent or Its bloody trail of Fullers. Smiling, the BlackHeart liked that. Not because It worried about the consequences of those two uncovering the Truth; that would simply be two more fools to add to the list. No, It just wasn't in the mood to deal with them, not when the pain of loving and hating was becoming more profound and distracting. Not when the goal was so close to achievement that It could sense victory.

The BlackHeart started the car, yanked it in drive and cruised off, heading for Mattie's. Not Mattie's per se, rather, driving by Mattie's headed to its real destination—Black Hill.

Like Mattie, the BlackHeart had come to appreciate the sincerity of the place. The dead Fullers knew the real deal, eliminating the need for subterfuge or games. The BlackHeart exited the car, softly slamming the door. It trotted over a few fallen leaves, over sticks and gravel, through the iron gates that still hung crookedly even after Governor's many fixes. It stood in the middle of a path worn to dirt by many years of shuffling feet and called Mattie's dead-in-the-flesh sister, Helen, and her prematurely-dead brother, Willie, to show their spiritual selves. Both victims of the BlackHeart's wicked ways, they appeared, not at all intimidated by Lucifer's seed.

In the natural world, had anyone been present to witness the exchange, they would have seen a teenage girl whose mouth and hands moved and whose eyes glowed, animated. Yet alone she stood in silence. In the spiritual world, however, the back and forth between three beings was loud, reaching the stars and beyond.

Helen, who'd been soft, tender and loving in life remained so in death. She cried angel tears and screamed at the BlackHeart from the onset, "Leave us! We've suffered enough."

Feeling cocky and victorious, even though the Truth still eluded It, the BlackHeart replied in a silky voice, "You know I can't do that." It smiled, loving the power, the hold It had on the living and the dead Fullers. "Well..." It teased, "...at least not until Governor delivers the Truth to me. Then, they'll all be free to worship me."

"Never!" Helen declared. "Never!"

"Governor won't fold," Willie inserted in the fight, even though he wasn't sure of the veracity of his statement. "You'll slink back to Lucifer's dark, heartless, bloodless lair, defeated."

"You can repeat those words to your baby sister once I send her to you." The BlackHeart projected an image of Mattie's body, tortured, twisted and covered in blood, along with an image of the white Holy Bible lying on the ground in Mattie's front yard.

The sights sent Helen into a full wail.

Willie couldn't stand the sight either. He had to go. Encircling his sister's spirit, he led her away to their home in the sky.

Really full of Itself now, the BlackHeart laughed all the way to the car and continued laughing as It sped by Mattie's property, tooting the horn and spraying the air with pebbles and rocks. It sobered finally when It glanced in the rearview mirror and saw Mattie step out of the shadows and stand proudly in the middle of the road like a warrior. The BlackHeart quivered at the sight, lost some of Its bravado. It would not be easy besting Mattie. It would not be without mutual pain and anguish. Better to focus on bending Governor to Its will and securing a different ending for all. Pressing hard on the accelerator, the BlackHeart went to do just that.

Which is why, at the stroke of midnight, It was sitting outside Governor's house. The old man had finally made it home from Dallas not long ago, and he now sat in his comfy reading chair in his living room, reading the biography of some lesser known U. S. war general. The BlackHeart initiated Its intrusion, sifting into the unconsecrated home and for the first time, It entered the man, lovingly touching him here and there. With this visit, It also added a voice—Cora Jean's voice. It spoke as convincingly to Governor as It had spoken to Charles Fuller those many generations ago.

"Come to me, Governor."

His eyes had fluttered shut moments ago at what he thought was Cora Jean's first touch, and now he moaned at the invitation. His body responded, growing warm and sensitive. Any barriers he thought to erect were now banished as his heart, mind and soul willingly opened to what felt like Cora Jean, in the flesh.

"Do you want me, Governor?"

Governor nodded, happy to be lost in the sensation of her. He moaned again and the book he'd been reading slipped to the floor, landing at his socked feet.

"You can have me forever, Governor. Would you like that?"

Again, his head bobbed up and down. Again, he moaned.

"You can have this feeling all the time. That would be nice for both of us."

"Cora Jean," Governor rasped, "Cora Jean." Her name became a chorus for the man who worked hard and loved deep.

"I'm yours," *she* whispered, touching him more boldly. "Give me the Truth and I'm yours—always."

§

Governor faltered here, but with the right touch and a vivid memory of *her*, resistance fell, and he stood. He molded his hands in the air, as if tracing the curves of the real Cora Jean. Pleased, he hugged her tight, pulling her close, loving the feel of her in his arms. He kissed her temple, inhaled the floral-flavor of her shampoo, knowing she used that fragrance because it was his favorite. He moaned at that, a sign of her love for him, and he pressed her softness into his hardness. He ached for her, had to have her. Confused in love, he nodded, agreeing to the terms of having her forever.

"Go get me the Truth. Get it for me, Governor, so we can be together for all time."

It took some time for Governor to peel himself away from her. Even then, his hand lingered in hers, the last touch for a short time. Then, they could touch forever. He smiled at that and it gave him strength to let her go, for now. Still caught up in the mirage, Governor hurried through his rooms to the back door. He pulled his truck keys off the peg board by the door and then ran as fast as his aged bones would allow. He didn't bother to lock his door, grab his wallet or turn off the few lights he'd been using. The truck engine rumbled to a start and he backed out of his double-wide driveway before the engine had settled itself. What consumed him as he reversed down the steep incline was Cora Jean's lovely face, smiling at him, urging him to hurry so they could reunite.

Encouraged thus, Governor completed the twenty minute drive to Mattie's in half that time.

Mattie had a bad feeling about this visit. Governor was acting like a rabid dog, crazed out of his mind. She sensed it more than she saw it in the weak light from her porch. She sighed and hung her head; she didn't want to fight him. She loved him—as much as she loved her immediate family. She didn't want to kill him, either. Nor did she want to die by his hands. She didn't like this one bit.

There again, pounding on her locked screen door. Looking up, down, all around, fidgeting like he had ants in his pants and twitching like he'd taken some badly compounded street drugs—all of which confirmed to Mattie that he'd lost his natural black mind to the BlackHeart.

This broke Mattie's heart. She thought he'd been *the one*. Thought he'd be her replacement, the next Keeper of the family records. But apparently, her mind had lost its way too. Had been so desperate to escape the secret of the curse and life on earth that she'd made him out to be something he wasn't.

Fortifying herself, calling on "In-Me," she unlocked the front door. With only the screen door separating them, she looked her nephew up, then down and then up again. He towered over her, standing over six feet tall even with his crooked body, to her four foot eleven. And even though he was thin, he was hard and muscled. That was to be expected since he shoveled, weeded, fertilized, watered, stocked, unloaded and loaded all day long at the cemetery while all she did was walk around and sometimes tussle with her strays.

For sure, he had the physical advantage. She, however, had the mental edge—plus years of coaxing good out of people who were controlled by another world's creation. So, taking a deep breath she unlocked the screen door, and as she'd done when the BlackHeart first visited with her mother, Mattie stepped out on the porch. But unlike the first time, Mattie was ready for whatever this turned out to be.

"I gotta have it, Mattie."

Calmly, she instructed, "Call on 'In-Me' Gov'nor. You can do it."

"Cora Jean—" he croaked, still wrapped in the dream.

"Go deep, Gov'nor, find yo'self."

He balled his fists and took a step toward her. His brown eyes had lost their natural shine. "Gone in there and bring it to me."

"You want it, go git it." Her voice rang firm, challenging. She took a step forward, already tired of this nonsense and reached a hand in her outer pocket, wrapping her fingers around the handle of a big, nasty-looking butcher knife.

"I cain't."

This was true, a fact she could use to sway him. While the BlackHeart possessed him, Governor could not enter her hallowed home. This rule served as an extra layer of protection designed by God's ambassador to protect her and the Truth. So no, he couldn't just waltz in and retrieve it, but there existed two other ways he could gain possession of the Truth: divest himself of the BlackHeart—in which case he wouldn't need the Truth—or kill Mattie. She tightened her grip on the knife, not sure yet which way he would lean.

"Why cain't you, Gov'nor?"

A flicker in his dull eyes told her he struggled with the question. That raised hope in her, but still she held tight to the knife.

"Why cain't you go inside my house, Gov'nor?" she persisted, making sure to use his name again and often. Hearing it, she thought, might help him remember who he was and why he was here.

He knew. It came slow, the answer to her question and his true identity, but finally it surfaced to his consciousness, rising above the feel-good memories of his lost love, the affection and warmth of their shared past, and the constricting hold of the BlackHeart.

He knew…and he came out fighting.

Twisting and turning his torso, he moved violently to oust the evil inhabitant that had played with him all day. When his physical moves to divest It didn't work, Mattie saw him plant his feet, close his eyes and with Herculean effort force himself to stillness.

Soon, she heard words familiar to her, and she joined in as he chanted: "*Perfect love casts out all fear… Perfect love casts out all fear… Perfect love casts out all fear…*"

A short time passed and then the Governor she knew returned. The one who had, indeed, been chosen as the next Keeper of the Fuller's Curse. She loosened her grip on the knife.

Images of a white Holy Bible being ripped apart by some unseen force filled Deborah's dream. The torn pages flew through the air, oozing black-red congealed blood as they floated to the dry, dusty ground. A fat, gray mockingbird perched in a nearby tree trilled and warbled as the soiled pages landed in a circle. At first, fluffy white clouds filled the sky, but then they gradually darkened until they were midnight-black. Then, at the exact moment the final page landed, the mockingbird flew away, expanding and growing at such an explosive rate that it quickly exceeded the bounds of planet Earth. But the final image, the one that caused her sleep to flee, was that of her daughter, Hope—her face, specifically. It had the same black-red blood trickling from her forehead, temple, and cheeks and her eyes were closed as if they had been permanently glued shut like a corpse in its coffin.

Deborah awakened with a start, but didn't move. She laid there breathing deeply, with sweat pooling on her forehead. Finally, she moved, reaching up to wipe away the sweat while listening to her heart drumming loudly in her body.

It's just a dream, Deborah, she coached herself. *Just a dream.* But knowing this as fact didn't make it easier to shake the heaviness of the nightmare, especially the image of Hope in death. It upset Deborah, nearly scared the life out of her. Taking deep breaths, repeating the fact it was just a dream helped Deborah relax to the point where she could ease past the image and focus on the now. Now, her daughter was alive, spending the night at her friend Dinnie's house, according to Samuel, whom she'd spoken to late last night. Now, her daughter was active, well, and on the path to an outstanding college experience and eventually a career as a medical researcher—and Deborah planned to keep it that way.

Spurred into action by this thought, Deborah sat up in bed. She dried the wet spots on her face with the sheet and pushed back the covers. She noticed the time: *1:38.* The numbers on the digital clock flashed red in the gray-black darkness, the only other light being the dim glow of the lane's lone street lamp through the window. Something about the lateness of the hour gave her the creeps and she shivered involuntarily, even as perspiration soaked her nightgown. Reaching out, she tapped on the bedside lamp's base, causing light to shine in a lopsided circle that barely touched the edge of the bed.

Drawing up her courage, she swung her legs over the side of the bed. Then standing, she stepped tentatively to the overhead light switch on the opposite wall, her heart speeding up as she glanced at the shadows in the corners of the unfamiliar room. She reached the light switch without incident and soon, the rest of the darkness in the room fled. Odd shapes that had previously been shaded in varying degrees of black and gray appeared normal now and familiar. In one corner, a box kite. To the left of the bed, the closed closet door with a shirt sleeve stuck in the crack. A clothes hamper in a corner, along with a TV that did not have a gaming system attached—their Nintendo resided in the family room where Mary could supervise and control it. Comic books, as well as copious amounts of toy cars and sneakers littered the floor and dresser. All things common to a young boy's existence. Deborah smiled faintly at the thought, thinking how different it must be to raise a boy than a girl. With her thoughts still on children, especially her girl, she lifted her briefcase off her duffle bag which sat on a chair in a corner and took it to bed with her. She didn't think she'd be able to sleep so may as well work on her project.

Yesterday, behind the morgue staff's backs, she and Ester had smuggled copies of death reports, autopsies, and police accounts that detailed causes that had affected death. Deborah pulled out those copies now and began reading. She had not been reading long when she ran across Mattie's name listed as a witness on a report. Not an eyewitness, mind you, but one who could attest to the discovery of the body and the crime scene.

This caused Deborah to pause and backtrack to what Mary had declared yesterday and what Shandra had said all along—that Mattie knew everything about the Fullers. Somehow, without leaving her house much or interacting with the clan, she knew. Curious, Deborah pulled out a legal pad which contained notes she'd taken yesterday at the morgue. How many times did Mattie Fuller's name show up on witness lists? Deborah wanted to know, and she quickly counted. A handful of times. Compared to other Fullers? Another quick count. More than any other Fuller. Even compensating for her longevity, she still outwitnessed others.

Deborah lifted her head and stared straight ahead at the wall in front of her. A poster of the Power Rangers had been tacked to it, but Deborah didn't see that. Her mind was fixed on Mattie, and after a time she came to the same conclusion as Mary and Shandra. The oldest living Fuller knew things—people, facts and situations—that put her around death a lot. And given that fact, Deborah felt sure she *could* help them disassociate Fullers and death. There no longer existed an *if* or *possible* in Deborah's mind. Mattie knew, and Deborah's job was to find her and get her to talk.

Again, Deborah consulted the clock: *2:13*. She seriously considered dressing and rushing to Aunt Mattie's to speak to her now. Surely, the woman was home at this hour. But then, Deborah came to herself. It was far too early in the morning and Imogene Fuller had raised her far too well. She would not disturb Aunt Mattie's rest, nor would she be an inconsiderate houseguest by coming and going at strange hours of the night—or morning.

Leaning back against the headboard, Deborah restated the plan to be at Aunt Mattie's house as early as feasible. She hoped and prayed that their elder would be home, but if not they would wait. The old woman would have to appear at some point, and when she did how would Deborah get her to talk?

Deborah wasn't naïve. She knew that cornering Mattie was one thing; getting her to open up would range from hard to impossible, even with Deborah being one of two people Aunt Mattie wasted words on. Her track record with Aunt Mattie confirmed that: her and Hope's first visit to Aunt Mattie when she'd only verified what they already knew; at Black Hill when Aunt Mattie had shared valuable information but had walked away before Deborah could delve deeper; at Shandra's funeral when she could not decode Aunt Mattie's message.

The trick would be getting good, useful information out of her, and that thought sent Deborah's mind scurrying for the right approach. Maybe if she used the 'love of family' angle? But as soon as she thought it, she nixed it. Dear Aunt Mattie avoided the other Fullers like some people avoided black cats and cracks in sidewalks. Maybe Governor's influence? That might work, but it meant they'd have to rustle up Governor first, win him over to their side, and then approach Aunt Mattie as a unit. Not the most efficient approach, but capable of producing worth. Deborah put a thumbtack in that idea and moved on to another approach—honesty. *Yes*, Deborah thought, *that might work*. Even though she didn't know Aunt Mattie through and through, Deborah felt, given the woman's inclination for plain, unfiltered speech, laying the facts out bare might appeal to her.

She would start with the family tree, present it to her as she'd done for Mary, with one exception—expand the presentation to cover all eight major family lines. Hopefully, that would begin softening Aunt Mattie's heart. She would follow that and end with Ester's damning charts, making sure Aunt Mattie understood the threat to their family. She didn't worry that Aunt Mattie would run off and alarm the Fullers. Aunt Mattie made it clear she preferred to ignore family, and family made it clear they preferred to be ignored by her. What concerned her was if those documents would be enough to completely melt Aunt Mattie's heart and cause her to share any knowledge about deaths and accidents.

Deborah sighed, an acknowledgement that if honesty failed they still had

Governor.

Last night after dinner, while sitting around relaxing, Mary had let slip that Governor worked Saturdays, off on Wednesdays. And while Deborah would prefer not to interfere with his work duties, she was not going to leave Partway this weekend without learning something about the accidental deaths.

Plumping up her pillows, Deborah settled in for more reading and note-taking. Not too long afterwards, the words on the pages began blurring; the pen in her hand slipped out of position, and when one page of a report slapped her softly in the face Deborah didn't feel it. She was asleep, resting comfortably in a dreamless state.

Sitting in Hope's car in the middle of Governor's driveway, the BlackHeart seethed. Twice now, It had lost. Twice now, the elders had been right there, right at the crossover point, yet had somehow culled inner strength to retreat and thwart Its plans.

The BlackHeart fumed. It raged. Throwing a tantrum, as It had done after losing to Mattie, would not satisfy this time. Fuller blood is what It wanted, what It demanded as compensation for Its loss.

At this hour of the morning, selections were slim, but not impossible. Like most earthly families, the Fullers divided into segments. There were those who attended church on Sundays, Wednesdays and any other day when they needed a word from the Lord. Then, there were those who liked to party on Fridays, Saturdays and any other day when a strong drink would do. And finally, there existed a cross section that did both, any and all days of the week. One of the partying Fullers would do just fine as payment. Someone so drunk out of their skull, so high as the sun that they didn't know their left hand from their right—and the BlackHeart knew just where to find one of *those* Fullers. It started the car, backed recklessly out of Governor's drive and headed deep, deep, deep into unincorporated Partway.

There, in the middle of a circle of mature trees stood a two-level stone house. On the top level lived the owners—a scruffy husband and a plump wife, both with long, greasy, gray hair that he wore in a braided ponytail and she wore loose about her shoulders. Occasionally, a grandchild or two moved in with them, but never for long, probably because of the activity on the bottom floor—loud music from two jukeboxes, free-flowing illicit and prescription drugs, and the ever-presence of both legal and bootleg alcohol. Local authorities knew of the place, but since deputies and state troopers were known to partake of a drink or two, or down a pill or two, or snort a line or two at the no-name place, the house was allowed to operate as is.

At 1:38 the BlackHeart eased onto the grass and dirt path that dead-ended at the house. It doused the lights, both blessing and cursing Hope's car choice. The car, her sweet sixteen gift from her parents, was capable of speed that allowed it to escape and dodge. But the BlackHeart hated how the Mustang stood out. When killing or murdering, it was best to be as inconspicuous as possible, which the car's color—red—and classification—classic sports car—did not allow it to be. Not that it would be a problem if the BlackHeart, as Hope or any other Fuller, was ever pinned with a murder charge. The BlackHeart would simply inhabit another Fuller body, leaving Hope or whoever to deal with the consequences.

Going less than twenty miles an hour, It bumped along, hearing the familiar sounds of night creatures and the thin sounds of good-times through the open window. When the outline of the house distinguished itself from the outline of the trees surrounding it, the BlackHeart swerved off the trail, mowing down tall grass to angle out of sight behind the trees and cars, motorcycles and even a bicycle—vehicles parked in random fashion between the trees. Satisfied It had effectively hidden the Mustang, It cut the motor and got out. Inhaling deeply, It almost choked on the obnoxious mélange of smells: liquor, pine, sweat, charred wood, vomit, freshly mowed grass, cigarette smoke and piss.

Shaking Its head at the unpleasant odors, the BlackHeart crab-walked toward the yellowish-white light that streamed from the house. It paused between a pecan tree and a Camaro to scope out the house, cars and scenery. At this distance and angle, It had a good side view, allowing It to see both the front and back of the house. It appreciated that and settled in to wait and think about what type of Fuller It wanted this time. Male or female? Young or old? Dark or light? Since a female had been Its latest victim, in all fairness, a male should be next. Then again, eliminating a person was part chance, and It decided to see what chance would offer.

While It waited on chance, the BlackHeart tried not to think about the pure internal strength of Mattie and Governor. That was an attribute Charles Fuller had not possessed, so it must have entered their bloodstream from another source family or perhaps a recessive gene. Now that It thought about Charles and hand-me-down attributes, the BlackHeart wondered what they *had* inherited from him. Charles had been average in height, powerfully built with nothing crooked on him. Mattie was short and thin; Governor, tall and lean. One had a crooked finger from battles fought and won; the other a crooked body from years of hard labor. And they had beaten It! The BlackHeart's anger grew so overwhelming It could barely contain Itself in the girl's body. Yes, a Fuller would die and soon, It promised Itself.

As if Its anger had materialized a victim, a man stumbled out the back door, or rather was pushed, tossed or kicked out given the arch of his back and the windmill-like propulsion of his arms. Feeling the vibrations that told It the evicted man was indeed a Fuller, the BlackHeart studied the man further and noted the generous gut, the one good hand.

It whispered to Itself, "Step-Uncle Billy."

Not the one It would have preferred to kill, with Step-Uncle Billy being a fan and all—and not even a blood relative, but married to one so long he'd taken on their vibrations—but somebody had to pay for Mattie and Governor's unbendable wills.

Again crab-walking, the BlackHeart angled toward the drunken man, who now cursed loudly and bumbled about in the dirt, searching for what It didn't know or really care. While still half a football field away and yet contemplating how to attack the retired Army sergeant, the front door opened and out walked a pair of lovers, arms linked, eyes only for each other.

The vibrations were strong, telling the BlackHeart that both were Fullers. *Hmm. Kissing cousins? Two kills as payment for two losses?* The BlackHeart liked that. Liked it even more when It realized It had never killed in tandem before. Liked it immensely when It realized the lovers were headed Its way, which would put them further away from the house into dark shadows. In a snap, the BlackHeart settled on the pair, and just that quickly Step-Uncle Billy recovered his life, never knowing how close he'd come to losing it.

The BlackHeart watched as the couple closed the gap between them. They veered away after some steps, heading toward a late model car, which was parked close to the path. The young couple, who looked to be in their late twenties, laughed and smiled at each other and nibbled on each other's lips as they walked, unaware that a murderer stalked them, moved with them and who was now only a few yards away. When they reached the car, the young man opened the unlocked door, and instead of seating his lady in the front seat he flipped forward the passenger seat and climbed in the back after her. The BlackHeart had been around since God breathed life and therefore knew what was about to follow. Too bad they would not finish their bout of carnal pleasure.

They had to pay.

The car door had creaked when the man opened it earlier and it creaked again when the BlackHeart opened it. The woman, who straddled her lover, lifted her head and torso at the noise—and the surprised look on her face at seeing a pretty, teenage girl staring back at her with dark, hate-filled eyes would stay on her face even after they buried her.

"This is not for pain," the BlackHeart explained, knowing she wouldn't understand. "This is for losing the Truth."

The BlackHeart struck so quickly and so powerfully that Its hand was like the strike of a snake as It crushed the woman's larynx. With a gurgling glottal sound, she crumpled forward on top of her man, and within the next eye blink the BlackHeart pressed the front seat forward, closed Its hands around the confused man's throat and pressed hard. All this took place in little time, giving neither man nor woman time to emit a cry for help. A few minutes later, the light in each of the BlackHeart's victim's eyes dimmed, and soon their souls released from their physical bondage, and travelled across woods, creek and fields to sojourn with the family matriarch. Two kills that surprised even dear old Aunt Mattie.

About the time that Deborah fell back asleep, the BlackHeart left the scene of a double homicide undetected. Feeling vindicated, It pulled onto the black tarred road that fronted the path and headed for the nearest county road, singing loudly and off key until It suddenly realized something.

Blood. No actual blood spilled.

In Its attraction to the idea of a double killing It had forgotten that It had wanted blood, actual Fuller blood, to spill on the earth. Feeling cheated again— never mind that It had cheated Itself this time—the BlackHeart screamed and beat the steering wheel so violently that the column almost snapped. Anger devoured It, causing It to break free of the vessel that housed It.

It wanted more. It *demanded* more.

Approximately four hours later at half past 6:00, a surprise visitor woke the three occupants of Mary's house with loud banging and repeated peals of the doorbell. In her borrowed bedroom at the front of the house, Deborah, disoriented and groggy, sprang up in bed. It took a full minute for her to realize where she was and to identify the noises. Someone wanted in. Someone was determined to get in.

Deborah looked at the clock and heard Mary's loud and impatient, "Hold on. Shit! I'm comin'."

Relieved, Deborah fell back in the bed, snuggling under the covers, eyes closing in sleep. But before they closed all the way they popped back open, and she jackknifed up in bed.

"Aunt Mattie," she croaked in a sleep-heavy voice.

Within seconds, she was on her feet and scrambling to her overnight bag. She wondered if Ester had slept through the noise and decided not, since Ester slept lighter than she did. But just in case she still slept, Deborah crept to the bathroom and quietly began her morning routine just as Mary gave entry to her boyfriend.

Within the hour, both Deborah and Ester had showered and dressed for the day, as well as consumed a healthy portion of the big country breakfast Mary had cooked for them plus one, her boyfriend who had come directly from the jailhouse specifically for that purpose. According to him: "I think they fed us dog food."

Even though Mary had begged them to stay longer, Deborah was keen to start her mission of pinning down Aunt Mattie and Governor. So, after hugs and cheek kisses for everyone, including Mary's boyfriend who looked every bit as if he'd spent a few days in lock-up, they gathered their bags and those briefcases filled with that God-awful study of death and settled into the SUV. Amid shouts of "thanks" and "bye-byes" and "see-you-soons," they pulled away from the sunny house and summery hostess.

Driving down Mary's chipped and littered street and soon skirting the outer edges of downtown Partway, Deborah prayed success would be theirs. Too much happiness depended on these visits, too many futures that needed to remain bright and unshackled. Deborah didn't realize that with each prayer, each petition, her foot inched further and further down on the accelerator, advancing her vehicle to well beyond the speed limit.

"Whoa! Where's the fire?"

Deborah snapped to the present at Ester's warning. Consulting her dashboard she eased her foot up, frowning slightly. "Sorry, I'm just anxious to get to Aunt Mattie's."

"I can tell. I wanna get there too, but intact."

Ester returned to searching her cell phone. Deborah felt sure she was looking for calls or texts from her soon-to-be-ex-husband, Lewis. She felt like the worst friend in the world for relegating Ester's domestic troubles to the back of the line, but Deborah promised herself that as soon as they beat back death, Ester would have her complete attention.

"Did you think of anything else that'll help us?" Ester asked. "My subconscious came up with zilch."

"Actually…" Deborah shared with Ester the revelation about Aunt Mattie and the witness list. She also filled her in on the recommended approach.

"Sounds solid."

"I hope to God she's home. For some reason, I feel like she's the key. That she's important to unlocking the mystery of our charts." The magnitude of their visit pressed down hard on her. Subconsciously, in response, she clutched the steering wheel and again her foot eased toward the floorboard.

Ester's own face reflected caution; her words issued to tamp down Deborah's expectations, just in case. "I know how important this is, Deborah. But I wouldn't expect too much. She *did* lie to you about having family records. Mary confirmed that she has them. I'm not calling your aunt a liar, maybe she's just old and addled in the brain, but I don't want you to think of her as a miracle pill."

"I know, Ester, I know." Deborah stopped at a red light and sighed deeply. Ester's words made plenty of sense. They always did, but Deborah elected to hang on to her gut feeling on this one. "Tell me what you think our approach to Governor should be. I was so focused on Aunt Mattie I didn't even consider an opening for him."

She shifted toward Ester, interested in what the doctor thought. But a spot of red and the smooth thrum of a sports car engine hooked Deborah's attention. She turned back to the front, straining toward the dashboard, watching as a strawberry red classic Mustang turned right onto their street a few blocks ahead of them.

"That's Hope!" Deborah shouted, "That's Hope!"

Ester looked up too late to see all that Deborah saw. By the time she narrowed in on the target car she saw taillights, a splash of red and a vague silhouette in the driver's seat. "It's probably the same car we saw yesterday, Deborah. The town's not that big. Of course we'll see it often."

Sure she was right on this point too, Deborah argued, "No, Ester, that was Hope. I know my daughter. I know her car."

Deborah had been planning to turn left onto the FM road that eventually led to Mattie's road, but she clicked her signal off, maneuvered her truck around the sedan in front of her and plowed through the intersection, uncaring that her light remained red. Thankfully, no opposing traffic existed, but that didn't stop Ester from screaming out.

"Deborah, are you—" She bit the rest of her sentence off after looking at the strain on Deborah's face.

The same fears from yesterday surfaced and seized Deborah, causing her heart to beat erratically and her breathing to stall and stutter. And yet she sped on, intent on getting to Hope to discover the tragedy, whatever it might be.

"Ester, call my people," Deborah demanded. Trepidation and deep concern for those she loved degraded the quality of Deborah's voice and set her expression to tragic. "Why didn't she call me? Why is she here? What's going on?"

Reasonable, sensible questions for an absent daughter, but rhetorical questions for all others, and yet Ester took a stab at answering while pulling Deborah's cell phone out of her purse.

"I'm still not convinced it's her, but if it is, she must be delivering the type of news—" Ester clamped her lips together, recognizing she'd said too much again. "Sorry, Deborah. You know me and my mouth."

Normally, Deborah forgave easily and she would have this time too, except Ester's words hadn't registered. Deborah's mind had blocked them, immersed instead in inventing dark, turbulent deaths for loved ones near and far. Those deaths were the ones parading through her mind that caused her usual dark coloring to turn ashy and gray.

Looking at Deborah and understanding her state, for it was hers too, to a lesser degree, Ester moved on reporting, "It's ringing."

"Get out the way," Deborah yelled at the driver of a small import who dallied along, obviously in no hurry. Stomping her foot on the gas pedal, the Suburban responded, lurching forward, allowing Deborah to shoot around the car.

On the passenger side, Ester grabbed the "oh shit" bar and held on. "Whoever it is, is in one helluva hurry. I can barely see her tail end." She paused, ending the call on Deborah's cell phone. "Hope's phone went to voicemail."

Two pieces of bad news in a millisecond birthed fresh fear and panic within Deborah. She kept her foot planted firmly on the gas, ignoring the needle as it leaned steadily to sixty, sixty-five and kept going.

Previously one block ahead of them, a mother-mobile mini-van now occupied the space three inches in front of Deborah's bumper, creeping along slower than the thirty-mile-per-hour speed limit. She pummeled the steering wheel and fumed. "What *is* it with these people? Can't they at least drive the speed limit?"

If her mind had been in its usual fair state Deborah would have empathized with the mother, for in her back seat were four riotous boys in four different team uniforms. Baseball gloves were either tossed up and down in the air or bopped against another child's head. Occasionally, the mother would swivel her head, move her lips, then turn back around or she would raise a fist in the air, shaking it meaningfully. Usually, Deborah would have backed off, extending space and sympathy to the mother, but not this morning. This morning someone in her family may have died—and she needed to get down the road to find out who, what, when, where, and how.

Leaning long and hard on the horn she tried to intimidate the mother into turning, moving over, anything that would allow Deborah to skinny past her. The mother glared at her in her rearview mirror. Deborah sent her a pleading look, which the woman turned down flat. To doubly affirm the refusal, the mother rolled her eyes and neck.

She left Deborah no choice but to pass her, illegally, as she'd done the other vehicle moments before. Unfortunately, it wasn't possible this time, given the super-size of her SUV and the wide body of the aged mini-van in front of her, at least not on this major street with only two lanes and oncoming traffic. Not enough room or time.

"No answer at your home or Samuel's cell phone. Not the same results as yesterday, but it is Saturday, and some people aren't as diligent about monitoring their cell phones on the weekend."

Again, that was not what Deborah wanted to hear. The lack of responses compounded fear with worry and desperation, making her try one more time to pass the woman. Before she could make a move, however, the mother turned onto a side street out of Deborah's way, but too late. Up ahead, the taillights of the red Mustang she'd been following winked out of sight.

"If it was her, where do you think she was going? I'm so confused by all these country roads. Who lives this way?" Ester used Deborah's cell phone as a pointer, pointing straight ahead.

Deborah was ahead of her and already knew this way led to Governor's. But what stumped Deborah—other than the reason for Hope being here— was that Hope knew the way. The two of them had been to Aunt Mattie's but never to Governor's. Months ago, when she and Shandra had been working on the family tree at the Partway library, Hope had wiggled out of every one of those visits to Partway, negating the opportunity to learn about her relatives or her way about town. And yet from the little bit Deborah could see of Hope's driving today, the girl seemed adept at navigating the area. Deborah supposed Hope could be GPS'ing his location from her cell. But then she would have to know his address and since the postal service hadn't bothered to give him one, other than a rural route, she wasn't sure if that were even possible.

Her confusion came out in her voice. "Governor. Hope would go to him before Aunt Mattie. She would only go there if she had no other choice."

The tires on the Suburban screamed as Deborah executed a not-well-planned turn at an unnamed street off one of the main arteries edging downtown. A few miles down that street they crossed railroad tracks, and the cement street turned into loosely packed gravel which forced Deborah to slow down or risk losing control of her truck. She cursed the city and county—might as well throw in the state—for not paving all of Partway and for not investing in the gold and black signs that warned of curves and twists, for there were enough of them to be mindful.

They continued on slower now, scouting every driveway, turnoff, field and grove for a red car with a lone teen driver. Soon, the houses thinned and those that sprang up here and there were older than those closer to town. They'd reached rural Partway, that territory shaped like a man's loafer that extended out in all directions from Partway proper. Not to be confused with unincorporated Partway where Mattie lived, this area boasted tame roadside vegetation, sophisticated fences and relatively mannerable roads.

And still Ester complained. "God, this is a hellish mess. Who—Ohhh!" Ester's words were impaled by her own abrupt exclamation, brought on by Deborah's wild right hand turn into Governor's dirt and pebble driveway. An unexpected dip into and out of a rut bounced the women to the right, almost out of their seats. A steep incline followed, forcing their backs against their seats and providing them with a landscape view of the white hood of Deborah's truck. Finally, finally the driveway leveled out to present an unobstructed view of Governor's yard and house. Deborah braked abruptly, not believing what her eyes saw or didn't see.

"Where's Hope?"

Again, slower this time, Deborah searched the front yard, the side yard and the double driveway next to the house. No little red Mustang, only a broke down rusted truck left for dead out back next to a sparkling white storage shed. "She should be here. She was way ahead of us."

"Probably got lost," Ester fussed, straightening herself back in her seat.

"You definitely have to know *how* to get here to get here."

Slightly relieved by Ester's perfect logic, Deborah put the SUV in park and left the motor running. "You're right. She probably took a wrong turn. We'll wait a few minutes."

The wait was hard; the wait was slow; the wait almost drove Deborah nuts. Scenarios great and small, all involving death, grated at her, keeping fear intact and worry, too. While they waited, while these scenarios played like re-runs in Deborah's mind, Deborah made check-in calls to the rest of her family and—wouldn't you know it—not a soul answered home or cell, except her father, who assured Deborah he and Imogene were fine. Not wanting to put anyone else at unease, Deborah kept the conversation short, hiding the true prompt for her call.

As she disconnected Deborah wondered if the passing of extended family ranked high enough to bring Hope to this place. Maybe a fourth cousin, an in-law or a "play" aunt or uncle had met with death. As soon as she questioned it, Deborah knew that wasn't it. Not only would those outer-circle relatives not warrant a two-hour drive, but knowing Hope's selfish teenage tendencies she would not have volunteered for the drive even if a death *had* warranted the drive. Arise early on a Saturday? Drive to a dead-end town? No, that was way beyond Hope's caring capacity. So why was she here? And where was she, for God's sake? For Deborah knew that as sure as her name was Deborah that the person she'd seen had been Hope, and that the red Mustang she'd seen had been Hope's car. No one could tell her otherwise.

Needing a break from the endless questions that came without answers and scenarios that disturbed her, Deborah turned to Ester who was talking on her own cell phone. She looked down at Ester's lap and saw that while she had been dialing family Ester had dug out a file folder on death and was making research calls. She tried to focus on Ester's side of the conversation.

"...Dr. Joseph Wilson in Humble. Residence."

Deborah could hear the automated system provide the number and then dial it automatically with Ester's agreement. Seconds later, "Yes, Dr. Wilson, please," Ester asked in her professional voice. A brief pause followed her request and then, "Joseph, Dr. Joseph Wilson." Another pause, then with less patience in her voice, "The one who worked in Partway at..." Ester glanced at Deborah and rolled her eyes. She rushed through an explanation for Deborah's sake. "Two Dr. Joseph Wilsons. Father and son. They're getting the right one. Hopefully." Ester rolled her eyes again.

Deborah nodded and remained silent, looking all around and in her rearview mirror for her daughter. Suddenly, waiting wasn't enough. She opened her truck door and tossed words at Ester, "I'm going to walk around, check the house and street."

"Road," Ester corrected as Deborah slammed the door. Raising her voice so it penetrated beyond the closed door she repeated, "It's a road not a street…and barely that."

Throwing a hand up in the air at Ester's faint words, Deborah circled Governor's house, checked out the space behind his storage shed, looked past the tree line that separated his property from his neighbors and saw nothing of interest. She returned to the front, walked past her truck noticing Ester remained on the phone and sidled down to the road.

She stood in the middle of it, shading her face with her cell phone while looking to the north, south, east and west. No Hope. No red sports car. In fact, no cars at all. She stared across the street at Governor's neighbor's house, one of only three on this vein of the road, and thought about knocking on the Fortneau's—according to the stenciling on the mailbox—door and asking if they'd seen a red sports car pull in at Governor's.

She switched back and forth on going or not going three times before she finally crossed the road, walked down their long drive and lifted one of the knockers attached to the eight-foot tall double doors. As Deborah waited for someone to help her, she assessed the Fortneau's possessions: expansive, two-story brick home; giant timber, iron and glass doors; massive ceramic pots, one guarding each door and both filled with Texas sage; and elaborate porch furniture with weather-resistant flower print cushions. Her assessment told her two things about the Fortneau's: they had money, which they advertised through oversized material goods and they were obviously city people pretending to live country. This last observation she gleaned by comparing what existed on Governor's side of the road.

His one level house probably measured 1,300, no more than 1,400 square feet. His doors, both screen and front, boasted plain white paint and for interest peeling paint competed with cracked paint in certain places. Rusted vintage gliders rested out back under a mature pecan tree for those wishing to soak in the great outdoors. And for decoration, Governor used metal water buckets and plastic milk jugs with the tops sawed off, which also served as herb pots for birthing basil, dill and rosemary.

Guessing enough time had passed for a Fortneau to show, Deborah lifted the treated-to-look-like-natural-rust knocker again, thinking uncharitably: *At least Governor has a doorbell.* More moments passed letting Deborah know that no one could help her here. She returned to her side of the road to her truck to wait some more.

Ester glanced up when Deborah entered the vehicle and remarked, "I can tell by your face. No Hope."

Screwing up her face in response, Deborah settled in and checked her cell phone for the hundredth time. Still no return calls from family. Wondering where everyone could be, why no one bothered to return her calls, why Hope was in Partway and a million other whats and whys, Deborah turned to watch Ester, hoping the statistician or the study of death could distract her from worry and wondering.

She watched as Ester made notes on a page, then flipped a few pages back to write on that one as well. Her frustrated, anxious silence must have disturbed Ester, oppressed her work, or made her more outwardly aware than usual because Ester halted her note-taking to stare at her friend. The defeated look on Deborah's face apparently hit Ester hard and square in the chest. Dealing with emotions was Deborah's forte, not Ester's. But seeing the slumped shoulders, the threatening tears, that beat-up look seemed to force Ester to stretch beyond her norm to offer a remedy she hoped would restore their roles.

"Maybe we should park on the road and wait for her there," the doctor suggested. "If she's lost, she won't be able to miss this monster of a truck."

The suggestion worked. Deborah's face lost some of its sag and her, "Great idea!" came out sounding almost normal. She yanked on the gearshift, made an efficient about turn, and the huge truck rocked to a stop at the foot of Governor's drive yet politely nudged the road so its visibility was unmistakable.

One minute of searching both ends of the road turned to ten. Still no red car or car of any kind, for that matter. As Ester had stated earlier, this road was one you planned to travel. One did not aim to come here without a map or local in hand—which was good for maintaining residential privacy, but bad for the soul who had no guidance because that meant a tour lasting many, many hours given the extensive backlash of branch-offs and secondary roads, not to mention trails and ruts.

Deborah couldn't wait many, many hours for Hope to *eventually* make it to Governor's. She needed to see Hope, talk to her, touch her, find out what was on her mind. Fear still cradled Deborah in its arms, but tension, rooted in the unknown, inflicted the greatest pain.

In spite of the pain, the not knowing, the fear, Deborah forced herself to sit there, afraid to leave to go hunt for her daughter but also afraid to stay and wait. Trapped in this conflicted state Deborah thought she should at least use the time well and assist Ester. It was, after all, her family's death study. But she knew herself, and in this state of unrest she would not think logically and would make mistakes, which would then force Ester to clean up behind her, grumbling and complaining during the entire fix.

That left Deborah with only two activities she could not screw up—listening for return calls from her family and watching for Hope. She did both. With both ears tuned to her cell phone, she scanned one end of the road to the other end and then took a break to watch a pair of birds fly from branch to branch, tree to post, ground to air. Turning back to the road she searched its graveled length as far as she could see before investing a few seconds in checking for missed messages or texts. A third time she examined the road, then turned to nature as a diversion, watching butterflies as they looped and fluttered. The fourth time as she scrutinized one end—

Deborah sat up straight and stretched her neck. Yes, there to the northwest a cloud of dust, the sure sign of a vehicle in motion and now heading their way. Deborah smiled, nudged Ester who looked up and followed Deborah's pointing finger. Neither spoke, just watched anxiously as the dust cloud moved closer and closer and then…veered away from them. Disappointed, Deborah slumped back in her seat and felt like crying.

She didn't. Stuffing her tears, she picked up her cell phone and began a dialing marathon to family all over again. First call to Hope and last call to Reggie, Hannah's husband. Voicemail reached at every end. Deborah didn't leave a message. Not only did she not trust her voice but she also didn't want to misspeak and pull the rest of the family into her distress.

Laying her phone on the console, Deborah laid her head against the headrest and closed her eyes. But she couldn't relax, and they popped right back open as she undertook another ten minutes of the same mindless activity of watching the road, listening for the ring of her cell phone and being entertained by nature. When the digital clock on her dashboard flipped to 8:30 Deborah could not do it any longer. With her foot on the brake, her hand gripping the gearshift and her mind made up, she turned to Ester, knowing her friend was not going to like her words.

"Ester, I need for you to get out and wait here. I'm going to run by Aunt Mattie's."

"WHAT?!"

One would think she'd asked the statistician to plagiarize a report. Heated red undertones mixed poorly with her tan coloring, giving her a splotchy, sickly appearance.

"I'm not staying out here among all this…this…countryness. You must be crazy!" The screeching of her voice filtered through the closed doors and windows, scattering birds and butterflies.

Deborah, too, wasn't happy about the choice. She would prefer that Hope was right there with them explaining herself. But since she wasn't…

"Ester, I have to find Hope. She hasn't called back. No one's called and I hate to leave too many messages and raise worry."

"But you don't even know it was Hope!"

Deaf to that argument Deborah offered diplomatically, "It's either stay and wait here, or I draw you a map to Aunt Mattie's house. You pick."

"I can't. I won't." Ester crossed her arms under her breasts.

Deborah stated doggedly, a look of hostile determination on her face. "I'm going to find my daughter."

"But you…you don't know it was her." With every spoken word the steam in Ester's voice evaporated. Oh, she still obviously believed in her position, but seeing the fire and desperation in Deborah's eyes wilted her usual mulish will. "It could be like yesterday. The same car. Same driver. With all the family at home safe," she finished weakly.

Deborah didn't respond, just looked at Ester with hard eyes and a harder will. Ester knew that look and that set face. She'd shown it to her plenty of times in the past when Deborah had run her section of The Lab with the same inflexible rigidity and more recently during the last eighteen years of raising Hope.

"Oh Jesus!" she exclaimed as she folded. "Shit!"

Ester was so transparent. Deborah could tell that she had backtracked to Deborah's initial offer, waged a short pro/con debate inside her head and knew the exact moment Ester, her dear friend of thirty years, made her decision. "I'll wait for her here, but you owe me, Deborah. YOU OWE ME!"

A relieved breath spilled out of Deborah. "Thank you, Ester, thank you. And yes, I do."

Heat from a mean Texas summer quickly overtook the manufactured air-conditioning as Ester climbed out of the truck, grumbling. She snatched folders, her phone, purse, and bottled water and barely moved out of the way before Deborah peeled off.

On the twenty minute drive to Mattie's Deborah kept her eyes moving, searching for any red or small car. As she took the curves, sometimes on two and a half wheels, she prayed that God would give her a break and let her meet up with Hope on one of the roads along the way. But God didn't seem to care much for Deborah's prayers this morning. She drove the distance to Mattie's without sighting Hope or her bright car.

At Mattie's cattle gate, the only gate on this stretch of road and the only gate in the county that had a sign that read: BEWARE. STAY OUT, Deborah climbed out of the truck, unlatched the gate and swung it open. When she drove past the gate she didn't bother to get out and pull it to. Not that she was being disrespectful to the owner. Just anxious to find her daughter. Again, she petitioned God, "Please be here. Please God, let her be here." In a few minutes she would know if God still loved her.

In case the gate and sign weren't deterrent enough Mattie had allowed tree limbs to overgrow the dirt path that led to her front door. The limbs swatted and scratched at the roof and sides of Deborah's Suburban as if they were playing a game. That wasn't all. Deep ruts in the path caused the big truck to rock side to side as in time to a catchy tune. The truck groaned its disapproval; Deborah paid it no mind. She was on a mission, focused on finding Hope. Half a curved and twisted mile later, with the truck still rocking and swaying, Deborah motored around a pile of lumber, bricks and porcelain—throwaways from a time gone by that Mattie had piled up instead of hauled away—and past an elm tree with as many roots above ground as under. Finally, a netted view through the branches of a weeping willow of Mattie's yard and house. And there...

"Oh, thank God! Thank you, Jesus!" Deborah cried.

There was Hope's car and there, on the bottom porch step, was Hope.

Tension and worry finally freed Deborah. Her shoulders and neck muscles relaxed, the lines in her forehead smoothed, and she even smiled through grateful tears, though she knew not the reason for Hope's visit. She was just glad to see her daughter alive.

That gladness lasted only a few more rolls of her tires. With a closer view, Deborah saw the scene was...off. Something wasn't right. Hope was gesturing wildly, looking like a threat to Aunt Mattie who stood in the shadows of her porch, close to her screen door. And in Mattie's hand—a big, ugly-looking butcher knife.

Deborah felt like she'd tumbled into the story Mary had told last night at dinner. Aunt Mattie with a butcher knife threatening a little girl. Except in this case, it was Hope doing the threatening, if Deborah correctly interpreted the girl's raised arm, the finger-stabbing in the air and the jerky neck movements. And all this from the back. No telling how marred her pretty face must be from the front.

Not understanding what she saw, Deborah strained forward as if trying to merge with the steering wheel. "What is going on?" she whispered, wiping her face clean of tears. "What's happening?" It looked like... More strands of the weeping willow scraped across her windshield, blocking her view for precious seconds. Then, beyond its thin leaves, in full view again, Deborah watched as first Hope and then Aunt Mattie eased closer. Hope, one step up and Aunt Mattie, one step forward. They were not drawing together in love. If the gestures and weapon were not clue enough Deborah could ascertain as much from Aunt Mattie's face. It twisted as it had when first they'd introduced themselves to her—pained, yet closed-off.

"Oh, Lord! I hope that girl's not saying or doing something stupid." She and Samuel had raised Hope to respect her elders, regardless of whether she liked them or not. And yet, from what she saw, it looked like Hope had slipped in her upbringing. Deborah's anger flamed at the thought, and she silently issued a threat of her own: *If that girl has upset Aunt Mattie for nothing, I'll be the one—* A sudden thought sliced through her words, extinguishing her anger. *Something* had brought Hope to Partway and that *something* must be so devastating, so damaging that it caused Hope to sweep aside her normal good manners *and* her usual teenage tendencies.

The now familiar emotions—fear, worry, desperation, uncertainty—returned falling hard on Deborah. What was it? What had turned her daughter into a child she didn't know? What made her argue like that with Aunt Mattie?

As if Deborah's questions had floated through the air and tapped her on the shoulder, Hope turned around, focusing on the forward moving white truck. She smiled at Deborah, the smile that always caused Deborah's heart to melt in love. Then, the young girl lifted her hand, waved and did the oddest thing. She walked ladylike to her car, got in and then fishtailed around, barely missing the edge of the porch and moments later barely missing Deborah's front end. Indeed, if Deborah had not swerved, Hope would have connected.

"WHAT IS WRONG WITH THAT GIRL?!" Deborah screamed as she twisted in her seat and watched the sashaying taillights of Hope's car through the rear window. She couldn't believe it! Could not believe Hope had left, had almost hit her, had ignored her, but mostly that she had disowned her by leaving. It was worth repeating. "What the hell is wrong with that girl?" The question looped continuously through Deborah's head as she sat in the idling truck staring backward, held hostage by surprise.

The slam of a door rattled Deborah out of her stunned stupor, and facing forward she saw that Aunt Mattie had retreated inside, firmly communicating to Deborah and the rest of the world: *Beware. Stay out.*

Deborah got the message but silently promised: *I'll make it up to you, Aunt Mattie. Just let me go get my daughter, and we'll be back to apologize and explain.*

Then, she turned around in Aunt Mattie's front yard as Hope had done earlier. Proceeding with caution, Deborah bumped along the one-way in and one-way out drive. She felt sure Hope had continued on and would wait for her on the road that ran in front of Aunt Mattie's house. This assurance she deduced from the narrowness of the drive which did not permit one to pull over and from knowing Hope. Hope wouldn't tolerate being on Aunt Mattie's property longer than she had to. Even before today's scene, Hope had made it clear Aunt Mattie was not one of her favorite people. So, Deborah crept along as fast as she dared, babying her vehicle along the tortuous path, past the cattle gate and finally stopping to take the time to secure it, an action meant to be the first peace offering to Aunt Mattie. There would be others. Had to be if she wanted to get information out of her later.

Deborah climbed back into her truck, made a right onto the road and stopped. The road was clear! No sign of Hope.

"Now, where the hell did she go?" Deborah screeched.

Earlier, her anger had flared, but only for a short time. Flared did not begin to describe the degree of anger that consumed Deborah now.

Steaming, she turned to face her back seats to search the road behind. There was a slight chance Hope had taken a left instead of a right. Deborah knew left was a mistake because the road dead-ended at the woods and fields that led to Black Hill. But Hope, less familiar, might not know that. Unfortunately, there was no sign of Hope that way, either.

Tamping down her anger just a notch, Deborah acknowledged the possibility that Hope could have moved on to the FM road up ahead where a soft shoulder existed for legitimate pull-offs. There, they'd be able to have a conversation without disrupting traffic—not that that would be a problem on this road, either. Who, besides hunters, Christmas tree buyers and Governor used this road, anyway? No one.

Again facing forward, Deborah decided she would give Hope exactly two minutes to make an appearance, which was more than enough time for the girl to discover the dead-end and execute a turnaround, if indeed she'd gone the wrong direction. If she was a no-show, Deborah made up her mind to proceed to the FM road. And the girl had better be there. It was *way* past time for a conversation.

As she marked time by her dashboard clock, Deborah's mind flipped back and forth between why Hope was in Partway and how she would ever manage to get Aunt Mattie to talk about Fuller deaths when her own child, the one whose life she worked so hard to free, had been so disruptive and disrespectful. Deborah groaned her misfortunes and turned back to stare out of her rear window.

Clear. And time was up. Feeling certain now of Hope's location, Deborah drove the C-shape of the road to the T-intersection of Mattie's and the FM road. Looking first right, then left, Deborah saw no sign of Hope. Her face screwed up as she surveyed the road again—a disabled combine on the shoulder, a pick-up coming from the west and a jackrabbit with twitching nose and ears, but no Hope, no Mustang.

"No, God. Please, no," Deborah half cried, half choked.

No longer able to hold her own against the dark emotions that had been shadowing her for months, no longer able to withstand the unmerciful attack of bad news, death and sorrow, Deborah fell against her steering wheel. Her arms draped across the top and cushioned her head, which rocked to and fro. Deep, anguished sobs gushed out so violently it hurt her inside, and tears so hot, so heavy and so plentiful mixed with saliva from her open mouth that they drenched her steering wheel. Total surrender, leaving her with nothing but pleas.

"Give me my daughter. Please God, I'll even take my boring, unhappy life back, just give me Hope."

After shutting out the world, Mattie trudged through her house to throw the butcher knife in the kitchen sink. She leaned against the counter, not knowing how she should feel—glad to have skirted a round with the BlackHeart or sad to have to live another day to deal with It. No doubt in her mind, they had been headed for a showdown and, if not for the timely or untimely arrival of Deborah, a final breath would have been taken today. Her final breath.

With the end being yea close, Mattie felt conflicted. Yes, that's the best she could describe the feelings swirling within her. Conflicted, double-hearted. She was ready to go home. She wasn't ready to go home. She was ready to die. She wasn't ready to die. She was tired. Well, no conflict there. She was tired. Tired of covering up death all these years. Tired of lying. Tired of inventorying lives. Tired of secrets and of new beginnings to the same ole tale. Tired that the final ending, the one act that would save the Fullers from the BlackHeart and restore them fully to God seemed so difficult for loved ones to carry out.

Disappointed in her family, Mattie hung her head. Reversing her steps, she returned to the living room and took her usual seat in the rocker by the front window. She pushed off, slowly rocking while staring through the see-through curtains. The playful sway of the trees in her yard and the nonsensical flight of birds offered a gentle background to Mattie's troublesome thoughts.

The BlackHeart had lost control, killing lovers who'd been down-the-line cousins of Mattie and each other. Not a good thing. The Fullers were already an endangered family. No Fuller was safe when the BlackHeart's pain exceeded Its threshold, forcing It to extract Fuller blood to end the pain. They could not afford for the BlackHeart to add revenge kills or any other type of kills to Its pain killings. The loss of lives would be too high. Even the BlackHeart must recognize that. Surely It was smart enough to know It could only control the Fullers as long as there were Fullers to control.

Mattie shook her head, wondering if the BlackHeart *could* even return to Its original pattern of killing now that It had Its first taste of killing for something other than releasing pain. Had this new loss-of-control killing been a one-time thing? Or did It already crave it like It craved eternal glory? If It did, Governor would have a hell of a time covering Its many deaths and such telling deaths too—*a double homicide! What was the BlackHeart thinking?* Now that the police acted like they gave a damn about the deaths of black folks they might actually start figuring correctly, and that would be bad. It would be even worse when the family figured it out. Why, there'd be "Willie" situations all over the county; killing mobs doing more harm than good.

Mattie closed her eyes, thinking about the increasingly difficult job she was handing off to Governor. Not only would he have to worry about this new type of killing, but also more dedicated investigators and police. Their task of covering-up the BlackHeart's kills got harder and harder each year, which is why when Deborah and Ester had come knocking yesterday Mattie had hid herself in the woods. Not out of fear of discovery, but because she simply had not wanted to waste either of their time with hard lies. She sighed, thinking she didn't have long to deal with the after effects of the BlackHeart's killings. But Governor, poor Governor...

With her head pressed against the wooden chair she fast forwarded through the earlier scene of the BlackHeart's visit. It had come to boast of the double killing; a revenge kill for not getting Its way. It had come to repeat Its offer from weeks ago for Mattie to hand over the Truth, and in exchange for the favor she could choose her own manner of death. It had come to threaten the current Record Keeper. Mattie had been on the verge of telling It to go to Hell, but Deborah's arrival had made that unnecessary.

All this thinking, worrying, wondering and re-hashing scenes burdened Mattie's soul; she felt it growing heavier and heavier, which took her naturally to thoughts of escape and home. But no! She quit rocking and sprang forward in her chair. She would not give the BlackHeart the satisfaction of belittling her last remaining days on Earth.

Standing, she reached for an optimistic thought, a saving plan, one that might save the Fullers and lighten Governor's load. As her mind went to work on that she walked through her house, exited the back door and headed for Black Hill. During the short walk there, the idea came to her that it was possible that once the BlackHeart grew tired of using the teenager's body, It might not be inclined to act shortsightedly, like a teenager. Maybe when, if It returned to using adults, It would be smarter and more thoughtful about Its kills. Mattie recalled how the BlackHeart had boasted at a past death scene that part of the fun was killing in secret, outsmarting the authorities, getting away with what mere humans could not, which is why It preferred accidental deaths to homicide or any other class of death. It proved Its superiority in that manner. Now that that tidbit had returned to Mattie she smiled, promising to share it with Governor. Using that knowledge, he could bounce it against the BlackHeart's ego and control the BlackHeart's killings in that way.

Mattie's smile broadened. Yes, she liked that. That idea would be her last gift to Governor. When he visited later for them to talk through his moment of weakness, of being used by the BlackHeart, she would brighten his mind with this, a saving plan.

Activity happened on three sides of Deborah. Above her, the tropical white ceiling fan bullied the refrigerated air, forcing it down to cool the den. In front of her, through the patio doors, the mechanical pool cleaner snaked quietly through the Caribbean blue water, looking to feed its plastic jaws with invading foreign particles. Behind her, pork fried in a non-stick skillet. Deborah was oblivious to all of this. Sleep had its arms around her, protecting her from all activity. But gradually, Sleep's rule over Deborah expired; time for Sleep to give its charge over to the cruelty of her life. When it would linger to shield her from cares for a bit longer, Consciousness growled and angrily bit Deborah awake. No gentle release. No softly whispered name. No kind shaking of her shoulder. Awake and aware instantly of the troubles from the previous day.

Aware of driving for hours around Partway and eventually Dallas, searching for the AWOL teenager. Aware of returning to their empty house and calling half the phone book searching for Hope. Aware of her and Samuel driving around all afternoon and half the night, stopping in at all of Hope's friends' houses and hangouts, praying for even a glimpse of the girl. Aware of pacing the den, channel surfing, running to the windows and doors every time a car sounded. Aware that her body had given up and passed out when she had willed it not to.

Now fully awake and aware that the troubles of yesterday had followed her to today and that the questions still remained: Where was Hope? ...in her bed? ...at Dinnie's? ...at another friend's house? Why had she been in Partway? Was she dead, a victim of the chart?

Deborah popped to a sitting position, resolved to obtain answers today, and she would start the search for answers in Hope's bedroom where she prayed to find the girl. As she untangled her legs from the Indian blanket someone had thrown over her while she slept, her daughter's laughter reached her.

Deborah stilled, not sure she had heard correctly.

It had come from behind her, from the kitchen where the smell of bacon and coffee mixed to tease her olfactory glands. Deborah whipped around to confirm the truth of her hearing just as another laugh sounded, and there was Hope, alive, in the flesh, giggling at something her father had said.

If she hadn't been fully awake and aware of the activity surrounding her she would have sworn she dreamt the cozy family scene before her: Samuel pouring orange juice; Hope with a metal spatula in hand—how many times had she told that girl not to use metal with her non-stick cookware—and Ester whipping eggs into a creamy consistency. But she *was* awake and aware, so that meant that while she slept Hope had come home and Samuel and Ester, aware of this fact, had not bothered to wake her! And furthermore, all three of them had decided to let her sleep while they cooked breakfast?! Deborah sizzled, unsure who to direct her anger toward first—her daughter or the adults? Quick decision—her daughter.

"Hope!" Deborah called, her voice sounding strained yet wired.

All three occupants in the kitchen ceased their light banter, the pouring and the whisking to stare at Deborah. She, on the other hand, only had eyes for Hope, and they bored into the girl like lasers.

Hope, seemingly unaware of Deborah's mood, smiled prettily and said, "Good morning, Mama."

Kicking the blanket aside, Deborah launched herself toward the kitchen, aiming for the one who'd caused such grief and heartache. "HOW CAN YOU STAND THERE HAPPY AND SMILING WITH WHAT YOU'VE PUT ME THROUGH?"

Hope's good morning smile vanished; her eyes widened. Turning to her father she pleaded with her eyes for his help. Interpreting her look correctly, Samuel mumbled something Deborah could not decipher, and in turn Hope mumbled something meant for Deborah.

"What's that?" Deborah challenged as she drew nearer; her voice slashed at the girl. "You want to apologize for all the hell you sent us through? Is that what you're trying to say?"

Hope scurried to Samuel's side for protection, but Deborah felt no empathy for her daughter. She needed the girl to understand the danger she'd put herself in, the worry and fear she'd evoked in others so that in the future she would act with care. And if the lesson could only be learned with a heavy dose of fear accompanying it, then so be it.

Crashing through the kitchen with sparks shooting from her eyes, Deborah stopped at the island in the center of the kitchen. Standing toe to toe, eye to eye, breath to breath with Hope, she leaned into the girl and raged. "What the hell were you thinking? How could you leave Aunt Mattie's without talking to me? Are you crazy?"

§

Hope had learned over the years which questions were meant to be answered and which ones weren't. She'd also learned when she had miscalculated her mother's love, and this proved to be one of those times when answers would not be appreciated and an apology was the only thing that would correct her misstep. "Mom, I'm sorry. Really, I am. And I promise I won't do it again. Ever. I'm sorry."

§

"It's too late for sorry! Do you know how worried I was? …your father and Ester, too…" Deborah shot a confirming look at her husband and friend, discovering they had abandoned the kitchen and the girl and now watched from a safe distance at the bar. Reminding herself to deal with them later, she continued her tirade. "We were all worried sick about you. We feared for your life! Do you understand that? And just what are you sorry for? There's so much—"

Finding herself about to slip into yesterday's fears and all the ugly outcomes it could have held, Deborah stopped. Her daughter was here, at home, safe, no missing limbs, no scratches, no bruises…

Suddenly, relief gushed from a source unknown, washing away anger. In a move that surprised herself, Deborah yanked Hope to her, folding her tight within her arms; she whispered words of love and thanksgiving that flowed sincerely and naturally out of her. "Thank you, God. Thank you for bringing my baby home safe. Thank you for saving her from that death chart." Tears filled her eyes and squeezed between her lashes to make slick her cheeks. Kissing her daughter's temple, stroking her back, the words of gratitude kept flowing. "Thank you, thank you, God. My baby, my baby is home. Thank you."

"I'm sorry, Mom," Hope whimpered, "I wasn't thinking, but I won't do that again. I promise."

Still clutching her daughter Deborah nodded her head, an acknowledgment of Hope's apology.

They stood that way, heart to heart, until Deborah's words and tears dribbled to nothing. Then sniffling, she leaned back, allowing only a handful of space to separate them, to stare into her daughter's eyes. What she saw in them made her heart melt—love, pure, unadulterated love. An overwhelming, reciprocating love flooded Deborah's being and urgently she pulled Hope back into her arms for more hugs, caresses and shared heartbeats. *God, I love this girl. I can't fathom life without her.* This truth she proclaimed within her soul and outwardly with words. "I'm sorry for screaming and yelling at you, Hope. I was scared. I love you and I'm so glad you're home and safe."

It was Hope's turn to nod acknowledgement of an apology.

With love and harmony residing again within the walls of their home, Samuel reentered the kitchen. He joined his girls in their love fest by briefly hugging and pecking each one, and then he raced to the stove to rescue the bacon. "Glad you girls got that worked out. Now, how 'bout some breakfast?"

Even though she wanted to continue to hold her daughter captive in her arms, Deborah let go. It was time to turn to lesser worries and answers now that the big worries of Hope's whereabouts and her state of being were sated. Donning the role of disciplinarian, Deborah asked, "What was going on yesterday? Why were you in Partway?"

"Daddy and Aunt Ester already fussed at me and told me I was wrong."

Ester, still standing at the bar, the dividing line between den and kitchen, confirmed the girl's words with a nod. And Samuel, checking on the biscuits in the oven, supported the teen's assertion with, "That's true."

"I feel really bad, Mama. I'm sorry."

With gratitude for the safety and life of her child lingering like a watermark, Deborah was able to block impatience and anger, even though they twitched to life, wanting to be loosed. To quiet the unwanted emotions Deborah needed to hear a rationale and thus commanded, "So, quit saying you're sorry and explain." Stepping on her own words, she demanded, "What happened to make you drive all the way to Partway and then ignore me as if I were a ghost?"

"It's like I was telling Daddy and Aunt Ester, I feel stupid now, but yesterday it seemed so real." Hope paused, then explained, "I woke up early from a nightmare. I dreamt you were in danger at Aunt Mattie's. Something inside me said, 'Go check on your Mom.' I didn't even question it. I just dressed and left."

Deep scowl lines sliced Deborah's brow in half. Her head cocked in confusion. "So, nothing happened? You just…had this…dream?" One of her hands flapped around like Step-Uncle Billy's good hand, trying to draw out more, sure there had to be more.

"That's it." Hope's head drooped in embarrassment, her cheeks glowed in shame as she voiced a weak defense. "But it felt so real, Mom. I wish I could explain it to you."

Ester, who had deemed the kitchen safe again, reached for the bowl of eggs and handed it to Samuel, remarking, "Same thing she told us. No more, no less than that."

Hearing the girl's explanation and having it confirmed didn't resolve a thing for Deborah. Unsettled her more, actually. But hanging up the Partway issue for now, promising to revisit it, Deborah moved on, picking at the other dangling issues. "Okay, so where were you when we finally got back? Surely, you must have known we'd be concerned. We called all over town trying to find you. Your Dad and I must have driven a million miles looking for you!" There it was again…anger, kicking, trying to burst free.

"When you showed up looking fine, I came on home. I figured you'd be with Aunt Mattie all day."

"Hope, that doesn't make sense. *Your dream* told you I was in danger at Aunt Mattie's house and yet you left me there?" Deborah's scowl line returned and then vanished as quickly as it had surfaced. "Never mind that—" she waved that issue aside. That was not the important one right now. "You haven't answered my question." Her voice rose, a sign that anger was about to be loosed. "Where *in Dallas* were you?"

Hope looked everywhere but at her mom when she answered. "At the mall. With Dinnie. We were on our way home when we ran into Monica and her boyfriend. We ended up going to his house to listen to music and to dance. We weren't drinking or doing drugs, Mom."

Anger was free! It wrapped around Deborah's vocal cords, making her voice spiral higher than the price of freedom. "So, while you were having a good time, hanging out with friends, dancing and singing, your father and I were running around frantic, out of our minds with worry, wondering if you were alive?!" Deborah breathed hard, staring at her teenager as if she weren't her child, couldn't be hers. Frustrated that she was, Deborah shouted, "YOU DIDN'T THINK TO PICK UP YOUR PHONE AND CALL?! YOU DIDN'T THINK TO RETURN OUR CALLS?!"

"My phone… I forgot to charge it. I didn't know…" Hope's voice trailed off, which did nothing to ease Deborah's anger.

Counting slowly, as Imogene had done when raising her three daughters, Deborah sought to ice down her anger and its sister-emotion, frustration, but found that by the time she reached ten, she couldn't do it. Perhaps she could have if she'd been able to share with Hope what she'd shared with Samuel last night about the death charts and its inherent dangers. But she couldn't bind her child with that type of knowledge. She wouldn't hang that curse over her daughter's head.

Oh, it was all too frustrating, so unfair, and that pissed Deborah off; angered her even more that their efforts to diffuse the power of the charts had been thwarted. First, by the slow-going research at the morgue, and second, by the missing elders whom Deborah and Ester had had to forgo interviewing yesterday since they'd used all their time tracking down Hope—who'd been their final obstruction to refuting the charts. And now, given yesterday's objectionable interaction between Hope and Aunt Mattie, it would probably take a Mount Sinai experience to get Aunt Mattie to open up, let alone score time with her. So, because the charts still existed with all their dark power and because the obstacles stayed stubbornly fixed—other than the now-found Hope—Fullers' lives remained tentative, questionable. And that was the source of her current anger.

Closing her eyes momentarily to sort her different sources of anger, Deborah decided there was nothing she could do about the charts. Not now, at least. Maybe never, but she wouldn't think about that now. Top priority for the moment—resolving her anger surrounding Hope's actions of staying out past curfew, not returning phone calls or texts, and not bothering to speak face-to-face with Deborah. Those actions were inexcusable, disrespectful and needed correction. With fake calm in her voice Deborah asked, "And what time did all this fun *without booze and drugs* end last night? I know it was after midnight because that's what time we finally made it back here after driving around looking for you."

Eyes fixed on a seam on Deborah's blouse, Hope answered, "I don't know the exact time. I didn't realize it had gotten so late."

"And how late is *so* late?"

"Around 3:00, I guess. That's the last time I remember on the clock." In this, the teen told the truth. A life-stealing accident on I-35 the previous night had slowed traffic down around Waco. Traffic had moved at seemingly one inch per minute, causing Hope to pull into their driveway at exactly 2:58. "I know that's past curfew, Mom, but I'm eighteen. Headed to college soon."

"I know how old you are, and you're not going anywhere! Our agreement stipulated no more missed appointments and now, with you acting like you've lost your mind, you're staying right here." Deborah pointed at the floor, punctuating her position. "Right here!"

Proclaiming death to the Spelman dream pierced Deborah's heart. Oh, the dreams she'd had for her daughter and now, most of them gone, lost to charts, with only one remaining—keeping Hope safe, alive.

"But Mom! You can't do that. Spelman, my medical studies—"

"Will be pursued here in Dallas. There're plenty of good pre-med schools around."

"Mom, are you kidding?"

Looking at Deborah's stubborn, sad face, Hope turned to her father, who quickly jerked his thumb at Deborah. Samuel's non-response and pointing thumb meant Deborah had the authority, the final say.

Stuffing her pain and disappointment deep inside herself Deborah, still operating as disciplinarian said, "And just because you're starting college doesn't mean you have new rules. You're still my child and I don't care if you're forty. If I tell you to be in *my* house by midnight, your butt better be here. You were disrespectful, Hope. Not only to me, but to Aunt Mattie, your Dad and Aunt Ester, and that makes you grounded. Two weeks."

"MOOOOOMMMM!" Hope drew the word out, apparently thinking the longer the stretch the shorter the probation time. "You can't do that to me! What about 'The Last Hoorah?' It's next weekend and the last time our senior class will be together—maybe forever."

"Guess who won't be there?"

Deborah glared at Hope and folded her arms in an *I have spoken attitude.* She didn't think she would ever learn to live without fear or worry, not knowing what she knew, and because of that Hope could expect to feel buttoned up, tied up, suffocated. That could not be helped. She'd already lost one child in this lifetime and she could not lose another. And if she did, if the charts remained unkind to her, well then, she might as well die too, because she would never recover, would forfeit her sanity to grief.

Shaking herself of the damaging thoughts before she sank so low revival would be impossible, she sought and clung to a positive thought. Coveting Hope would only last for a short time. Only until she, Ester and now Samuel figured out how to invalidate those cursed charts or find another way to save the family. With three great brains on the task it should be a simple matter, only a small measure of time before they achieved success, granting the Fullers the happily-ever-after they deserved. That one endearing thought was enough to help Deborah regain balance, to again embrace hope.

Softer now, in a pleasing tone, Deborah re-enforced her position, tacking on a mini-lecture. "Hope, this could have been avoided with a phone call or a few words at Aunt Mattie's. But since *you* chose to act irresponsibly, then *I* choose to act responsibly."

§

"Mom, please! Two weeks?!" Playing the role. Just like times before. The BlackHeart didn't care about being grounded, Hope's senior class, or some silly party. It cared about leaving this house, driving to Partway and destroying the Truth. "I told you, my phone died. That's not fair."

"And it was fair to worry us to death yesterday?"

The BlackHeart opened Its mouth, all set on a response, then snapped it shut. Covertly, It glanced at the kitchen clock and then the phone. Sometime today, probably this morning, a phone call from Partway would upend the adults in this house. Before that happened It wanted to be tucked away in Hope's room and hence, the reason for keeping Its retort to Itself; It would not be the one to delay Its own escape.

Deborah obviously had no thought to delay, either. She held out her hand, beckoned with her fingers. "You know the drill."

The BlackHeart stared at Deborah's hand, reading the sign language. It checked the clock again, knowing It had to beg at least one more time; Deborah would expect it. "Mom, please, give me something else." Clasping Hope's hands together in prayer position, begging with Hope's eyes, then giving Deborah that look that promised a whole new, better daughter, the BlackHeart offered, "I'll do all the cooking and cleaning. I'll wash your car, do the laundry, go to the store. Please, Mom, I'll do anything. I'll even apologize to Aunt Mattie. I'll do anything you ask, please, not two weeks."

Not even tempted, Deborah wiggled her fingers again.

Holding on to Its pleading look, the BlackHeart streamed a final, "Moomm..."

Deborah shook her head, stretched her arm out farther.

Recasting Hope's face to defeated, the BlackHeart reached in Hope's pajama pants pocket and pulled out Hope's cell phone. It laid it gently in Deborah's outstretched hand. As soon as the plastic made contact with flesh, Deborah closed her hand around it and pointed toward the back staircase saying, "Laptop, TV, iPod, car keys, everything…on my bed."

It took a few seconds for the BlackHeart to move, as if It deliberated another round of begging. Then, dragging Its feet, head hanging low, It left, headed down the hall and up the oak staircase.

§

Deborah and the other two in the kitchen listened to the echoes of Hope's departure. When she could no longer hear the girl's movements she sighed heavily and exchanged Hope's cell phone for a coffee cup. She felt Ester's judgmental eyes on her as she filled it to the rim. Avoiding Ester's eyes she handed her the cup and then turned back to the cabinet to retrieve a second one. Behind her back she heard Ester speaking.

"If you didn't know about the accidental deaths you wouldn't have been so restrictive."

"But I do know, Ester," Deborah snapped back and immediately regretted it. Ester had been a good, supportive friend these last few weeks, going way outside the lines of friendship. She didn't deserve Deborah's fear, masked as anger. "I'm sorry Ester," Deborah sighed, "I am afraid for her. I want her home, out of a world of danger. Does that make me a bad mother?"

As Hope had done earlier Ester opened her mouth but then closed it, obviously deciding to keep her words to herself. She turned and exited the kitchen. Claiming a stool next to Samuel, who sat hunched over his plate eating, she brooded in silence.

Deborah, also deciding to keep her words locked in, went to the bar to join them. Coming to rest on the other side of the bar facing Samuel and Ester she praised the benefits of a long friendship. Even without a spoken agreement she and Ester knew when to allow peace to fill a space. This, Deborah cherished. Because during times like now, when she needed time to be inside her own head, she could do so without guilt.

And where did her mind go? To the charts and her family, of course. With all the driving, calling and disappointments yesterday she and Ester had not had a chance to discuss the study of death other than to share with Samuel everything they knew. Samuel's external reaction had been much like Ester's, objective, unemotional. But Deborah, having lived with him for twenty plus years knew he'd taken a hit to his heart. She could tell by the way he'd pounded Ester with methodology and process questions as if he filled the role of a Ph. D. dissertation committee member, and by the way he'd taken control of the Hope scavenger hunt, commanding Ester to wait at the house in case Hope showed up and driving Deborah from house to house, place to place.

Deborah looked at her husband, wondering about the source of his strength. When they'd lost Rachel he'd taken solicitous care of her and Hope while handling most of the burial arrangements and maintaining his professional responsibilities. When The Lab siphoned off her physical, mental and emotional health he'd dashed on to the scene, told her boss she quit and dragged his wife home. Initially, she'd been resentful of his cavalier actions, but as she'd begun to piece herself back together, she appreciated him, loved him deeper. Only in the last few years had she come full circle to resentment and disquiet. Brought on, not by Samuel forcing her out of her career, but by Hope's expanding life which would not include her parents, primarily her mother, in the lead role. It surprised her to realize she'd never asked Samuel how he felt about their diminishing influence in Hope's life, and that revelation carried her right back to the source of his strength. *If* the chart claimed both her and Hope would his strength remain intact, or would he fall under the blow of having his entire family wiped out? And if he succumbed, would family support be enough to pull him out of the dark dredges of sorrow? Oh, she knew her parents, his parents, her sister and…

"Oh, shoot!" Deborah's exclamation captured everyone's attention. She stood up straight as if she'd been jabbed in the spine with a needle. "I forgot to call Hannah back."

As she stepped quickly to the kitchen phone she thought about how she'd rushed Hannah off the phone last night. She and Samuel had just pulled into the driveway of one of Hope's friends at the time of Hannah's call and after learning Hannah and her immediate family were fine, Deborah had promised to call back. She hadn't…until now. She reached for the phone and just as her hand touched the unit, it rang.

"Oh—" she gasped, startled, snatching her hand back. Recovering quickly, she damned her unraveling nerves and answered without even checking the Caller ID.

"Hello."

"Deborah—" Mary Fuller's voice came through clearly, but it didn't sound right. The cheeriness and laughter that seemed hard-wired into her voice and life had been replaced with dreary dread. As if suddenly psychic, Deborah knew someone had died. They'd lost another Fuller in Partway.

Clutching the phone Deborah asked, "Who is it, Mary? Who died?"

"Martin Fuller, Margaret's boy." Mary's stuttering sobs told Deborah that the grieving mother was reliving the news of Shandra's death while sympathizing with the newest stricken mother. "His body… They found him this mornin'… On the county road."

All the matter in Deborah's body seemed to congeal in her feet, and with nothing substantial holding her up she slumped against the cabinets, then slowly sagged to the floor. Lustrous tears shone in her eyes, and finding a circuitous route of escape they plopped onto her blouse, soaking the front.

Mary continued, her voice growing stronger with every spoken word as she distanced herself from her own grief. "Near as they can tell, his truck fell on him while changin' a tire. Every bone in his chest crushed flat. Didn't even waste gas goin' to the hospital. Straight to the morgue. I panicked, thinkin' it might be you. Glad it wasn't…but poor Margaret…" Her sobs returned now, loud and sloppy, piercing more holes in Deborah's heart.

Despite the twisted wreckage of her emotional and physical self, Deborah's scientific brain churned, forcing her to brokenly ask, "How old is…was…he?"

For seconds Deborah listened to the sound of de-escalating cries and then Mary's sniffling response, "Older than Shandra. Mid-to-late thirties."

Deborah had known that. Before Mary confirmed it, she knew that the charts had claimed their latest victim—a Fuller between eighteen and fifty. But like all good scientists and researchers she'd needed confirmation, and now that she had it she released the logical and fell to grief. Trembling, tears flowing faster and snotting as well, she keened, rocking back and forth. So cowed under by heartache she wasn't even aware of Samuel and Ester posted on either side of her.

A click on Mary's end of the line reached the tiny portion of Deborah's brain that still functioned. It registered an incoming call; someone needed to speak with Mary. "I'm sorry Deborah, it's probably about Martin. I'll call back." Mary clicked off, leaving Deborah with a burst and bleeding heart.

In that miniscule space after the final word, Deborah had an epiphany. The charts, the Fuller's curse…it was all true.

She, Ester and Samuel could research until the moment they exhaled their last breath and still, they would not disprove the Fuller's relationship to accidental death. A truck falling on a grown man—indisputable. A young woman falling off a cliff—indisputable. Another drowned and yet another shot. They would not save anyone. The Fullers were cursed.

Inside her mind Deborah screamed this truth over and over.

We're cursed. We're cursed. The Fullers are cursed.

So shell-shocked by her new truth, Deborah didn't feel Samuel's gentle touch as he wiped her tears and held her. Didn't realize Ester took the phone out of her trembling hand, dialed the last phone number and spoke briefly with Mary, who re-told Martin's fate and added to it the latest news of the double homicide.

Deborah didn't know that upstairs her daughter lay on her bed in her blood-red and yellow room, smiling a sick, sick smile. Lost in the images of accidental deaths, charts and funerals, she only knew that her family was cursed.

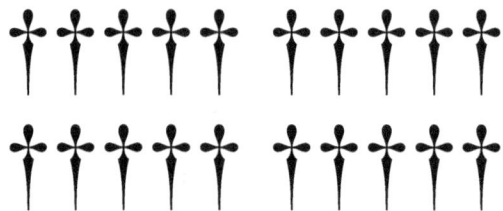

It was a soft shaking. Gentle enough to arouse without aggravating or offending, yet effective enough to cause Deborah to moan. The tender hand shook her shoulder again. This time, her eyes cracked open, even though her mind still struggled to break free of the chemically-induced sleep.

Inside the master bedroom, despite the late morning hour and the brilliance of the sun, it was dark—but not so dark Deborah didn't recognize the form, didn't know the girl she had given birth to.

"Hope?" Her sleep-deep voice cracked on that one syllable.

"It's time to go, Mom. I can't delay any longer. The pain is building fast; it's consuming me."

The slim figure backed away from the bed. She stopped at the threshold; the light from the hallway cast her in silhouette. "I'll meet you in Partway, Mama. Everything you need to know is there."

A few steps more and she was completely swaddled in light. "Get up now, Mama. It's time to end this."

She left the door standing wide open, an invitation.

Even though Hope was now gone Deborah raised a hand, vaguely reaching for her daughter. But she couldn't sustain the effort, so her hand fell, a soft thud against the covers. In her drug-corrupted mind the visit registered— the brief words, whispered; Hope, by her side, touching her; a command given. She wanted to react to the visit, to do as requested, but the sleeping and nerve pills had disconnected mind from body causing Deborah to lay limp and unresponsive.

But Hope needed her. She felt that need vibrating, reaching out to her, calling her to action.

Hope needed her.

She had to move.

Fortifying her weakened mind, Deborah coalesced her energy and with great effort, managed to rise to a sitting position. Humped over, head dangling, she waited for the black-and-white dots and the swirls dancing before her eyes to dissipate. Then, using the same force of mind and energy, she slid one leg and then the other to the side of the bed so that they hung carelessly, like discarded sneakers over a wire. With even greater will she scooted to the edge of the bed. Scooted, slowly scooted until her feet rested on the thick carpet.

She sat there, inhaling deeply, thinking fresh air in her lungs might eliminate the psychedelic patterns in her vision and reduce the ringing in her ears. It seemed the right cure because after a while the symptoms diminished, and she felt ready for the next big act—standing.

Pushing off, she failed the first time and the time after that. With the third try, aided by gutsy determination, she made it. Swaying slightly, she held her hands out and stayed upright, maintaining that position until she felt somewhat steady.

As challenging as the previous efforts had been, Deborah knew the really hard part had come: finding Hope and filling her need. Squinting, Deborah focused on the doorway and like one who groped through the dark, she held her hands out before her as she stepped, a safety measure more than anything else because she quickly discovered her reflexes and mind remained strangers.

One step after another, she made it to the threshold, the same spot where Hope had paused. She stopped, arrested suddenly by conflicting thoughts. *Had it been a dream?* she wondered. *Hope needing me. Had she mentioned Partway? And something about pain?* Pressing a hand to her forehead, Deborah searched her mind, trying to recover the words she thought she'd had a lock on, and failed.

Frustrated, she leaned against the door frame rubbing her brow, hoping the action would stimulate her memories and bring Hope's words back to her. It worked, but not in the way she hoped. Memories did return, but not the one of Hope's visit. Mary's phone call reporting first one and then two additional deaths in Partway over the weekend, embracing the truth about her family, freaking out—not as totally as she had with Rachel's death, but bad enough that Samuel had force fed pills to her. Those memories, the ones so heavy she'd fallen under the weight of them had returned and even now she felt herself succumbing to them, slowly sinking to the floor, fresh tears in her eyes. But then, she felt it. The vibrations on her skin, the pull on her heart, and she knew it was Hope. Hope needed her. Dangers seen and unseen stalked the girl. She had to save her.

Deborah straightened and hurried, as fast as one could who fought the after-effects of strong drugs, to the south end of the hall to Hope's bedroom. Because the hallway curved in a crescent pattern she could not see whether Hope's door stood open or closed—an indicator of Hope's presence or absence. Speeding past her office, a guest bedroom and the upstairs living room she finally reached Hope's bedroom and a closed door. This usually meant Hope wanted privacy, and therefore she should knock. But excusing conventional rules, Deborah flung open the door calling out "Hope!"

That precious name echoed off the walls with no corresponding reply. Walking into the room she called a second time. No answer. A thorough search of the bathroom, closets and balcony did not reveal the girl. Returning to the center of Hope's room Deborah stood there figuring her next move. An easier task, since the haze in her mind had evaporated enough to allow her to clearly distinguish facts. One such fact being a logical place Hope could be if not at home—work. Pivoting, Deborah stumble-walked to Hope's desk, snatched up the cordless phone and dialed Samuel's office. She turned, exited the room and headed back down the main corridor as she listened to the rings.

Between the fourth and what would have been the fifth ring, Loren answered in her always friendly tone. "King and Associates Neurosurgery."

Desperation and fear reflected rudely in Deborah's voice. "I need to speak to Samuel now. It's an emergency. I don't care what he's doing."

"One moment, Deborah," There was no offense in Loren's voice, just the same pleasant tone. "I'll get him right away."

Loren's or Samuel's right away did not match Deborah's right away. She'd expected a one or two-minute delay, not this extended time of listening to advertisements. She used the time to descend the stairs and check out the rooms on the first floor, searching for Hope.

No Hope.

Returning to the kitchen Deborah retrieved her cell phone from her purse and scrolled through it, seeing no calls or texts from Hope. Trying to ignore her rising desperation and expanding fear Deborah dialed Hope's cell phone as she headed to the mud room, intent on checking the garage for Hope's car.

"Baby?"

Finally, Samuel's deep voice.

"Samuel, what… Is Hope there? How long did I sleep? Why did you give me those pills?" Deborah rattled off the jumbled questions as they formed in her head.

"Whoa, baby, slow down. How are you feeling?"

"Is Hope there?"

"I told her to stay home and look after you."

Hearing this, Deborah's heart dropped, then began an irregular beat as fear and panic took control, one squeezing her heart, the other causing it to race. And on top of that, the intense feeling that Hope needed her.

"She's not here, Samuel. I think she went to Partway."

Deborah stood in the mud room with her hand twisting the knob, not understanding why it wouldn't open. Seconds later it came to her…the family rule. For extra security they kept the door locked, but always left an extra key in the deadbolt. Twisting the key violently, she turned the knob and yanked open the door. Only her SUV and the family car occupied the four-car bay. But somehow, she had known that already.

"Deborah, calm down. She probably just ran to the store. I'll call her—"

Crying now, knowing it was not as simple as running an errand, Deborah shook her head. "No, Samuel, no. She needs me. I can feel it."

Before Samuel could respond, Deborah's cell phone beeped. Eagerly, she scanned the incoming call detail. "Oh, thank God," she gushed and promptly answered, leaving Samuel hanging. "Hope, where are you?" she asked through her tears.

"Partway, Mother, I told you that."

That was all the girl offered before disconnecting.

The First Ending: The Demise

2 Thessalonians 2:10b (NRSV)
...they refused to love the Truth and so be saved.

How does one spend their last morning on earth? How does one knowingly prepare for the transition from the physical to spiritual? For Mattie, these were not difficult questions. These questions she did not agonize over since she'd known for many decades this day was coming and since she was so intimate with death.

This morning when "In-Me" woke her, informing her that *this* was her last day on Earth, Mattie did not concern herself with the questions that would have caused others to stumble and fall. She'd smiled, grateful that the day she'd held tenderly, eagerly in her heart had finally come.

She felt sadness at leaving Governor and, yes, the promise of pain scared her, but even those feelings did not supersede her joy at the thought of finally going home. In a while, she would unite once again with her family. The ones she loved best and the ones who loved her best.

To celebrate her homegoing Mattie had cooked her favorite breakfast of biscuits with country gravy and poached eggs. For drink, coffee. Then, she'd set out food and water for the strays that might stop in throughout the day or night. No telling when Governor would remember to care for her adopted family or if he would at all. Returning inside, she'd pulled the rocking chair onto the front porch. While rocking contentedly, with the Bible and Truth in her lap, she'd memorized the various greens of the trees shading her place, the caw and chirp of the birds that entertained her with song, the scent of pine and dirt that mixed to create a country smell like no other and the feel of wood, weathered and worn, on her rocker and the floorboards of her porch. After storing these sights and sounds of Earth, Mattie had turned to images of Heaven—the Pearly Gates, a city of gold, angels in flight and happy reunions.

A brilliant smile took ages off her flesh as she thought about everlasting time with Willie and Helen. She cried, envisioning the merger of her soul with Mama's and Daddy's. She laughed, anticipating her eternal time with Johnny and Floyd, her two serious brothers who had made Daddy proud. Oh, what a glorious end! She couldn't wait, except first….

She would have a hard finish with the BlackHeart.

As if her thoughts had conjured the evil one, Mattie heard the growl of the low-to-the-ground car and seconds later its bright red shine added color to the greens, browns and grays of Mattie's front yard. Before the Mustang screeched to a sideways stop, flinging dirt and gravel onto the front porch, Mattie was up, heading for the front door. The Bible with the papers of Truth she carried inside, shelving the book in an upright position on her desk. She stared down at it knowing this was the last time she would handle it. She couldn't stop her fingers from walking over its beautiful surface. She couldn't tear her mind away from the printed pages of scripture and the hand-written pages of Truth.

"Mattie! Mattie Fuller! You *know* what I'm here for." The young girl's voice filtered through the screen door, disturbing Mattie's reflections. "Bring it back out here, you coward."

The old woman lifted her head and dashed away the heart-heavy tears that signified the end. Earlier, she'd been happy, ready to go home. And she still was, but the end was so much more than just dying and going home. The end meant no more service to family, no more lies or secrets, no more meditations with "In-Me"—requirements she'd given her whole life to fulfilling. How could she just let it go and turn away from it permanently? This question she had not anticipated, and she had no ready answer.

"Come on, Mattie," the BlackHeart challenged, interrupting her unplanned goodbye. "I don't have all day, and neither do you."

Wiping her tears, Mattie agreed with the BlackHeart. They didn't have all day, and because she didn't know how to say goodbye to her life's work she just reached for the butcher knife on the desk and tucked it in a pocket. Then, pushing her frail shoulders back, she closed her eyes and began to chant: *Perfect love casts out all fear.*

Emotions closed off tight. *Perfect love casts out all fear.*

Senses tuned and focused on protecting the Truth. *Perfect love casts out all fear.*

"In-Me" leading, directing, she braced herself for her future and exited her home for the last time.

The screen door hadn't even slammed shut behind her before the BlackHeart, sounding as cocky as the car engine had moments ago taunted, "Paid your last visit to Black Hill? Ready to make your journey?" It mocked, knowing they both knew who the victor would be this time.

"Don't waste yo' ego jus' yet," Mattie said, planting her bare feet firmly on the porch, her hands firmly on her hips.

"Don't you worry about me, old woman. You worry about yourself."

The evil one took a baby step forward. "I don't know how many times I've come for that..." It pointed at the w i n d o w i n d i c a t i n g the Bible, safe inside the house. "…when your Mama had it and the ones before her, but this is the last. As soon as you're dead, I'm going in there and get it myself."

"It ain't for you. I tole you b'fo, it for them in'stred in keepin' the Truth, like Gov'nor and thems that seeks the Truth, like yo' Mama."

The BlackHeart sneered. "You really think the people you're protecting give a damn about the Truth or *you*? The Fullers talk about you like you were a dog. They say you're crazy and mean and a killer. And *if* they really knew how you served them, how you keep them from losing their minds, do you think they'd appreciate it? Hell, no! If they'd turn from God, why not you? Silly old woman."

"May be, but I'ma still do what I s'posed to do."

The BlackHeart stepped closer to the porch, hovering at the bottom step, Its eyes glittering. "You're determined to make this unnecessarily hard, aren't you? I'm offering you an easy death, Aunt Mattie. Wouldn't you like to have a final viewing at your funeral? Just a little bit of pain, not much blood. The way you deserve to die…what you've always wanted…"

The Record Keeper moved one step forward toward the BlackHeart, placing herself solidly between Truth and bad. Three old and sagging steps separated good from evil. "You think it your'n? It in there."

The BlackHeart was quick, and Mattie was old. But Mattie had righteousness and smarts and years of conquering bad on her side. So when the BlackHeart charged, Mattie bent low, catching the BlackHeart around Its middle and pitching forward so they both flew through the air and landed hard on the scraggly dirt yard.

With the wind knocked out of It, It lay still for several seconds, waiting for the black and white kaleidoscope behind Its eyes to stop shifting. Mattie lay on her side, inches from the BlackHeart, wondering why her ankle felt like it was on fire. She looked down and saw that it was swelling and darkening.

That was her last thought for many moments because the BlackHeart launched a sudden hard elbow upward to Mattie's jaw and a second to her face. Well-placed, direct hits that hurt. Tears glossed the Record Keeper's cheeks as her hands instinctively covered the injured areas. Eyes closed against the pain, curled in a ball, she didn't see the BlackHeart stumble awkwardly to Its feet and rush to the passenger side door. It jerked the door open and reached inside, backing out moments later with car keys in hand.

Paying Mattie's writhing and moaning no mind, the BlackHeart stepped around her and fit the key in the trunk lock; the trunk opened easily. Digging in and tossing the contents of the trunk, It searched for the tire jack with which It planned to bash Aunt Mattie's head. All of this It did while making a mistake— ignoring the family's most dutiful Record Keeper so early in the bout.

Mattie wasn't out and she definitely wasn't through. Scaling through the pain she steeled her physical self for more fight, and then grabbed the

BlackHeart's ankles. With near super human strength, she yanked as hard as she could. The BlackHeart lost Its footing and toppled downward, hitting Its head against the trunk and the bumper. A shrieking cry full of pain and anger rent the air as It crumpled to the ground, cupping Its bloody, torn lip.

Using the bumper as leverage, unmindful of the blood smear on the chrome and a plug of hair dangling from the trunk latch like an earring, Mattie lifted herself until she was standing. Ignoring the shooting pains in her ankle that tendriled up her calf she reached into her pocket for her killing knife.

She pulled it out, lifted it high above her head and twisted around to stab it…into the dirt.

The BlackHeart, guided by instinct, had rolled toward Mattie, toward the car, managing to avoid the knife by a foot.

Mattie, however, was not so lucky. The gravity of the downward, twisting move threw her off balance. Again, she landed hard in the dirt near her knife and bunched tight as new pain rippled outward from her injured ankle, making the world change from color to shades of gray.

A fresh flow of tears tainted her face.

"You old witch," the BlackHeart bit out angrily as It scrambled up reaching for the keys dangling from the trunk. It snatched the keys out and limp-walked to the driver's door. "I'm sick of this," It yelled over Its shoulder at Mattie. "You're dead."

The car started smoothly, blowing hot exhaust out the rear toward Mattie's prostrate form. The BlackHeart gunned the motor—a warning for Mattie to get ready to meet her Maker. Mattie heard it, knew what came next, wanted to roll out of the way of steel and rubber but "In- Me" bade her be still.

Deborah's coming, "In-Me" toned, s*earching for Truth.*

Mattie cried harder as she rolled fully on her back and stretched out her body. She cried because of the anticipated pain, but mostly because the dream she had dreamt for so long that the Fullers would one day exist without evil ruling them would die with her.

Governor's nearly here, trying to reach you, to save you. Extend your spirit. Let him know it's okay, that things are as they should be. Tell him you love him, that you'll always be with him.

She followed the instructions of "In-Me" as tears, big and small, wet her ancient face.

That's good, Mattie. You were good; the best. Now, accept your end and come home.

Mattie cried for the good ones and for the bad ones. For all the Fullers, she cried…then knew no more.

§

Mattie was dead—finally.

The BlackHeart felt good, even though victory was still to be had. Complete victory, that is, which would come shortly when the Bible and papers of Truth existed no more.

It crawled out of the car with a vision of the Bible and its secrets in a heap of gray, flaky ashes. And after the burning—evil's permanent, unlimited rule of the families within its domain.

There would be no more pain from both loving and hating. No more threat of losing to a Record Keeper or the one who loved It best. No more tussles or interference from those who acted as protector. Like dear, departed Aunt Mattie.

Stepping around the rear of the car, the BlackHeart knelt to study Mattie's dead body. It had expertly run over the woman several times, crushing her as thoroughly as it had Martin Fuller. There would be no more breaths for Mattie. Her eyes were permanently closed.

She was forever still.

Another Fuller death and how fitting that this should be one of Its *best* kills, given the woman had been one of Its greatest adversaries. Success swelled Its veins, pumped triumphant blood throughout. It felt invincible!

On the verge of shouting and dancing, It forced Itself to remain calm. Not yet. One task remained then, the celebration.

Rising, the BlackHeart knocked dirt off Its clothes and scrubbed at the blood on Its arms and hands. It strutted the few feet to Mattie's front porch—oops, not hers anymore! She'd probably willed it to Governor—up the rickety steps and across the landing. The BlackHeart knew the sanctity of this house had departed with Mattie's soul, making it as normal a house as any. Still, It paused at the screen door with a hand on the knob. Taking a deep breath, It snatched open the screen door, as if expecting a deadly surprise. When nothing happened It crossed a threshold It would have never crossed if Mattie had still been alive.

Releasing Its breath, It stood in the foyer, quick-scanning both the living room and hallway. Feeling a tug from the living room It veered that way, knowing the Bible resided there somewhere. The tug became tauter, more intense the closer It got to a desk, an antique one which, if restored, would be beautiful enough to rest in any mansion. The BlackHeart saw It before It reached the desk. The Bible stood in full view on top of the desk, gleaming white with sparkling gold edges. Just the sight of it started a tremble in the BlackHeart—the anticipation and excitement of finally owning that which had aggrieved It for so many ages.

Since the taking of Charles Fuller's soul, It had come close so many times to possessing this book. Had even touched it a time or two, but to actually claim it, this was something new. Overwhelming. And emotional. This last one a surprise to the BlackHeart who discovered that tears had formed and now dripped onto the girl's t-shirt. A surprise until the BlackHeart remembered that the girl still existed deep within.

As Mattie had done earlier It drew the book toward It, admiring its beauty, fingering its craftsmanship. Prompted by knowledge of the destructive contents within, the BlackHeart set aside its aesthetic perusal to lay the Bible open. With great care It pulled out the papers from front and back covers and skimmed the Truth. With precise detail and accuracy the Record Keepers had recorded Its genesis and history and had laid bare Its work presented as names. Lists of names, names so plentiful the BlackHeart blossomed with pride, burgeoning even more at the anticipation of exponential growth after It put matches to the papers and the Bible.

Stuffing the papers back inside, the BlackHeart lifted the heavy Bible, wondering how Mattie had managed. The woman had been so old and seemed so frail. Of course, of that last fact the BlackHeart knew differently. The old girl had inflicted real harm, had drawn blood and not for the first time. But since victory had fallen on Its side the BlackHeart graciously forgave her.

Carrying the prize outdoors the BlackHeart dumped it on Mattie's remains before continuing to the Mustang. Wrenching open the passenger side door, It dug in the glove compartment for matches, thinking: *What a beautiful day for a bonfire.*

At the same time that It clutched a book of matches a lone gray cloud moved overhead, as if positioning itself for a better view of the things to come on Mattie Fuller's property. Birds which had been silent observers of Mattie's death flew off or dove for cover. Breezes which had broadcast the scent of death now escaped through trees, leaving the atmosphere still… eerily still.

Heaven and Earth seemed ready to position itself in either hiding or watching from afar—in anticipation.

The BlackHeart felt the change and understood it immediately—the new Record Keeper had arrived. Without lifting Its head to confirm with sight, the BlackHeart felt him jerk to a stop and rush out of his truck to the body of his mentor. With his hands clasped on either side of his head as he looked down at her, he seemed like a little lost boy and even more so when one foot began stomping the ground and tears, big and abundant, plopped down on Mattie's inert body. He stood there for long moments in that same position, doing that same thing—and then, he turned suddenly. His long legs had him back at his truck in little time digging around in the bed.

Seconds later he removed a heavy shovel. He examined it from handle to tip and then turned to face the Mustang.

The BlackHeart backed out of the car slowly, very slowly and then straightened to stand next to the open car door. Their eyes connected and It felt

Governor's pain so intensely the BlackHeart actually slumped a bit.

In fact, Governor shook so fiercely his vibrations almost knocked the BlackHeart over. Unsettled by this, the BlackHeart wondered how It had not detected his presence sooner; It wondered how he had kept his spirit so close to himself. While searching Governor's hard eyes for clues and noting his fighting stance, the answer came—Mattie had trained him well, extremely well.

The challenges It had put him through had been inadequate, pitiful, leading to an incorrect judgment on Its part that Governor would function well but only with Mattie's support. Now, It knew better. Now, It knew Governor would be every bit the opponent Mattie had been.

The BlackHeart took a deep breath. Time to buck up for a second fight. Culling everything evil within, It stepped toward Governor and was not surprised he showed no fear.

Instead, the man nodded at the matches in the BlackHeart's hand and stated unequivocally, "You ain't burnin' neither."

His voice did not shake, quiver or tremble. No part of him wavered, not even when he glanced again at Mattie's body.

The BlackHeart stopped, wanting him to strike first so It could gauge his strength. It would not underestimate him again.

"How you want it?" Governor asked. "Ain't that what you asked Mattie?" He tapped the pointy end of the shovel in the dirt, calling attention to the garden tool he used daily for work.

Again, the BlackHeart remained mute. It had detected something new in Governor's voice, something It liked even less than the steadiness. It sought to define it so It could learn what else It had overlooked in the man. Determination to avenge Mattie? Commitment to use his God-gift for greater good? Devotion to duty? The BlackHeart searched the man, seeking the what, and learned nothing—and that told the BlackHeart that the old man had given himself to "In-Me."

"You asked Mattie if she wanted a painful death or an easy one. Now, I'm askin' you."

The BlackHeart thought of a reply that would prompt Governor into action, but before It could speak Governor's potent energy reached out, encased It and squeezed painfully tight as It had done to him at the graveside cleaning months ago.

Amazing, the force of his spirit, as if he had inherited Mattie's strength and tacked it onto his own.

Learning too late that It should have struck first, the BlackHeart stutter-stepped like a punch-drunk fighter, trying to shed the constricting band that limited movement, staggered Its breathing and waylaid Its thoughts. Struggling to be free to initiate an attack of Its own, the BlackHeart missed the start of

Governor's next move. It learned of the strike when It felt a disturbance in the air and seconds later felt the slap of the shovel. The result: a hit against Its temple and cheek so forceful and crippling that the BlackHeart lost Its connection to spirit. It barely had time to reunite body, mind and soul when a second blow slammed the other side of Its face so hard It hit and bounced off the car like a pinball, spinning and twisting to the ground where Its tears mixed with dirt and blood to form a human paste of pain.

"STOP! NO!"

The BlackHeart heard the command, as did Governor.

Finally, Deborah had arrived—and so timely!

For the BlackHeart sensed Governor crouching over It with shovel poised over his head and pointed edge aimed at the back of Its neck, intending for this to be his final blow, the one which would have ended the girl's life.

"DON'T! NO! STOP!"

With Its face pasted to the ground, the BlackHeart used other senses to "see" Deborah running wildly toward them. The terror on her face could only be described as "love losing out to the worst fear imaginable."

"STOP!" she screamed.

By the third command the BlackHeart felt sufficiently recovered to at least lift Its dirty face off the ground. It would have grinned at Deborah if the pain hadn't been so bad. She was here and already playing her role as equalizer for moments like this when the Record Keeper had the upper hand. Deborah provided the opening the BlackHeart needed to give Governor what he'd been giving.

Dizzy with pain, contorted in agony, It moved in spite of, hooking Its hands around one of Governor's feet and pulling as hard as It could pull. Already perched precariously, the man lost his balance, lurching sideways and down, hitting the unyielding ground. A loud grunt testified to just how hard he fell.

Beating him to the ground by mere seconds, the shovel lay as a divider between good and evil.

Reaching the downed pair, Deborah raged into Governor, kicking and screaming, "Leave her alone! Leave my daughter alone! I'll kill you!" Frantic, her fists flailed into him as she tried to protect her child. "Leave her alone!"

There was no engagement from his side. Just a simple push that sent Deborah sprawling onto her backside near her daughter.

Unhurt, Deborah scrambled to her knees and then crawled toward Hope. She ignored Governor, seeing that his aggression seemed to have deflated since her arrival and bent down peering into Hope's face, gently fingering the discoloration, swelling, cuts and blood on her face. She cooed, "My poor little darling, are you okay? Where are you hurting? Tell me, sweetie."

Her heart ached looking at Hope's injuries. Tears collected in her eyes and began a steady downward flow. Not waiting for Hope's answer Deborah moved, gingerly feeling down the girl's body, relieved to discover no broken bones or gushing blood.

She returned to kneel at Hope's shoulder asking, "Can you stand?"

A brief nod from Hope and when the girl started to rise Deborah assisted. When she stood at full height Deborah saw a grimace on Hope's face, and a violent anger built within her.

She turned on Governor, fury spewing from her eyes and voice. "Are you crazy? Have you lost your damn mind? What kind of…of…of *person* shovel-whips a child?" Her voice became hysterical. "You could have killed her!"

"I was tryin' to."

"What!?" Deborah sputtered, her face twisted in confused outrage. "Are you—"

About to question his sanity again, Deborah answered for herself: *Of course he's crazy! What's the point of even asking?* And that being the case, she just needed to get her daughter and leave.

"Come on, honey."

Easing an arm around Hope's middle she tried to turn her toward the Suburban she'd left running, its door hanging wide open, but Hope refused to budge. Deborah stared at her, a pronounced "what?" hovering on her face.

Seeing Hope offered no answer, that her daughter's gaze remained fixed on Governor, Deborah came up with her own answer—Hope needed more time to stabilize herself. Giving her that time, Deborah turned again on Governor.

"I'm sorry I ever brought either of us to this God-forsaken place. Crazy?! All of you are crazy!"

"You gone be even sorrier when you find out what It been up to. Gone…" Governor, who had also risen to his feet challenged the BlackHeart, "…tell her. Tell yo' Mama what you been doin'. Gone… tell her 'bout yo' evil, black heart."

"Black heart?" Deborah stared hard at Governor, saw his serious expression and demanded in incredulous disbelief, her voice an octave higher than usual. "That's what this is all about? The black heart…from the curse? Are you *kidding* me?"

So captured by Governor's ridiculous assertion, Deborah did not notice that Hope shook off her arm as if she could no longer stand her mother's touch. Nor did Deborah notice when Hope bent to retrieve the shovel and then straightened with a sinister smile on her face directed at Governor.

What Deborah did notice was Governor's belief in his words. She took steps toward him, still angry but unable to shake her mother-nurturer role which demanded she teach and correct—regardless of the audience, regardless of the situation.

"Governor, you can't be serious?" She shook her head. "You're smarter than that. Surely you know that the Fuller's Curse is nothing but a myth?"

Behind her, Deborah didn't see Hope toss the shovel from one hand to the other. Nor did she see the devilish smile that twisted into a devious smirk. She did see Governor's return expression which promised a brutal end, and she misinterpreted the look. She correctly deciphered the fact that he wanted death—but whose death is what she got wrong.

And that incorrect assumption sent her blood rushing through her body, causing the veins at her throat and temple to pulse viciously. Her voice dropped way down deep when she said, "I can see you belong in the same sorry category as Step-Uncle Billy and Cousin Clarice—and to think, I thought higher of you."

Deborah turned from her mother-instructor role. Forget him! He was on his own, free to believe what he wanted. Just as Samuel and Ester had finally let her believe in the Fuller's Curse. Not the version Governor believed, where a black-hearted killer terrorized their family, but the version involving accidents and early deaths. Just referencing the verbal sparring the three of them had engaged in after Mary's debilitating call yesterday drained her of energy. And that, along with this current scene caused the heavy weight of darkness, of mental and emotional instability to tug at her again, trying to pull her under as it had yesterday.

"Ask her."

His words saved her, turned her mind back to the present. She watched as Governor stepped boldly forward, edging to the side to keep Hope on visual lockdown. Deborah noticed that his eyes never veered from Hope, not even while he was speaking to her.

"Ask her how many Fullers It's taken."

"We're not going to stay here and listen to this nonsense," said Deborah, turning from him and seeing that Hope was standing solidly on her feet and that she seemed alert, back to normal—as normal as a person could be who'd just sustained a serious beating.

Deborah reached out a hand to her. Assuming Hope would take it she swiveled toward Governor and said, "My daughter wouldn't hurt a soul. I raised her, and I didn't raise a killer. But that's not really the point. The real issue is you hurting her—and for no reason is that acceptable. I could press charges against you, and I will if you ever come near her or us again."

"Turn around," Governor spoke evenly, pointing past Deborah and Hope to the crumpled corpse of Aunt Mattie. "Look past her. See her latest handiwork."

It just so happened that Deborah had planned to turn anyway, with the idea of snatching Hope's hand and leading her away from this land of Fullers. So when she did turn, she had not planned to see death. But there, beyond Hope, near the rear end of the Mustang—an obviously dead Aunt Mattie.

"Oh, my God, oh God, no, no." Deborah pressed her hands against her mouth and doubled over as if someone had gut-punched her. "No, no, please, God, no." She collapsed to her knees, balling tight into herself. "No more death, no more."

She shook her head, denying that which lay before her, unwilling to pile another rotting body on top of the dead heap of Fullers from the weekend and those from the charts. Squeezing her eyes closed she prayed that they deceived her, but when she opened them seconds later, she realized that they had not lied. Aunt Mattie's body was posed before her, unnaturally still. In its lifelessness it had taken on an interesting color, supplying an artist's palette to the bold, dark bruises that dotted her skin.

Thinking that if she couldn't undo the death she could at least erase the imprint from her mind Deborah rubbed her eyes hard, really hard.

It didn't work.

It seemed instead to cause the image of Aunt Mattie's body to not only magnify, taking over her whole mind, but also acquire details that didn't exist in reality: swarming flies; buckets full of black blood; sharp, gleaming knives.

When the fictional images combined with reality, Deborah couldn't hold herself together. She vomited, missing Hope's canvas tennis shoes by a breath. Then, crying started and violent tremors. "No, no... No, no... No, no…" she repeated over and over, like a record needle stuck in a scratched groove.

With no trace of sympathy or feeling of any kind in his voice Governor said, "Mattie ain't the only one nor the first. Ask yo' *daughter* how yo' sister, nephew and Shandra really died."

Bent over in a child's pose with her forehead pressed to the ground Deborah cried out, hearing but not really comprehending Governor's words. "Another accident… The curse… Poor Aunt Mattie."

"Wasn't no accident. None of 'em. They all deaths by yo' daughter, the cursed one."

"No, no, no," Deborah sang her song, though muffled by her distorted position.

"Ain't it so, BlackHeart? Or Hope? Which one you wanna use?"

"Your choice, Record Keeper," said the BlackHeart.

Deborah heard her daughter's reply, but as with Governor's words she rejected them, sinking deeper and deeper into her grief-lost mind. Yet not beyond sanity. A glimmer of her motherly self parted the darkness, demanding Deborah protect both her child and the truth and the way to do that—get up, grab Hope and go. Leave this place of death, of images of Aunt Mattie, Shandra, Martin and so many others. Run away, hide from death before it took them too.

With great effort Deborah forced herself up to her knees. With her hands pressed to the ground on either side of her, eyes closed, still trembling, she prepared to stand. But then, she heard Governor's voice, farther away now.

"Tell yo' Mama how you made it look like SIDS took the baby."

This forced open Deborah's eyes, made her stare at him in stunned stupor. "How—how could you know that?" she demanded, wiping snot and tears from her face, her eyes reflecting the weariness of death. "Who told you about my Rachel?"

She'd been so absorbed with the recent Fuller deaths Deborah did not realize that Governor had found Aunt Mattie's butcher knife and retrieved it. Now, he held it loosely while Hope maintained control of the shovel. They faced each other, both looking wary and dangerous. In her sub-conscious mind she registered the standoff but consciously, she saw nothing.

"Nobody had to tell him, Mother," Hope answered for the man, cutting a brief glance at Deborah. "He's the new Mattie. He knows everything."

Deborah didn't follow. She looked at Hope, her face blank; her mind unable to comprehend.

"I killed Rachel," Hope declared and then sighed dramatically, as if losing patience with one habitually slow in understanding. "A pillow. Easy and quick." The teenager snapped her fingers to accentuate the fact and then continued boasting. "Anna and Curtis were just as simple. Anna I held under until she quit struggling. Curtis, he thought I'd unloaded the gun."

Deborah shook her head, denying Hope's words while trying to understand why her darling was saying such horrible things. What had Aunt Mattie said to Hope this past Saturday? Or perhaps it had been Governor. Was that the real reason for the beating? To force Hope to confess to such hideous acts? Anger flared suddenly, all-consuming, pushing grief and all other emotions out of range. She stood up then, her eyes red, hands balled at her sides, a hard set to her face.

"You did this." She shot the words at him, bulleting him with hate. "You messed up her mind. It wasn't enough to attack her body. You had to beat her mind, as well." She stepped toward Governor, her intention to protect and preserve clear. "You won't win. I'm taking her away from here. I'll get her the help she needs, and she'll go on to enjoy a successful life while you die in this God-forsaken place." Deborah stopped within inches of him, bordering on his personal space. "You're a mean, hateful man, and I'll hurt you myself if you ever make contact with her EVER again." Stepping backward with anger still disfiguring her face Deborah held her hand out to Hope, staying alert to Governor, to anything he might do to retaliate. "Come on, Hope, we're leaving."

"I'm not going anywhere," the girl replied, her voice full of sass. Deborah whirled, surprised at her daughter's words and tone, but even more astonished when she saw Hope—*really saw her*. A black dotted mist seemed to pulse about her from crown to sole; that mist caused Hope's skin to not only appear darker in hue, but also to vibrate, similar to the wave effect of intense heat coming off desert sand. More than that, Hope's eyes looked fevered, yet intensely focused, and at the moment, those insane-looking eyes pinned Deborah with impatience, disgust and something darker that Deborah couldn't define.

Her reaction to this new Hope: fear. A fear that filled every cell of her body and made her heart crumple. Breathing became troublesome as she divined the fact that this new Hope had replaced the old one—and the old one was gone forever. Deborah shook her head, disavowing the new Hope.

§

"No, not going anywhere. Not until I'm through with Governor—and you're in the damn way," Hope sneered.

Deborah's tears suddenly rose from their storage place and exposed themselves.

"What, *Mother*?" the BlackHeart asked nastily, witnessing Deborah's weakness and becoming angered by it. "You don't believe I am what Governor says I am?"

It laughed as It had on the day It collected Charles Fuller's soul and family. When Its loud, cruel laugh thinned, It confessed in a deep, exploding voice, "I *am* the BlackHeart. The cursed one. Born with Fuller blood from you."

"No. I don't believe it." In spite of the strong evidence in front of her, Deborah refused to see Hope as anything but her sweet little college freshman.

The BlackHeart shrugged. "That's your problem, Deborah. You put more faith in charts and analysis than in what's before your eyes. You rely on research and logic when you need to listen to your inner voice. The one that's telling you now to believe. The one that's trying to warn you of the truth."

§

Deborah covered her face with her hands. She couldn't stand that dark shield that was shrouding Hope. She couldn't absorb that foreign voice issuing from her daughter. She couldn't comprehend the vibrations that pulsed off Hope and crowded her. And yet, she could not give up, could not let her daughter go.

"He's playing on your grief, Hope." Deborah spoke between her fingers. "You're stressed from all the death you've known. You're young, impressionable. Please, ignore him," she pleaded.

§

"Now you're just lying to yourself, Deborah." It stepped into the space separating them. Not that Deborah knew. She remained closed. No eyes for seeing. No ears for hearing. Determined to hold on to her truth about Hope, to what she knew and had learned from living with the girl for eighteen years. "Logical to the end, and yet here I am offering you the truth, giving you the answers you and Ester ran around trying to find."

Savagely, It snatched Deborah's fingers from her face and pressed Deborah's face between Its own hands. "I am *not* what you think I am. I am a killer. I have been killing since the beginning of this world."

Crying painfully now, Deborah desperately wrapped her arms around Hope, holding on as tightly as she held on to the belief in Hope's goodness. "No, Hope. Samuel and I couldn't have produced such a child. It's not your nature. You're—"

Violently, It shook loose of Deborah's embrace. Hate made Its eyes hard, dark, uncaring, like those of a snake.

§

But Deborah's love ran deep. Deeper than the BlackHeart's hate. She matched Its backward steps, determined to keep them connected, to keep them close. Again, she hugged Hope to her, cradling the young girl within her loving arms.

"You're good and sweet, Hope. I've seen you with kids, with your grandparents. You're smart and…and you have a great future. Don't believe Governor's—"

It wrestled free again, this time flinging Deborah to the ground. Deborah landed on her side with a hard "umph" as the breath was knocked out of her. Quickly, she sucked it back in, scrambled to her feet and moved toward Hope, reaching out to her.

Love glowed so brilliantly from Deborah's eyes that it obviously pained the BlackHeart, causing It to stumble backward, as if scorched.

Then, a forceful grip on her shoulder halted Deborah's progress before she could reach Hope. She tried to shake off the hand, to ignore the silent command to stay put, but her efforts only made the grip more viselike. She turned, ready to attack Governor physically and verbally, but when she met the butcher knife a scant distance from her eye, she forgot the pain and her plan.

"You can stop It, Deborah," he spoke solemnly. "You got the power. That's why It hates you, most of all."

"Shut up, old man," the BlackHeart spoke from behind Deborah.

Governor gave the BlackHeart no mind. He kept his eyes on Deborah, his words for her. "You can stop the curse and save the Fullers. All you got to do is kill It. That'll end the curse forever." He lifted the knife higher, attracting the sun's rays, making the dull blade shine.

"Shut your mouth!"

"It has to be killed by the Fuller who loves It most. That's you Deborah."

"SHUT YOUR FUCKING MOUTH!"

"You been searchin,' tryin' to find a way to save the Fullers. This yo' chance. Save us all from Satan's own."

Deborah stared between him and the knife, hearing but not accepting.

Kill Hope.

Kill her child.

Her only remaining child. Deborah shuddered and closed her eyes.

"That's not yo' daughter," Governor said calmly, guessing her thoughts. "You see the evil 'round It. You hear the soun' of Its true voice. The soun' of thousands of deaths. That's the BlackHeart. Not Hope."

Deborah shook her head, insisting on denial. She refused to believe, to accept the truth or her role in saving the family.

"It knows yo' perfect love can rid the fam'ly of this curse forever. That's why It fears you, hates you and loves you."

At the word love, tears coursed down her face. "I love her too," she choked out and stepping away from Governor she turned her back to him.

Governor moved with her, standing to the side of her, never ready to give up on the one who could save them all. "See that Bible on top of Aunt Mattie?"

Deborah shut her ears to him too late to stop the automatic glance in Aunt Mattie's direction. Again, the sight of death sickened her, but she wrapped her arms around her middle, controlling it, and for the first time she noticed the white Bible with splotches of red blood on its cover. An unexpected, odd thought flitted across her mind. *The two belong together—woman and Bible.*

"Gone look in it," Governor coaxed, "It's all there. The beginnin'. Every death. Those killed by the cursed ones and the cursed ones we Record Keepers had to kill. The limitations of evil and even how to stop It. It's all there in that Bible. The Truth."

The scientist in her wasn't fully retired. Just as the black vibrations had buffeted her, so too did the call of research. She felt it, couldn't resist it and wasn't surprised to find herself taking slow steps toward the Bible. Death, anger, killing, curses, and grief sloughed off with every step. She felt the old tingle at the possibility of knowledge revealed, of facts discovered. She felt the old increase in heart rate at the potential for learning.

In the background, egging her on, Governor issued words of enticement. "Records, old records. Pull the papers from the covers. Read 'em, get yo' answers. You gone see it ain't yo' daughter at all, but the BlackHeart."

Deborah squatted and gingerly lifted the Bible off Aunt Mattie without touching the corpse, without staring into Aunt Mattie's face. Moving away from the body, she planted the book on the ground, and on her knees, she followed Governor's instructions for retrieving the Truth.

"I'll give her that," the BlackHeart offered Governor in a false, benevolent tone. Pointing to Deborah who'd begun reading, It said, "I did as much for Charles. Gave him time; I can do the same for her. After all…" The BlackHeart's smile resembled that of a carved pumpkin—jagged, spooky, false. "…I'm going to win this one, too. I'll kill you and she's not strong." It nodded toward Deborah, who now sat rocking back and forth, hands covering her mouth, tears dripping in a steady procession. "She'll kill herself or lose her mind."

Governor did not acknowledge the BlackHeart's claims or Its digs. He watched It closely, but directed his words to Deborah, even though she remained glued to the Truth. "You can be the one to give this fam'ly back to God, Deborah. An Old Testament sacrifice will free us. Release us forever from the curse. Sacrifice It, and save us."

A fast reader, Deborah finished and then looked up with a stricken expression. She clutched the original Charles Fuller deed in her hand and stared straight at Governor. Her tears fell harder, faster and her voice fell apart, came together, fell apart again as she spoke.

"I…I don't know…This…Aunt Mattie…she couldn't possibly know. There're matches… Names on our charts and…and…the black heart references on the autopsies. But—"

Deborah stopped. The mental struggle to marry the natural to the unnatural, the logical to the illogical, the spiritual to the material overtook her speech. Sinking into her mind, she considered dismissing the information, chalking it up to an old woman's imagination, except there was corroboration by, of all people, she and Ester. The historical data recorded in handwritings that differed and reflected various dates throughout the ages; physical documents, the deed and Charles' oral testimony written by someone who could barely write; the list of dead Fullers, some of whom appeared on their charts; and a family tree that mirrored her own—all of this Deborah, the researcher, could not deny, leaving her with no choice but to accept the Fuller's Curse. And not her version of the curse, but Governor's version, with a black-hearted killer and the current killer—her daughter?!

"No," Deborah shook her head, stuffing the tender papers back in their holding slots as fast as she could. "No!" she denied the Truth again, refusing to believe the evidence in front of her, turning her back to research. "Not my Hope," she refused to condemn her daughter.

She brushed off her hands as if brushing away any evidence that she'd ever touched the papers, then backed away from the Bible as if it were Lucifer himself. As she scuttled toward Hope, she tried to block out images of Rachel, Anna, Curtis and Shandra, a distraught Hope beside each body. She tried to lie to herself about Hope's whereabouts on Saturday when the Fuller couple and Martin's lives were snatched. She tried to ignore the memory of this morning, Hope whispering in her ear, telling her to come to Partway and arriving here to more death, with Hope again on the scene.

"No," she lied, trying to stop her mind from tallying the facts as more proof that validated the Fuller's Curse and that Hope was the BlackHeart.

Standing, Deborah ran the last few feet to Hope. She would have grabbed her and kept running to the truck except her damn, well- trained brain, churning with facts, circumstances and data, blocked her exit. Breathing heavily, Deborah stopped in front of her baby, studying her as if she'd never seen her before, examining her from top to bottom. Hope, her darling daughter, top ten in her high school senior class, college-bound student, future doctor. She appeared the same—average height, brown eyes, caramel-coloring, thin body frame, long hair in a ponytail. She cocked her head, querying with her eyes as well as her voice.

"Hope?"

"She's gone, Deborah." Governor's words wafted from behind her. He slipped the butcher knife into her open palm. "Save us. Free the Fullers."

Deborah gripped the knife, brought it up to stare at it.

Through watery eyes, she looked at Hope again and saw a Hope she'd refused to see before—black, lifeless eyes; prominent veins on her face, neck and arms showing dark with the black blood pumping through them; and skin as dark as a Halloween night. This Hope was evil! This Hope was the BlackHeart! Every bit the killer It professed to be. The thing that played casually with Fuller lives, creatively picking off people as if they were no more than berries on a bush. All the heartache. All the pain, grief, and wasted lives—and for what? So the Evil One could attain unlimited, infinite control of their family?

Deborah looked at Aunt Mattie's body. She stared at the knife in her hand and wondered if she could be as cold-blooded. If she could take a life as the BlackHeart, through her daughter, had done. Taking a deep breath, Deborah lifted the knife over her head and made the mistake of looking into her daughter's eyes. Because now, the BlackHeart had changed Its appearance, evaporating evidence of Its nature, allowing light to return to Hope's eyes, skin, and personage; smiling that smile, the one that melted Deborah's heart every time. The one that caused unconditional love to sprout and bloom. Deborah didn't even register the instant metamorphosis. Just surrendered to love, letting it guide her hand down, allowing the knife to free-fall to the ground.

Deborah's perfect love proved imperfect as she returned Hope's smile and admitted to all the world, "I love you, Hope. I love you."

The strength of Deborah's love did it, caused the BlackHeart to strike out in hate. Deborah didn't see the shovel rise into the air because she was gazing so lovingly into her daughter's eyes. She didn't realize she was a target until metal connected with her so loudly that a passerby—if there had been one—would have attributed the sound to thunder.

Deborah flew backward, knocked off her feet.

She landed hard in the dirt on her back, stunned. Struggling for breath, she saw through watery, cloudy vision that the BlackHeart straddled her, blocking out the blue of the sky. Pain radiated outward from the point of impact and even though Deborah thought to roll onto her side, knowing that would help her breathe, the pain wouldn't let her move. Not even to blink.

Soon, she began convulsing, spitting up blood, and her eyes rolled back into her head. This continued for some time and then…peace. All movement ceased. Pain subsided.

Her eyes returned to normal and she blinked slowly, bringing her daughter's face into focus. Her precious, beautiful, intelligent, ambitious, talented and kind-hearted daughter. Tears rolled from the corners of her eyes as Deborah smiled up at Hope and held out her arms. Love made her eyes bright like midnight stars.

Even when Hope pierced her throat with the pointed edge of the shovel, Deborah continued to love her, accepting Hope's blows, accepting Hope the way she was.

§

Governor stood by silently on the verge of losing control of his emotions. Almost crying. Ready to change places with Deborah after witnessing such consuming love for evil. But "In-Me" nudged him, reminding him of his role. *It's okay, Governor. Deborah is in a good place. Pull yourself together. Do what you're supposed to do.*

Correcting himself, he picked up Mattie's abandoned knife and waited on the BlackHeart.

It stood over Deborah's cast-off form, breathing hard but smiling. The smile evidence of Its elation at striking down another Fuller. And not just any Fuller, but the one who could have ended Its control over all the families It possessed and sent It straight back to Hell.

The BlackHeart straightened from Its bent over position and still smiling, cut a daring look at Governor. Then, It visually measured the distance between It, Governor and the Bible. Governor was closer to the Truth.

"I tol' you, you ain't leavin' here with that."

"We'll see."

Governor was fair and alert. He allowed the BlackHeart the first strike and because he was alert, the shovel missed him, just barely. The force behind the swing, the uneven ground, and snagging a foot on Deborah's body caused the BlackHeart to spiral out and meet the ground, flat on Its stomach. The shovel skidded out of Its hand. Then, in one fluid movement, Governor kicked the shovel away from the BlackHeart and dropped his weight onto Its back, digging a knee in Its spine. In the next second, Governor grabbed Its ponytail and yanked Its head back, exposing Its young throat—slicing It from ear to ear.

The Second Ending: The Rise

1 John 4:18 (NRSV)
There is no fear in love, but perfect love casts out fear.

On such a beautiful day Governor sat inside his house in his favorite reading chair. Mattie's rocker, the same rocker she had used years, years and years long to record, cry and dream, resided across the room. He'd had to move a few of his pieces out to accommodate the extra seat, but he needed a tangible reminder of his aunt. Something besides the Bible and Truth.

As Mattie had done for so many years Governor sat with the latest paper of Truth in his lap. The Bible lay on the side table within easy, quick reach. In his right-hand scratch he engraved the truth, preserving it for eternity. He had almost finished recording the good and bad names when he sensed her spirit. She entered from the rafters, falling on him like a soft spring shower. His heart and soul received her gladly as she entered him, bringing with her a lightness to his heart and lovingly restoring his soul.

He smiled.

They communicated in the language of spirits through feelings, senses, and thoughts that were both within and without.

"*Ya' done good, Gov'nor,*" Mattie said, resonating pride. "*Handled it all real nice. The killin'. Throwin' my body on the highway so's a truck could catch the blame. Leavin' mother and daughter in the front yard to let the police figger what they can. Ya' done good lettin' 'In-Me' do the guidin'. You was strong, real strong.*"

"*I just did, no thinkin.' Like you said.*" He paused, and that spiritual silence told on him, telling of the hard time he was having after his first bout with the BlackHeart, even though he had done good.

Mattie understood and said, "*It ain't never easy, Gov'nor. Fam'ly's fam'ly, no matter what. You gotta 'member you was given this for a reason. You got purpose.*"

He nodded in agreement, but whys still filled his head. Why couldn't it have ended yesterday? Why couldn't Deborah's love have been perfect enough to end this forever? How many more BlackHearts would he have to face? When would it end? ...would it ever end?

In her spiritual state, Mattie knew the answers to all questions, but it wasn't her place to tell. *"The mysteries of God ain't for man."* She shared that much with Governor, adding, *"When you ascend and leave that cruel world behind, then you'll know. Then, you'll know."*

Governor didn't push. He knew Mattie had said all she could, and would say no more. The little bit she shared was good enough.

"We all proud of you, Gov'nor. Ever'body's proud. We all watchin'—yo' Mama and the lady you love—Cora Jean. My fam'ly. The ones you got on them papers, too. We all lovin' you."

"That's good, Mattie. I like hearin' that." Governor paused, smiling a handsome, rakish smile as he recalled yesterdays with his lady love. *"Cora Jean, you say?"*

"Lovely as ever. She'll be up at Black Hill, next time you visit."

"That'll help cover the loneliness. You, Mama and Cora Jean at Black Hill." He liked that; it made him feel good all over. It made him pick up the black ink pen and finish recording the names on the onion skin paper.

Mattie answered the question that rose with the task. *"Deborah and Hope are together as b'fo. They know God used Hope in a special way and so washed her clean. They happy, yet sad watchin' Samuel, Ester, Imogene, Daniel and others."*

Governor could relate to their sadness. Already, the yearning of his soul to be freed of physical restraint tugged at him. He'd only served the family one day as Truth Bearer and already his greatest desire was to be with his loved ones, to be home in Heaven. Governor shook his head, wondering how Aunt Mattie had endured it all those years, wondering how he would manage.

Because they were one, Mattie felt his desires, understood his doubts. In keeping with tradition, she extended a balm to soothe his yearning, which also served to paint a vision for the future. *"It beautiful here, Gov'nor. Glorious. No pain, no heartache, no evil or sin. Only purity, goodness, perfection. You'll love it when you come."*

Just as she had needed to hear those words and had relied on them over the years, especially when the troubles of the world threatened to overwhelm, so too would Governor. *"I gotta go now, Gov'nor. See ya' tomorrow at Black Hill."*

Then, she left his body as gently as she'd come, leaving behind a lighter, less burdened Governor.

Sighing with contentment, Governor tidied the paper, slid it in its proper slot and rose out of his chair. His seventy-something-year-old bones cracked and popped as he walked to the table that doubled as a desk. He positioned The Good Book just so, neighboring a chipped china cup filled with different colored rubber bands and a thin cardboard box of onion-skin paper.

§

Miles away from Partway, Texas, travelling over fields withering under the killing rays of the sun, through woods, thick and dark green, and into town to the only medical clinic within a sixty-mile radius, a dark spirit flew purposefully until it found what it had been looking for—a Fuller cousin had just given birth.

The baby boy, weighing in at nine pounds one ounce, measured nineteen inches long. Both Mama and Daddy cried happy tears and smiled lovingly at their son.

Outside in the corridor, news of the birth reached those who'd been waiting, and excited chatter erupted in the hallway. The newborn's uncle passed around cigars, making sure to hand the first one to the baby boy's green-haired grandmother, Clarice.

The doctor placed a stethoscope to the baby's chest, smiling at the strong, steady beat of his heart and the spirited cries from his well-developed lungs. A fine, healthy boy.

But then, just as the doctor straightened, he saw something horrible. The baby's eyes turned black with no spark of life. The veins in its face, neck and arms rose up, stretching the skin taut. Not only did the veins become more pronounced but also they writhed like a bushel of snakes. And finally, the baby's skin turned black as if black blood pumped throughout his little body.

Startled, the doctor jumped back and when he blinked, he was surprised to see the baby boy appeared as it had been before: coffee-colored with soft, supple skin and chocolate brown eyes. A perfect, beautiful baby.

Recovering his composure, he chuckled nervously then picked up the quiet baby and handed him to the nurse. He returned to his report, recording: *Exceptionally healthy. Good lungs. Strong heart. Unexceptional delivery.*

And although the delivery of this Fuller baby *had* been unexceptional, he couldn't help remembering a similar occurrence that had happened to him. Oh, when was that? Oh yes, about eighteen years ago when he'd worked in Dallas.

Perfect love casts out all fear!

About the Author

Ann Fields began her writing career in 1996 with the publication of her first romance novel, *After Hours*. Since then, Fields has published three additional romance novels, *Second Time Around, Love Everlasting,* and *Give and Take. Fuller's Curse* is her debut in the horror genre.

Fields also has published in non-fiction, authoring the book *Stop Stalling and Write* as well as numerous articles, which have appeared in *Teen Graffiti, Basic,* and other magazines.

Her short stories have been published in *A Legacy of African American Literature* and *Bouquet: A Delightful Collection of Mother's Day Romances.*

Visit her online at www.AnnFields.com.

Dear Reader,

Thank you for reading *Fuller's Curse*. You almost didn't have the opportunity to do so.

Fuller's Curse was a long time coming into this form. I started writing the story in 2000, finished in the summer of 2001, then spent more than ten years trying to sell the story. I have more rejections on this manuscript than the sky has stars. But, finally in 2012, I received an offer. I was elated! However, a year later—two months before the publication date—the publishing house closed and there was *Fuller's Curse*—not rejected, but orphaned.

Frustrated, I took a page from Deborah's playbook and said, "I'll prove to the publishing gods that this is a story worth publishing. I'll self publish. So there... (stick out tongue here)." Now, mind you, to self publish is something I never wanted to do—EVER! But, I did it and I'm happy I did. It has truly been a unique experience and as a recovering controlaholic, the process of self publishing allowed me to feed that addiction in a gentle, constructive way.

So in 2013, *Fuller's Curse* finally made it; transforming from a Word document to an actual book, and I'm so glad. I hope you are too.

Again, thank you for your patronage. It's because of readers that I continue to write, and now publish, with an end goal of delivering quality literature.

Sincerely,

Ann Fields

Author of Quality Literature

SPECIAL NOTE: *Fuller's Curse* is book one of the *Curse* series. Even though I don't have a publication date yet for book two of the *Curse* series, I hope you will keep an eye out for book two, *Tremont's Curse*. Ester makes a return visit in *Tremont's Curse*. As well, you'll learn more about Sap's interesting background and meet one determined, young lady of the Tremont family.

"Naming Rights" Contest

Are you the type of person who re-names characters?
Do you have a knack for matching names to personalities, places or things?
Are you the person everyone turns to when naming new babies?
Do you consider yourself creative?

Then the "Naming Rights" contest is for you!

The "Naming Rights" contest gives one lucky person the chance to name a character or two in the *Curse* series. Yes, that's right! You'll work with author, Ann Fields to create a name for a character or two.

Only three simple steps to enter...

1. Take a few minutes to write a review about *Fuller's Curse;*
2. Post your review to any book review site such as Amazon, Goodreads, Shelfari, etc.
3. Email afields121@yahoo.com with the date and title of your review as well as the name under which the review was posted. In the Subject field, type: Naming Rights Contest.

Then sit tight and wait for the "Naming Rights" winner to be announced.

Contest Details...

1. Contest runs from April 23, 2013 through October 23, 2013.

2. Reviews must be an original written work of the entrant (English language only).

3. Entrants must be at least 18 years old by October 23, 2013.

4. By submitting the required information to the official email address (afields121@yahoo.com), entrants agree to and accept the contest rules and decision as final and binding. Entrants also agree that they are giving the contest sponsor (Ann Fields and A New Thing Publishing) permission to add entrant's email address to the sponsor's database for promotional purposes. Entrants may opt out at any time.

5. Limit one entry per posted review.

6. A purchase will not increase or decrease an entrant's chance of winning.

7. The winner will be selected via a random drawing of all submitted entries.

8. One winner will be selected. The odds of being selected depend on the number of entries.

9. The winner will be notified by email by October 28, 2013; all other entrants will be informed of the winner by October 29, 2013 via email.

10. Those excluded from the contest include family and friends of Ann Fields (you know who you are) as well as employees, contractors, partners, interns and affiliates of A New Thing Publishing.

11. All federal, state, local and municipal rules apply. Void where prohibited.